KEN ALLEN | SUPER SLEUTH SERIES

HEROES EVER DIE

KEN ALLEN | SUPER SLEUTH SERIES

HEROES EVER DIE

J. A. CRAWFORD

CamCat Publishing, LLC
Ft. Collins, Colorado 80524
camcatpublishing.com

This is a work of fiction. Names, characters, places, and incidents are either products of the author's imagination or are used fictitiously.

Hardcover ISBN 9780744305920
Paperback ISBN 9780744305449
Large-Print Paperback ISBN 9780744305746
eBook ISBN 9780744305722
Audiobook ISBN 9780744305753

Library of Congress Control Number: 2022932162

Book and cover design by Maryann Appel

5 3 1 2 4

To the people who

told the stories that shaped me.

And to my hero.

Thanks, Mom.

WHAT!?
CRASH!!
HMMMM

WOOOOOW!!
YEAH!!

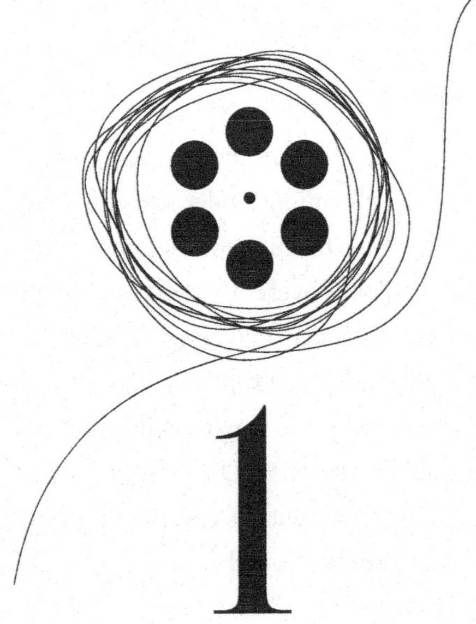

1

FALL HAD COME to This Town, the season where hopes spring eternal, with new productions shooting up to bloom or be nipped in the bud. I was on the studio backlot, gaping at everything like a tourist. There was a reason why I couldn't wipe the grin off my face.

I was about to meet my hero.

I don't often ask for favors. Whether it's a character strength or flaw, I am far more comfortable helping others than I am being helped. But when I heard Dave King was coming out of seclusion, I had to meet him. Just once. And thank him for doing so much for me, a person he didn't know existed.

Of course, the one man who could grant an audience with King was the person I owed the most.

Ray Ford was the "Magician of Make-Believe"—the premier special-effects expert in the entertainment industry for more than six decades. Last season, when the rest of the world pegged me a serial killer, Ray fabricated the host of gadgets that elevated me from mild-mannered to super. In return, he played spectator to my adventures and got to test his inventions under real-life conditions.

Ray was currently transforming mild-mannered actors into silver-screen superheroes. There were two major players—production companies with rival expanded universes—filming and releasing simultaneously in a box-office death match. The demand for spectacle and escalating budgets had led to Ray working both sides of the fence. I didn't want to imagine what his NDAs must look like.

I got far as I could without an escort—corralled with a crowd of fans waving their phones around in hopes of catching the barest whiff of a leak. There was no shortage of ex- [insert armed service branch here] private police personnel hoping to be discovered through a guarding gig, and my banner year didn't elevate my status to the height required to part a sea of badges. I took shelter in the shadow of a warehouse and drank in the October air. It was only seventy-five degrees, but my blazer was a sculpted sheath of ballistic gel. While nothing less than a bursting shell could penetrate its surface, the material also blocked the cross breeze. I dug out my phone and jumped back into the Dave King omnibus collection I had downloaded for long plane rides.

Ray located me via the bell he'd hung around my wrist. My custom-built smart watch had all the extras, including GPS, a heart-rate monitor, and a microphone which never turned off, for Ray's eavesdropping pleasure. You didn't think about how much you talked to yourself until someone was listening in on every word. He waved at me from the far side of the security cordon. An extra-large fanboy hard-blocked my route.

He ignored my polite requests and apologies, so I spiked his phone like a volleyball.

"Dude, what the hell?"

I shoved my way into the opening. "That's what you get for filming vertically."

He sized me up, decided I wasn't bully material, and went searching for his phone.

Ray admitted me through the gate. He was as I saw him last, muscle and gristle shrink-wrapped into a one-piece racing suit. His russet skin was free of stubble and his head was razored into a reflective surface.

"Well, well. If it isn't Ken Allen, the detective to the stars himself."

"Quiet, you'll draw a crowd."

Ray laughed. I had been a shamus for exactly two cases, one where I cleared myself for murder and another which had taken me overseas.

Security permitted me through after Ray presented a lanyard with a hybrid hologram/bar code. I hung it around my neck, and we wove through the time traveler's menagerie that was multiple-production traffic toward the soundstage.

Ray opted for chatter. "How was your flight?"

"Are you telling me you can't listen in when I'm on airplane mode?"

"Ken, help me out here. I've been practicing my small talk. According to those internet sites, I need to work on my people skills."

As someone who had been the subject of memes for more than a decade, I felt Ray's pain. "I warned you not to look."

When Ray replied, he kept his volume low. "It wasn't by choice. My last few gigs have had leaks. Been trying to track the source."

I knew which soundstage was ours from the drones. Constructs of Ray's design, they patrolled both the interior and exterior of the hangar-sized structure. Like any magician, Ray couldn't have the audience peeking behind the curtain. But time was catching up to him. Everyone had a camera in their pocket loaded with apps capable of instantly reaching millions. As kids, we were warned about the rise of Big Brother. What no one foresaw was that we would become him.

The guard at the door scanned our lanyards before letting us pass, including Ray, who had been gone five minutes. I stepped into the façade of a factory. A cauldron that could have boiled a tyrannosaurus rex belched molten metal into the air. A catwalk OSHA never would have approved ended over the cauldron like a diving board. The grated floor allowed a peek at a legion of killer robots idling below. Orange light glowed from off-screen sources. The light wasn't there to provide visibility, but instead to create shadows and suggest heat. Smoke machines added a haze of steam, enhancing the effect.

All the trappings of moviemaking were present: the light arrays, boom mikes, camera tracks, and monitors. At least one person was assigned to each object. Everyone had a badge hanging from their neck, even the saints stationed at craft services.

An average-sized white guy in a modern, tactical version of a Confederate army jacket stepped onto the catwalk. Clutching fighting sticks that resembled rolled-up scrolls, he inched forward like a dog who wasn't supposed to be in the kitchen.

I couldn't contain my excitement. "Bill O'Wrongs is the villain in this one?"

"Yeah," Ray said. "Wait here."

When you're a kid playing pretend, you either want to be a cop or a robber. Me, I was a cop all the way, right down to the embarrassing daydreams of saving my fourth-grade teacher from masked kidnappers. I've never been a rule breaker by nature. So, when Ray told me to stay put, I stayed put.

There was plenty to take in. The production was an expert operation, performed by a crew who had worked together many times, churning out franchise faire assembly-line style. I had appeared—not acted but appeared, you'd agree if you'd seen it—in exactly one movie, whose production wasn't exactly traditional. If I had my way, that flick would have stayed secret forever.

Then again, it was what got me here. I guess you could say I had a love/hate relationship with my origin story. Someone's assistant approached me.

I knew it was an assistant from the way he eased into my eye line, instead of confronting me as to who I was and what I thought I was doing. Which was good, because I didn't have a firm answer for either. Not now, not ever.

"Mr. Allen?"

"Mr. Allen is my father. Please, call me Mr. Allen Junior."

The assistant made a note in his phone, and I immediately regretted the joke.

"Mr. West would like to speak with you."

The assistant was unable to hide his curiosity over how a person of my station could possibly know Flint West. I waved up to Ray above me, but he was absorbed in his work. If he needed to find me, he could. "Then let's not keep Mr. West waiting."

The assistant led me outside while not taking his eyes off me, as if he were watching his kid. Mr. West's trailer was nicer than every place I'd lived up until three months ago, when my life took a ride on the roller-coaster that was the twenty-four-hour news cycle. The assistant waved a key fob across the door, and I heard a latch click.

"Mr. West is inside, Mr. Allen Junior."

A response would have only created more problems, so I stepped into a curtained landing area, stopping to ensure the door locked back into place. A deep voice boomed from the private side of the cloth barrier.

"That you, Ken Allen? Get in here!"

I pushed the curtain aside and ran face-first into Flint West. He squeezed me until I was ready to pop before pushing me back to give me a once-over.

"You miss me, Ken? You know I missed you."

Flint was in a silk robe, boxer briefs that could have been painted on, and nothing else. His smile made me smile.

"Your body sure didn't," I said. "You were so jacked in that last Civil Warriors flick people thought it was CGI."

Flint shook his head, smiling at suffering-gone-by. “Man, we had paramedics off camera with IVs ready. I looked like that for maybe an hour. They couldn’t get the lighting right.”

He gestured for me to sit before taking a seat himself. I’d never known someone who could maintain genuine, interested eye contact for as long as Flint could.

It forced me to say something.

“Becoming an ideal carries a cost.”

Even before computer magic, there were myriad methods to elevate a humble human to heroic status. One was extreme dehydration. In combat sports, competitors only had to be at their fighting weight for a scant moment on the scale. The best way to do so while maintaining your muscle mass was to eliminate as much liquid from your body as possible. Typically, by sweating it out.

It was a dangerous practice. People have died cutting too much weight, particularly those of Flint West’s proportions. And I was the one who taught him the trade. In my previous alter ego as the “Sensei to the Stars,” I had acted as both personal trainer and stage-fighting guru for the A-list.

Flint West was my masterpiece.

“So, Ken, you got a minute for the little people, now that you’re a big-time crime fighter?”

I leaned forward, elbows on my thighs. “Not sure where you’ve been getting your news, but I cleared my name and went on safari.”

Flint wasn’t buying it. “Mmm-hmm. Well, your safari buddy and I have the same agent. You saved her career, man.”

The way Flint said it, we could have been talking about his mother. The pedestal he was putting me on was high enough to end us both if I tumbled off. Flint’s emotions were as herculean as the rest of him. The intensity that had served him on the gridiron translated perfectly to the big screen. You felt what Flint was feeling.

“What’s on your mind?” I asked.

"I have a friend." Flint started having second thoughts. He crushed his lips together. His jaw was so muscular it had striations. When you are cast to wear a mask, it's all about the jawline.

"You have lots of friends," I replied. "Including me. This isn't going anywhere you don't want it to go."

Flint nodded at my reassurance. Around rep number five, he unflexed his mandibles. "This friend of mine, he's getting into something big. Real big. And dangerous. He's used to going it alone, but I think he could use your help."

The vagueness was giving me a headache. I massaged the bridge of my nose.

"I'm going to need more proper nouns here, Flint."

"If I were to hire you, would my friend have to know you were on the case?"

"I can't work for a guy who doesn't know I'm working for him. And I can't help someone when I don't even know his name."

Flint tapped a fist on his lips to acknowledge I was making some good points, so that was progress. When he spoke again, he kept his hand over his mouth.

"It has to do with Dave King."

Flint didn't ask if I knew who Dave King was. We had bonded over our love of all things King, years past. It was no coincidence Flint was playing one of King's characters on screen.

"What's going on with Dave King?" I asked.

"What you should do is meet him. See if you hit it off."

I managed to keep from throwing my hands into the air. "Sounds like a plan."

Flint nodded some more, adding a smile. "All right. All right. Okay, Ken. Look, they have to start getting me into costume."

"Has that process gotten any better?"

"A little. It's like having your own pit crew."

"Well, you did make your name in action vehicles."

Flint laughed to be polite, then switched right back to sincere. “Look, go talk to Dave. Keep it casual, tell him you and I are buddies.”

“I’ll do my best, but when it comes to acting, my track record speaks for itself.”

This time, Flint’s laugh was genuine.

Flint’s assistant played boatman and guided me back to set, where he pointed out Dave King, who I would have known anywhere. I strolled up next to the legend, strategizing how to break the ice, but King spoke the moment he noticed me.

“It’s too small.”

Dave King had once been a big man. Geometrically cubed, with a block head, a barrel chest, and boxy shoulders. You wondered how a pencil could have survived those scarred, square clamps he had for fingers. Age had taken its toll, shrinking him down and thinning him out, but in my eyes, he would always be a giant.

Dave King, the man who had birthed hundreds of heroes with nothing but a #2 pencil and some bristol board. Dave King, the greatest mythmaker of the modern age.

“I always dreamed big. These are titans we’re talking about.” I stood up straight when King glanced my way but stopped short of puffing out my chest. “Who are you supposed to be? One of mine?”

I was stunned silent.

The first thing I said to Dave King needed to mean something, without coming on too strong. The silence was getting uncomfortable, so I went with what I was thinking.

“I wish.”

Dave King boomed a laugh that turned heads in our direction. “If wishes were fishes, we’d all cast nets. So, who are you playing in this picture show?”

It wasn’t the first time my getup had been mistaken for a costume. While my jacket passed casual inspection, close-up, people realized it was closer to a bulletproof vest than a button-down blazer.

"Myself. I'm Ken Allen." In an attempt to impress him, I added, "I'm a detective."

Dave King measured my form with an artist's eye, fitting me for the role. Whether or not I was qualified, I looked the part. Seasoned, but still in shape and easy on the eyes. He might have drawn me in the role, once upon a time.

I tried to remember any of the hundred questions I'd dreamed of asking him over the years. The kind that demonstrates the depth of your devotion. That mark you as a True Fan.

"Well Ken, if you're looking for evildoers, take your pick. Here comes a grade-A pack of thieves now. Good to meet you."

Dave King offered his hand. I don't usually shake hands on principle, but for him I'd make an exception. His grip tremored as we touched palms, the thick fingers curled like claws. I let him lead, keeping my response a notch less firm. There was too much to tell him. I decided to start with the ending.

"Thank you, Mr. King. Growing up, your work meant the world to me."

King pursed his lips with a nod. He must have heard the same sentiment a billion times before. A sadness crept into his eyes. I'd blown it. Upset him, when I'd intended the opposite. We untangled hands. I did most of the work. Once his fingers had locked down, they didn't want to release.

The group Dave King had identified as suspect stopped an arm's length from us. I knew right away who was in charge, because he was rocking a hoodie and track pants. In a realm of suit and tie, the person in casuals bore the crown. His right hand was a Desi woman who wore a power suit as if it were armor. She studied me, so it was only fair for me to study her back.

In This Town, you had to realign the one-to-ten scale. There were too many tens. Her makeup was impeccable. Professional, with deniability. I knew right away she was smarter than me.

Not that it was a rare occurrence.

"Mr. King," said the tracksuit-in-charge. "So glad you could make it."

Only he wasn't.

A lifetime of taking hits had taught me to trust my instincts. Later on, I could dissect the factors behind my initial read. Off the cuff, my gut was enough.

Dave King's innards were synced with mine. "Save the speeches. I've got a shelf about to snap from worthless awards."

I wasn't sure what to do with myself. I hadn't gone looking for an awkward situation, it had found me.

Tracksuit read me all wrong. "I didn't realize you were bringing representation."

"He's not a lawyer," the woman informed him.

"Let's take this elsewhere, this isn't our shoot to start with," Tracksuit decided. When he went to guide Dave King by the shoulder, King shrugged him off.

Realizing my moments on set were numbered, I scanned around for my patron. Ray was above me, with Bill O'Wrongs, on the edge of the catwalk. Ray walked Bill through the stunt, pointing, soothing, and doing everything else he could to reassure an actor who was about to dive into a vat of lava.

The cameras weren't rolling, so Bill O'Wrongs wasn't in character. Unless his interpretation of the villain was a guy who nodded nervously between deep breaths. Ray turned Bill O'Wrongs's back to the pit, then reached out over the threshold and grabbed a handful of air. Try as I might, there was no making out what Ray was attaching to the actor's costume.

Ray wound his way back to me and guided us to his spot behind the firing line, where he had a battle station bristling with monitors, each displaying a different camera angle.

"I thought they wiped out the wires in post."

Ray snorted. "If you're going to do that, why not go ahead and make a cartoon?"

The crew took position, their stillness spreading a contagious tension. I wanted to watch it go down live but got a better view from the monitors. I leaned in, as if another six inches would help the ultra-high-definition images. I knew what was coming but not when. Sitting through the coverage for later editing was torture.

Flint entered from above, crashing through a skylight. Stopping to hover midair, he spread his wings to reveal the golden-taloned symbol on his chest below an eagle cowl. I couldn't help but play civilian. At least I didn't point and shout his name. Fortunately, Bill O'Wrongs had it covered.

"Flying Freeman!"

Ray had trimmed Flying Freeman's avian cowl to take full advantage of Flint's carved-from-ebony jawline. The sculpted brow accentuated his intense expression. I wasn't surprised they were still showing his eyes instead of the golden orbs from the comic. It was a dumb move to take away an actor's biggest tool, and anyone who could have won the role of Flying Freeman would have made damn sure of it in their contract.

Flying Freeman dove with a two-footed kick, which Bill O'Wrongs blocked by crossing his fighting sticks. It was the absolute dumbest way to defend such a massive attack, but it looked great. Flying Freeman drifted back with a beat of his wings and pointed at his foe.

This was where it would cut to a close-up hero shot—complete with a one-liner—in the finished film. But right now, the sausage was getting made, and we sat through twelve more takes of Flying Freeman's entrance. Ray's drones swept the set, vacuuming up the not-actually glass and installing the next doomed skylight.

Once the director got what she wanted, they moved on to shooting the rest of the fight scene. There had never been anything like it on film. Flying Freeman kept to the air, attacking Bill O'Wrongs from every angle. This sort of thing was normally done with computer graphics, but Ray had developed some new version of wirework. A technique which allowed the cameras to zoom, pan, and track to show that the actors were doing their own stunts. I could only make out the wires when one of the players was off their mark. They were woven into a network, like a three-dimensional spiderweb. Ray was playing puppet master via drones.

Bill O'Wrongs's scrolls were revealed to be chain whips—a little on the nose when fighting a Black hero birthed during the civil rights movement. But it was sure to generate an online debate, and there was no marketing like free marketing. I was blown away by the actor's skill in manipulating a pair of the most complex weapons in martial arts. Until I realized the whips were also tethered to the drones.

After the second meal break, the director made the decision to push forward to the ending sequence. The announcement caused some grumbles and groans, but she reminded everyone they had fallen behind schedule. Ray winced at her comment, which told me he had something to do with the shooting problems. I put a pin in it and kept quiet on the set.

The sequence came in two beats. In the first, Flint as Flying Freeman started on one knee, wings sheathed as Bill O'Wrongs rained down the chains with both hands. In a surge of determination, Flying Freeman spread his wings, casting the chains aside. From his crouch, Flint launched into the air, delivering an uppercut that sent both him and Bill O'Wrongs airborne. They ascended at two different speeds, Flying Freeman rising high as Bill O'Wrongs drifted weightless.

As Bill O'Wrongs hovered over the smoking cauldron, Flying Freeman flipped in the air and dove toward him. With a colossal hammering punch, he sent Bill O'Wrongs rocketing toward molten justice.

Usually, this kind of stunt was executed at low speed, then sped up in post. But that technique always showed. The little things added up: the steam drifted too fast, or the capes whipped around like flags in a storm. Small motions became jerky enough to yank the audience into the uncanny valley. Ray had created an effect performed in real time. It had me believing a man could fly.

Bill O'Wrongs plummeted at a rate that would have flagged a radar gun. He started dead center over the cauldron, but the angle was all wrong and he veered toward the lip. I reached out as if I could will what was coming to halt. Bill O'Wrongs clipped the edge of the cauldron. The back of his skull struck the rim, ringing the bowl like a gong. A blink after, he splashed into the faux liquid metal, sending a wave of glowing material into the air, where it cooled into sparks.

Behind me, Ray cursed, once and short. Under his piloting, the drones lifted Bill O'Wrongs out of the cauldron, a limp marionette, and lowered him gently as medical rushed in.

Ray stared into the circle of paramedics, but his thoughts weren't in the present. The paramedics went through the motions, administering CPR until an ambulance arrived. I caught a glimpse of an EMT trying to straighten Bill O'Wrongs's airway. I'd seen Pez dispensers with straighter alignments. It wasn't the first death I had witnessed. I didn't take it any better this time than the others.

The call came to clear the soundstage. Ray didn't budge. Almost imperceptively, he started shaking his head and didn't stop. An inch left, an inch right. He went back to his bank of monitors and loaded what looked like diagnostics.

"This was no accident, Ken. I don't make mistakes like this. Not now, not ever."

Every reply that came to mind, every consolation I considered, fell short, so I kept them to myself.

"I'm not responsible for this. I want you to prove it. I don't care what it costs or how long it takes."

Ray's gadgets had saved my skin ten times over. He never so much as asked for a penny. If the man needed me to tilt at his windmills, so be it.

"This one's on me, old buddy."

Before Ray could argue, security swept us off set. We had joined the pileup being funneled toward the doors, when I spied someone who belonged in an entirely different universe.

"Is that Foxman?"

Ray tilted his head, trying to get line of sight through the chaos. "Might be Flying Freeman's stand-in."

"Nope. Different capes." I started shoving a path toward the door. Being a detective meant noticing things that were out of place. Foxman didn't belong in this universe.

Or on this set.

I forced my way out of the exit into a packed mob. The chatter among the crew was rapidly drawing attention. Running from the scene would only draw more, so I walked with purpose, a guy late for his afternoon roundtable. Actor that I was, it didn't fool anyone. I raised my badge like a torch to ward off security. There was a lot of ground to cover with a throng of people in it, but it was hard to miss a guy dressed as a fox.

I finally broke free of the crowd and gave pursuit. Three guards tried to stop me to check my lanyard but not hard enough to cause a scuffle. I came around a corner to spot Foxman fifty feet away, taking a selfie with a fan. As the taller guy, he was holding the phone. His cape was wrong. It had four scallops instead of five, and his boots were brown when they should have been gray.

I drew the Quarreler—a fictional nonlethal pistol Ray had made real—and attempted to creep closer. I was inside effective range for the taser darts, but Foxman was cuddled up to a civilian and his cape looked sturdy enough to afford some protection. Foxman caught me out of the corner of his eye.

He was good. He dropped the phone and took out the fan with an elbow in the same motion as he spun toward me. I sent two shots center of mass.

Foxman swept up his cape, soaking both darts. When he completed his spin, he extended an arm toward me. His fluted metallic gauntlet sported twin openings reminiscent of a double-barreled shotgun.

I threw my arm over my face. Twin impacts slammed into my forearm and ribs. As I reeled, Foxman aimed his gauntlet at the ground between us.

Smoke exploded all around me. I forged ahead toward Foxman and clear air. I held my breath, but the cloud attacked my sinuses. My legs stopped working. I broke through on pure momentum only to wipe out on the pavement.

My airway started to close up. I went blind. The sun on my skin felt like a nuclear blast. I tried to call for help, but you need to be able to breathe to talk.

Foxman had taken me down without breaking a sweat. How could I have been so stupid? I forgot about his gadget gauntlet and now I was going to die like some two-bit villain.

2

MY BLOOD ROCKETED through my veins as my airway blew open. The world exploded from a pinprick to wide-angle. I had never been so happy to see Ray's face. He slipped glasses over my eyes and the world became the sepia of faded newsprint.

"Keep these on. Too much light could mean permanent damage." Ray yanked me to my feet. "We gotta go."

I was the mix of alert and exhausted only chemistry could create. "Someone needs to remind Foxman about his code against killing. What would his parents think?"

Ray kept his voice low. "We can banter back in the RV."

Not knowing where my volume was, I nodded. My eyelids felt like sandpaper against my corneas. I was expecting the panel van Ray used to outfit me for the climax of my first case, but he had gone giant-sized for the studio shoot. How the RV maneuvered through the cramped alleys between the soundstages was beyond me. Knowing Ray, it was secretly a hovercraft.

When he got close, a hidden door on the side of the RV slid open.

"Why not use the actual doors?" I asked.

"Because people try to break in through actual doors. You could use those façades for target practice, and we wouldn't hear a thing inside."

Ray preceded me through a hidden hatch thick enough to repel a howitzer. The outer door gave me a hot second to clear my fingers before it ratcheted back into place. Once we were nestled together in the airlock of the foyer, the inner door unlatched to admit us. Maybe Ray was overdoing it. Maybe not. No one locked away their secrets like a man who could build his own vaults.

The next chamber was a control center with a mosaic of monitors on one side and a tinkerer's workshop on the other. A spectrum of textured Technicolor fabrics was laid out on the surgical-grade table. Ray had been making costumes. His daughter commanded my attention before I could further take in the scene.

Elaine was half-Ray, half-mystery. She looked twenty-five, but nothing and no one was as they first appeared in This Town, myself included. She could have patented the clip she'd invented to bundle all that hair, blacker than space while shining like the stars. Her eyes, cinnamon and sparkling with mischief, came from Ray. Her chair belonged on the bridge of a ship on a five-year mission to explore strange new worlds.

Elaine glided toward me, her chair appearing to float on the air. "What's happening, hot stuff? Swooning over me already?"

I tapped my smart watch. "Good looking out. You saved my life back there."

Ray pushed a tumbler of liquid as cold and clear as ice into my hand. "I'll get something to take the edge off that skin irritation, hold on."

"Skip that and tell me what's going on." The glass trembled as I raised it. "Does this have any sugar in it?"

"Don't worry, big guy, we know how you like it," Elaine said.

Ray attached a canister with a coded label to an airbrush and removed my loaner sunglasses. “Open your eyes and shut your trap.”

A soft mist bathed my eyeballs. The relief was as immediate as every commercial promised their remedy would be. I took a drink. Whatever was in the glass turned my throat from a chimney to a waterslide. I drank some more. Ray guided me through the RV’s workshop area into a small sitting room and eased me into a chair. I shifted to keep the pressure off the side where I’d been hit.

“Only one seat,” I said.

“It’s okay, I brought my own,” Elaine replied as she floated in behind us.

Ray checked my vitals as if I were powered by an internal combustion engine.

“Ow. Are you a licensed medical professional?”

“I told you before, Ken. I’m a licensed everything.”

Breathing became my main focus. Thinking would have to come later. “In that case, I have no allergies to report.”

“Everyone is allergic to what you inhaled. Best part is, should there be a need to perform your autopsy, the cause of death would appear to be a reaction.”

At the time, I didn’t find it strange Ray wasn’t surprised I had encountered a fully functional Foxman. As I said, thinking came later. Shedding my armored blazer was as much as I could manage. There was a reason why it hurt so much on the one side. I had a souvenir stuck in my jacket: a fanged wheel, fatter in the middle, tapering to four scalloped points. When I moved to dislodge it, Ray tore the blazer out of my hands.

“Might be rigged. I’m going to look at it in the lab.”

Elaine stayed to keep me company. “Was that a Chinese Star?”

I immediately regretted nodding. My brain was a balloon bouncing around in my skull. “Shuriken. A wheel-style one. Not sure how those things got stuck with the Chinese label. They hail from Japan.”

"Ninjas use them." Elaine was getting excited. Ray enjoyed living vicariously through someone dumb enough to run into a poison cloud. It looked like the apple didn't fall far from the tree.

"Maybe." I didn't know much, but I knew martial arts. It was up for debate if ninjas were ever even a thing. If they were, they weren't called ninjas. That label gained steam the eighties. "The guy behind Foxman's cowl knew his stuff."

Sitting wasn't getting me anywhere. I eased to my feet and stretched out to evaluate my condition.

Elaine leaned in. "How do you know?"

"This for-real Foxman did everything right. When he stopped to take that selfie, he turned to watch his backtrail. On spotting me, he cleared the fanboy, in case the guy was part of the ambush."

I started flowing through techniques, closer to tai chi than kata. I wasn't trying to show off. It brought me back to baseline, physically and mentally, regulating my breathing while testing my equilibrium. Before dropping out of high school, I had dated a cheerleader who did the same thing, miming internalized routines while we loitered in her kitchen.

"He was smooth. His defense flowed immediately into offense. And professional. His objective was to escape. He didn't get caught up in the moment or take my ambush personally."

Elaine's chair also served as a technological battle station. She listened to me while working at the touchpad built into her left armrest, directing us back toward the workshop with a glance. Ray was on the analog side of the space, studying the projectile embedded in my jacket.

Elaine turned toward the computers as the monitors awoke. Footage of the fatal incident was frozen on display. "We're queued up, Dad."

Ray locked eyes with me. "What we're about to show you, you can't mention to anyone. If the cops saw it, they would open a file and I would get sued for a billion dollars."

Before becoming sleuth to the stars, I had spent five years working in their homes, conducting an all-inclusive action-star master class—body sculpting and stage fighting with a healthy dose of What Not to Do, drawn from personal experience. Not once had a sliver of anything I witnessed hit the tabloids. Ray knew this and still felt the need to voice a disclaimer.

I did my best to not take it personally. "This where you hand me a pen that uses my blood for ink?"

"Ken's a stand-up guy, Dad," Elaine said.

I set my fists against my hips. "Truth, justice, and the American way."

"You're right, you're right," Ray said. "And there ain't no other way to show you this wasn't my fault. It was sabotage, plain and simple."

"Your word is all the proof I'll ever need."

Ray's jaw tightened, which was as close to apologetic as I had ever seen him.

"Start with the medium angles, Elaine," he said.

The monitors swapped windows to show a half dozen views of the soundstage, all from above. The footage was more closed circuit than cinematic. But unlike security cameras, the shots weren't from a static angle: they panned, swept, and zoomed.

"There are cameras in your drones?"

Ray nodded. "I record my own footage for later study. Always have, one way or another."

Which was a major breach of contract. If the studios found out Ray had been filming illegally on every production he had ever worked on, he was looking at hundreds of lawsuits.

"Don't worry. I'll die before I talk."

We watched the god's-eye footage, ten times over. Knowing what was coming didn't make it easy. None of us caught anything until Bill O'Wrongs was six feet from the afterlife.

"There," Ray pointed at the edge of the screen. "That's not one of mine."

I could make out maybe three inches of another drone, blurry at the edge of the screen. "I'm not doubting you, but how do you know?"

"I haven't used hex bolts going on five years."

"Let's go through the footage again," I said.

This time I focused on the background, particularly the crew, looking for anyone out of place. Ideally, someone holding a remote control.

In the shadows next to the entrance, I caught the edge of a cape. "Pause it."

"Looks like Flying Freeman's double," Elaine said.

"Flying Freeman has a winged cape. That's a scalloped cape," I replied. "Foxman snuck on set prior to the big finish. He wasn't drawn in by the hubbub."

Elaine turned from the screens toward me. "But Foxman isn't in the same cinematic universe as Flyman Freeman."

"Yep. Flying Freeman is a Tachi Productions property. Foxman plays for the rival team. Is Duquesne Studios filming nearby?"

"Yeah," Ray confirmed. "Real close. Which is nice, with Elaine and me switching back and forth."

"Maybe we can find more footage of this faux Foxman. There are cameras everywhere on the backlot."

Including the cameras carried by everyone in This Town, all the time. Pivoting from the screens toward Ray's bench made my head rumble. "Foxman snapped a selfie with that fan he took out. I need my blazer back."

It wasn't only for protection. The jacket also concealed a harness strapped on underneath. Along with the holster for the Quarreler, I had matching nonlethal grenades and other tools of the trade. Handy but conspicuous stuff.

Ray turned his attention to my damaged jacket. I had never seen him at work. He went from a vibrating stress-engine to a precision timepiece, extracting the shuriken as if he were performing an operation. The projectile was beautifully forged, with beveled edges on each curved blade. “Give me a minute to seal up the punctures, or the gel layer will balloon out.”

Elaine juggled tasks on three screens simultaneously. “If that fan got dropped as bad as you said he did, maybe someone called for medical help.”

Through a celebrity gossip feed, Elaine discovered an ambulance had indeed shuttled a man from the studio lot to the nearest hospital in the matching time frame.

The room started tilting. I grabbed the door frame for support. “Coat or no coat, I gotta go now. I’m not the only one who’s going to be chasing that bus.”

Ray grumbled through a quick-and-dirty patch job on my jacket. I ripped it out of his hands and headed to my vehicle as fast as my shaky legs would carry me.

Fortunately, my ride happened to be a motorcycle. It was also the White Stag, one of the most famous fictional vehicles of all time. This particular model was a living piece of cinematic history, gifted to me by way of an apology. Everywhere I went, the bike drew its fair share of attention.

But sighting me wasn’t enough. People needed to take a picture to prove it on social media, which led to them swerving constantly in my direction. Unending vigilance was required on my part to prevent being run off the road. I sheltered next to an empty passenger bus that was going my way. This phenomenon also meant my up-to-the-minute whereabouts had become public knowledge.

Clearing myself of two high-profile murders had shifted me from “has-been” to “is-a-thing.”

When it came to Ray and Elaine, my Bluetooth was always open. "Any way to figure out what room this guy is in?"

Elaine replied for my ears only. "Hospital systems are closed."

"Then I am forced to employ my irresistible charm."

My irresistible charm and a hundred bucks got me the fanboy's location. The security guard I bribed must not have liked blondes. In fact, a non-blonde had beat me there: the woman from the Dave King showdown who'd known I wasn't a lawyer. Foxman's copyright holders had sent their best to put out the fire.

She was wearing a cream jacket-skirt combination which cost more than my mortgage payment. Currently, the jacket was draped over her arm. By the look of her neck, shoulders, and calves, she fought a daily battle against her curves. Her dark satin hair was twisted into an impenetrable labyrinth. She was sitting on the end of the hospital bed, indicating an area on a leather-wrapped tablet.

"So, sign here and here and we can issue payment." Her voice was perfect.

Casual and filled with promise.

I butted in before it was too late. "Nondisclosure agreement?"

Either the woman was expecting me or she was flawless at faking she had foreseen my arrival. "Good to see you, Mr. Allen. I was hoping we'd get a chance to talk."

"You have one for me in there?"

"Duquesne Studios is still interested in acquiring the rights to your life story. I'm fully authorized to negotiate from our prior, generous offer." The woman extended her hand. "Zaina Preeti."

I gave in and shook her hand. People always took my dislike for the practice the wrong way. I kept it light, as if I were taking something hazardous from her. Her skin was hot. Guess all that radiance had to come from somewhere. Good thing I was wearing dark glasses.

I looked past her to the fan that faux-Foxman had elbowed into unconsciousness. His medical treatment included shaving the back of his head. He was lucky to be alive. Pavement was one of America's deadliest weapons.

"She's offering to buy the exclusive rights to your story? How much?" I asked.

Preeti answered for him. "The amount is confidential."

It was an old hush-money trick: Buy the rights to bury the story. And deductible as a business expense, like every other dodge the studios used. I moved to the other side of the bed so when the fan was looking at me, he wasn't also looking at Zaina. She would win that contest every time.

"I know an entertainment lawyer who handles the A-list. She could look over this contract for you. Make sure your story fetches what it's worth."

Zaina jumped in before Fanboy could think about it. "Once you involve representation, any further fraternization would be strictly forbidden."

I had to snap my fingers to get his attention. "You couldn't have hit your head hard enough to believe she's actually into you. The studio wants to pay you off. Fine with me. Go for it, but this is your chance to milk every dollar you can get."

Fanboy turned inward. The exploration didn't last long.

"I need to think about this," he decided.

Preeti betrayed nothing behind her veil. She wrote on the back of a business card with the kind of pen that required refills. "This is my personal number. I don't mind late-night chats."

As Preeti turned to leave, her eyes swept across mine to inform me I was on her radar. I shut the door behind her.

"Okay, before I give my lawyer a call, we need to know what we are working with. How did those pictures turn out?"

"Uhhh . . ."

His face told me everything I needed to know. "What happened to them?"

Fanboy dug his phone out from where he had stashed it under his leg. The screen was dead. "I think it broke when I dropped it."

I needed that phone. I decided to borrow a page from Zaina Preeti's playbook and sat on the bed. "I have a tech guy. See this watch? He built it."

It was a lie, but one Ray would have wanted me to tell. Elaine was his closest guarded secret. It took Ray eighteen years to tell me he had a daughter, and only then because he had no choice. Sitting had pushed my blazer open enough to give Fanboy a look at the pistol slung under my arm.

"Is that a Quarreler?" Recognition smacked the fan across the face. "Wait, you're that Jove Brand guy!"

"Guilty as charged."

"Oh man, I saw a post about you. You're like, a detective now."

"That's right." I did my best to nod the way a competent investigator would. Being thought of as a detective was magnitudes better than being remembered as the worst portrayal of Jove Brand, superspy, ever featured on film.

Fanboy started to get excited all over again. "Is this part of some case?"

Best to let him reach his own conclusions. "I'm not allowed to discuss the details. Speaking of details, what happened before I got there?"

"Not much. I thought that Foxman was part of the cast. Like a stunt guy. He caught me filming and asked if I wanted a selfie. How much do you think my story is worth?"

"That depends on if we can recover those photos."

I handed him one of the special cards Ray made for me. They were fancy things, able to act as flash drives. They were also tagged and bugged. If Fanboy ever plugged the thing in, Elaine was going to run wild all over his devices. "Get a new phone. Text me, and I'll get this back to you as soon as possible."

When I tried to tug the phone out of his grip, Fanboy locked down. He didn't know who to trust. He rubbed his head, wincing.

"Look, man, it's not like you can take it to the Apple Store. You heard Preeti. Last year, I had a chance to sell out and sell out big. I didn't take it. I'm not one of them."

Fanboy nodded, which made him dizzy enough to shake his head. His eyes rolled like his skull was a slot machine.

"The guy that did this to you almost killed me too. If I can find him, I'm going to even the score. For both of us."

That made up Fanboy's mind. "Okay, dude, but on one condition."

"Name it."

"When I get my new phone, we take a ton of pics together. And I get to post them."

When I got back to the parking structure, Special Investigator Ava Stern was leaning against my bike. Our dynamic during my inaugural adventure had been me failing to convince her I wasn't a murderer, and her failing to convince me to stay out of her way. As the only law-enforcement professional present during the thrilling climax, all the medals were pinned on her. It must have been hell getting Stern to hold still for it.

"What are you doing here, Allen?" Stern, unconcerned with concealing her pistol, was wearing a blouse a few ruffles from a baby tee and slacks fit for free climbing. She'd been working out but knew her body and had stopped short of creating harsh angles. Her copper hair was up in the type of gold coil queens employed in fantasy films.

"You chopped your hair," I said. "Not too much though. Looks good."

"It was getting in the way. You down here playing pretend?"

"We are in the land of make-believe."

Stern didn't like the way that tasted. "Your pusher isn't in any trouble. You're redder than usual, Allen. Haven't you ever heard of sunscreen?"

Leave it to Stern to figure out who had supplied all my gadgets. There was a reason why she was allowed to play lone gun: the woman got results.

"They didn't have my brand in Africa. Did you know lions kill a hundred people a year? It doesn't sound like a lot, but that's twice what lightning does, and lightning really gets around."

"Yet here you are. How come fortune never smiles on me?" Stern took a slow circle around the White Stag.

"Is everything in order, Officer?"

Stern shifted her attention back to me. Every time she did, I felt like I'd won a prize. "Somehow this prop you galivant around on is street legal. And state police are troopers."

"Ain't that the truth."

I knew the White Stag would pass muster. Back in the mid-1970s, Ray had built it for a Jove Brand movie, and he prided himself on achieving both form and function. Stern blocking my bike maybe counted as detaining me. Looking back, I don't think we had ever had a conversation that wasn't also an interrogation.

"Who did Duquesne Studios send?"

"Zaina Preeti."

Stern had converted her cigarette case into a nicotine gum holder. I wondered how much credit I could take for her quitting smoking.

"Good," she said. "Let her handle the housekeeping. Some asshole cosplayer punches a guy, and I have to drop my real case for fluff."

I relaxed a degree. Stern didn't know the Foxman impersonator was present at Bill O'Wrongs's demise. So far, his death was still an accident. If she got involved, she wouldn't display the same bias I did toward Ray. "Not enjoying the spotlight?"

Stern blew a smokeless exhale. “Your case got a lot of airtime. Now anything left of weird gets tossed on my desk. Everyone at headquarters has started calling me ‘X-Files.’”

“It’s the red hair.”

“What I have is a real case no one cares about that I can’t pursue because I’m on Ken Allen detail.”

“It really hurts, you wishing we had never met.”

“Every day and most nights.” Stern stopped leaning against my bike. She was the perfect height. Her eyes were ocean green. The gum made her breath chilly. “You look like hell, Allen. What happened to your jacket?”

I fought the urge to button my coat. Stern had never gotten a peak at the rig concealed underneath. Everything she knew about my gadgets was from secondhand accounts, like when she rounded up a mercenary company hired to discourage my inquires. According to Ray, everything in my loadout was legal. The only time the Quarreler possessed lethal potential had been when Ray chose the ammunition himself.

Fortunately, Stern kicked that pistol off a cliff and saved me from a choice I never wanted to make.

“I was the victim of an animal attack. This Town crawls.”

Stern didn’t hit me as she stepped past. Striking me would have been an abuse of authority. She just stretched her elbow into my ribs, real sudden-like. I didn’t feel it much, but not because I’m so tough.

“What’s that jacket made out of, Allen?”

“Send me your size. I’ll get you one for Chanukah.”

Stern was impressed but covered up quick. “How’d you figure me out?”

“That sweep you hit on me last spring was slick. You didn’t learn Krav Maga in a strip mall. I’d wager you put in your time.”

“It’s nothing I advertise. You never know how people are going to react.” Stern threw out the next three things she wanted to say. “My name's a tell but I didn't change it. A lot of us do, and not just in This Town."

"I like your name." I thought it and said it at the same time.

"I have actual crimes to solve. Good-bye, Allen."

I climbed into the saddle and unlocked my helmet. "If you need me, all you have to do is whistle. You know how to whistle, don't you?"

Stern didn't bother to turn around. "Yeah. You blow, Allen."

Ray was really choking up on the leash. His RV was waiting for me outside the parking structure. On the bright side, him breathing down my neck saved time playing catch-up. He snatched Fanboy's phone out of my hand and whisked it back to his workbench. Elaine was working on something that took at least four monitors. So much for being the center of attention.

"As a henchman, should I be doing push-ups or something?"

Elaine didn't look away from her multitasking. From what I could tell, she had a side gig as an air traffic controller. "I'm sure Stern will appreciate you keeping it tight."

The temperature in the RV dropped a degree. Any reply was probably wrong, so I let it go. In my book, Elaine was five stars in every category: talented, empathetic, funny, and gorgeous. She was also absolutely off limits. Ray guarded her like a dragon's hoard. Her chair might have played a part in that.

Ray rolled his stool over to Elaine. "I'm not getting anything off this phone."

Elaine plugged the device directly into her chair. It took her thirty seconds to reach a conclusion. "It's bricked."

"There isn't a scratch on the damn thing."

"My guess is a localized EMP, like the one we built for Ken's place."

I had an idea about that. “Maybe our fake Foxman did it. He caught Fanboy filming him.”

“Why not smash his phone then?” Elaine asked.

“My guess is he’s trying to stay under the radar. Foxman didn’t leap into action until he scoped me closing in. Fanboy also mentioned Foxman was the one who proposed taking the selfie. It gave him a reason to fry the phone without drawing attention.”

Ray was a stress cleaner. He started straightening up his workspace. “So where does that leave us? We got no way to prove Bill O’Wrongs’s death isn’t on me.”

I decided against a reassuring hand. Ray wasn’t the touchy-feely type. “Hey, don’t worry. We’re only getting started, and no one is pointing fingers yet.”

“It was my stunt, Ken. Not only did I design it, I was at the wheel when a man died. It’s only a matter of time.”

Elaine’s screen flashed with a call alert. Ray took it through his Bluetooth, so I only heard his end of the conversation, which amounted to, “I’ll be right there.” When the call ended, Ray put his head in his hands.

“That was Duquesne Studios. One of my stunts went wrong. Foxman is dead.”

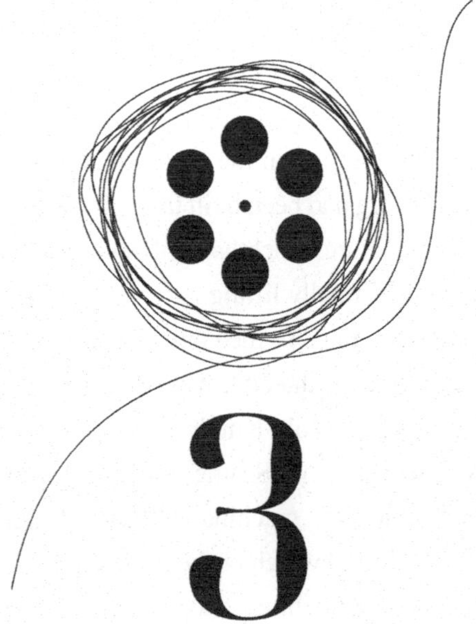

3

THE REMAINS OF the Foxcar kindled inside a shroud of smoke. Emergency services had to let the fire run its course. The heat was so intense no one could get within fifty feet of the wreckage. Rocket fuel burned hot. I eavesdropped as Ray talked to the crew. It wasn't an easy conversation to overhear.

"You could hear Mark screaming," said one crew member.

"Being strapped in like that was supposed to keep him safe," said another.

"He shouldn't have been driving the damn thing to start with."

Mark Caldwell was dead. The method portrayal of Foxman that rocketed him to the top of the A-list had claimed his life. I told myself that he probably didn't feel anything. That the smoke got him first. I also told myself I couldn't smell him roasting through the smoldering rubber and steel. In a space of a day, a hero had followed a villain to the grave. I turned in a slow circle, taking in the scene, scanning for any out-of-place extras or errant drones. This was as close to Knight

City as you were going to get in the real world. Powered by coastal storms, the sleepless berg had been built to draw lightning, with industrial age Gothic architecture which had only ever existed in the pulps.

At least the fog was finally lifting.

The way it was explained in the comics, coastal doldrums locked a permanent cold front over the city, while the west wind delivered a constant warm draft. As a result, Knight City was blanketed in neverending fog. It was definitely not Seattle, for legal reasons.

Here, on the backlot, fog machines of Ray's design provided the proper mood: a light shroud which broke into tendrils and wisps without blocking the shot, slightly blued and nonreflective, which was crucial considering the amount of light required for filming.

I got nowhere with my surveillance. Even if I knew who belonged and who didn't, fires had a way of drawing a crowd. When Ray finished blowing the crew's houses down, he came back huffing and puffing.

"They think it was a backup in the rocket boosters, but that's impossible. I built that car from the frame up. The afterburner is a closed system. So is the cockpit, for that matter. I'm gonna get a look at the dailies."

I followed in Ray's wake as he bullied his way to the monitors. He ignored the director's protests and started a playback. Knowing this would be our only chance at the footage before it was sealed in a vault protected by a division of lawyers, I pointed my video watch at the screen under the guise of cupping my chin in thought.

The scene started with a chase shot: Foxman turning away from the camera and running toward his ride so we could see Mark Caldwell was actually in the costume. It took three takes for Caldwell to vault into the cockpit. It wasn't just the cape. The costume had to weigh thirty pounds.

The cockpit locked into place without a hitch as the tracking shot swung behind to frame the retro-rockets. The Foxcar blasted off, stayed straight for about a hundred feet, then careened into a Victorian façade. The Foxcar didn't explode. It turned into an oven.

"No soap," Ray said. "The cockpit has a manual release in case the pneumatics fail. Mark should have been able to get out."

"Was he belted in?"

"I'll find out when I get this heap back to the compound."

A familiar voice chimed in behind us. "It goes to the lab first."

I spun around to find Ava Stern peeking over our shoulders. "This wasn't what I meant by morning, noon, and night, Special Investigator."

"You should be careful what you wish for, Allen."

Behind Stern, the studio personnel and local law enforcement were engaging in a turf war. Security special forces parted the mass to admit the suits. Zaina Preeti led the charge, backing Stern off with a cease and desist. "Could you please provide the documentation that gives you cause to seize this vehicle?"

Stern and Preeti were the same height, which put their game of "don't blink" on equal footing.

"The State of California needs to determine if foul play was involved."

"You've seen the footage. It appears to be either operator error or equipment failure."

They weren't exactly touching noses, but it reminded me to pick up some breath mints.

"I guess I'll just have to come back with a warrant."

"No need to guess, Special Investigator. We at Duquesne Studios will await the proper paperwork."

Stern didn't break eye contact. "Want to walk me out, Allen?"

"Sure."

I decided offering my arm would have constituted a conflict of interest. Preeti turned from us like a lioness who already had a full belly. When we were back on the cop side of the accident scene, Stern took the lead. She kept her voice low.

“This is the second time today an incident with Foxman came across my desk, and both times you’re at the scene. What gives, Allen?”

“I like you thinking I have a clue. You’re going to respect me yet.”

Stern shot me the same look she maintained last spring when she was pretty sure I had killed two people.

“Not believing me is your problem,” I said. “I’ve always told you the truth.”

Stern went for her gum. “But not the whole truth.”

“Good job, putting down the pack.”

“It helped me add muscle. In anticipation of our rematch.”

I backed toward the set with my hands up. “We’re on the same side this time. Promise.”

Preeti passed me on my way back to Ray. Ray didn’t look too happy, but who ever did, after talking with a lawyer?

“I gotta hold off until the investigation wraps.” Ray rubbed his head. “They’re going to fight the cops every inch of the way, but the whole inquiry will be documented. Which means ten engineers will get an intimate look at my designs.”

“Aren’t they patented?”

Ray rolled his eyes. “So, my life becomes me paying lawyers to prove I’m getting ripped off. If I’m ripped off in a country that even cares. Or if it’s not the government itself doing the ripping.”

“What would the government want with the Foxcar?”

“For military use.” Ray shook his head at the thought. “They’d love an excuse to take a run at my designs. They’ve been courting me for fifty years, but I’ve never wanted to make weapons.”

I straightened my cuffs. “Except for me.”

“You don’t count. I know you’re a good guy.”

My bulletproof blazer weighted heavily. It was getting on dark. Two people were dead, and I had almost joined them.

“I need food and sleep. We’ll get at this fresh tomorrow.”

Motorcycles are less fun when it's dark and you're tired. Fortunately, in the era of phone-distracted drivers, I was guaranteed an adrenaline rush from a near collision every fifteen minutes. My heart rate was returning to resting levels when I pulled into the spot outside my two-story office/condo.

Overlooking the strip, the building's exteriors were vintage This Town. The interiors were freshly remodeled under Ray's supervision, who assured me none of the security systems violated California's booby-trap prohibitions.

Dean Calabria was waiting on my doorstep, sitting on a backpack that would have seen him across the Pacific Crest Trail. He half shielded his eyes, half waved as I killed my headlight.

"Welcome home."

Dean went to offer his hand, changed his mind, and stashed it in his pocket instead. Either it was my imagination, or the kid had grown in the three months since I'd last seen him, when I'd saved his life and cost him a few billion dollars.

"Sorry I didn't call first. I, uh, didn't know what to say."

Neither did I. Half of Dean's DNA was mine. I knew it, and he knew it, but neither of us had the guts to say it out loud. In my defense, I'd only known for a few months, around the time I first met him and consulted my romantic history. He'd had a couple of years to prepare, after watching me star in one of his family's past productions on home video and doing some math of his own.

"Hope you don't need a lift to the airport. I didn't opt for a sidecar."

Dean cleared his throat. His voice had deepened. An emergency tracheotomy would do that. In my defense, it was my first. "I was hoping to stay with you, actually."

My life started flashing before my eyes.

In addition to being a power player in the industry, Dean's mother was fully capable of committing murder.

"Where are you supposed to be, Dean?"

"On my first camping trip."

There was no way Dean's mother didn't have him LoJacked. I hadn't spotted any security, but I assumed that was because they were competent.

I used my fingerprint to unlock the door panel, trying to decide the right play. This meant a lot to the kid. Was I going to mess him up more by saying no or saying yes? Dean hovered in the doorway while I took my time disarming everything and bringing up the lights.

"All right, kid. You'll have to take the couch. I don't have a spare room."

Dean hopped through the doorway off his right foot, same as me. "Couch is cool with me. I brought a sleeping bag."

Having grown up in a cliffside fortress that would have kept the Mongols out, Dean wasn't used to closing doors. I shut it behind him. He followed me upstairs, where I stored my gear and took stock of what munitions Ray would need to refill. While it felt good to shed my detective trappings, I noticed the burden less and less every day.

"Cool office," Dean said. "Wait, is that Keeper's desk?"

"It came with the place." Dean didn't seem to know the last guy who lived here had been murdered, or that said individual bought and furnished the place by blackmailing Dean's mother.

I led him back down the stairs, into a family room I mainly used to store all the movies I would never get around to watching. Dean dropped his rucksack at the end of a shabby couch a decade past its useful life.

I thought I had made peace with my lifestyle, but watching Dean judge my nest made me self-conscious. A shabby couch in a tiny condo, the result of a wastrel life whose highlight was headlining the film that anchored the darkest chapter in his family history. Whatever stories Dean had told himself about my choices were sure to clash with the drapes.

"This is great," Dean said.

"There's a half bath next to the foyer. You'll have to shower upstairs."

Dean looked at me like his place didn't have running water. "Okay."

"Kitchen through the door next to the half bath. You might have to hit the market. I don't eat carbs."

Dean gave his bag a kick. "I packed food."

We shared an awkward silence. None of my gears would turn. "I'm going to get cleaned up and hit the sack. Foxman almost killed me today. I'm still getting over it."

Dean made the same face I make when someone tells me they are losing weight on the cookie diet. I hauled myself up the stairs and trailed clothes to the master bath. Ray's renovations included a shower that could make slushies or boil eggs. It assaulted me from all sides like a masseuse with no mercy.

It had been a day. My thoughts ran the spectrum, but they swirled together to form a gray paste. I fell into bed face-first and stuck there.

Dean was a morning person, a trait absolutely inherited from his mother, a prototype A that out earned my net worth every day before breakfast. He was in the nook, sitting in the wraparound booth—the closest thing I had to a dining table—gnawing on a meal-replacement bar. I gave him a thumbs-up and slammed sixteen ounces of water.

After I came up for air, I said, "Make sure you drink plenty. Those things are designed to clog up the pipes."

Dean nodded and kept on chewing. I gathered supplies and started tracking my macros. Being on a case meant eating out, and eating out meant gaining weight. Not that that would hurt Dean any. He was still a growing boy.

"You want a smoothie?"

"Sure, and coffee if you're making it."

I'm not sure I approved of Dean drinking coffee with a voter's registration still warm from the press, but it wasn't my place to say so. It had been two decades since I'd lived with anyone, and that had been in temple. Monks were not the talkative type. For as long as Dean had been alive, I had spent the first few hours of my day in silence. Dean tried it out. He lasted two minutes.

"Did you get clawed by something? Your ribs look gnarly."

I talked between pulsing the blender. "It gets hot in Africa. I made the mistake of taking my jacket off. Live and learn."

"Were you on a case?"

"Yep."

Dean got up to take his tumbler from my hand. "But you won't talk about it."

"I can't talk about it." I sipped my smoothie while getting the coffee going. "Part of the deal is keeping people's secrets. The biggest part."

Dean considered that over his glass. "Must be hard."

"I've had practice."

It wasn't meant to be a comment on Dean's family history, but that's how he took it. At least he liked the smoothie. Three gulps and the tumbler was empty. He was watching everything I did.

"You put butter in your coffee?"

Having given my extra travel mug away, I was forced to drink from a measuring cup. "Grass-fed. Evens out the caffeine and helps supplement absorption. But that plus and the smoothie equals breakfast for me."

According to my watch, no messages or voice mails had come in while I slept the morning away. Dean did his best to pretend he liked coffee while I washed our dishes. After some soul-searching, I found a way to get us back into my comfort zone.

"Going to go through a workout, if you want in."

"I'll get changed," Dean said, skipping toward his bag.

There wasn't enough space in the condo, so we went out into the shared atrium usually reserved for sunbathing and smoking pot.

"This is just my daily maintenance check," I told Dean. "When I'm on the job, I need to know how my cylinders are firing."

Dean mimicked me through a series of movements I had refined over the years that were half stretching and half agility training. I slowly added speed and footwork, measuring how much almost dying had cost me. My inhales were shallow, which meant restricted oxygenating. I felt tired and my synapses were sluggish. Physically, I could handle short bursts, but anything sustained was going to total me. Fortunately, so far this job required racing against death rather than jogging alongside it.

Stopping to explain and correct Dean's form doubled the time the routine normally took. My old Sensei to the Stars—not a self-bestowed title—habits died hard.

At conventions, people would always comment on how nice it must be, getting paid to work out with famous people. But when you're teaching, it's about them, not you. Your workouts are on your own time. Between Ray and Dean, keeping sharp was going to be a challenge. And it took a razor's edge to survive playing knight errant.

A voicemail from an unknown number was waiting on my phone. I contained my excitement long enough to suit up. After an internal debate, I loaded concussion fléchettes into the Quarreler. They were intended for hard targets a taser round couldn't breech, faux-Foxman from yesterday being a prime example. Putting one into an unarmored person was rolling the dice.

The voice mail was from Zaina Preeti, requesting a meeting at my earliest convenience. I called back and left a voicemail of my own, telling her my earliest convenience was hers. I came downstairs to find Dean dressed in a light gray blazer, khakis, and shoes made by venerable Italian hands. My first morning playing surrogate parent, and Dean was hoping it was Bring Your Child to Work Day.

"My schedule is booked. I'm waiting on a call, then I'm out the door."

"Thought I'd tag along."

"No go. I almost died from a chemical weapon attack yesterday."

Dean rankled at the suggestion he couldn't handle himself, which he couldn't. The only killer he'd faced off against had collapsed his windpipe without breaking a sweat. I spared his pride by telling him the truth.

"Look, I've managed to fool everyone into thinking I'm somehow qualified for this job. If I show up with an unequipped recent minor whose mother owns a rival film company, it's all over for me."

Dean sucked it up and put his best foot forward. "No problem. Got dinner plans?"

I took two steelhead fillets out of the deep freeze. "Yeah, I'm grilling fish with my houseguest."

That brought Dean's smile back. As I was returning it, a call alert came into my Bluetooth. I flashed him a salute and headed out the door.

Preeti's time was too valuable to waste on salutations. "Can you come to me, Mr. Allen?"

"Yeah. Address?"

The coordinates pinpointed a location inside the same studio backlot from yesterday. Ray and Elaine were listening in, because my GPS set itself. Preferring two-way communication, I called them after Preeti hung up on me. Ray answered with a question.

"What do you think she wants?"

"The lay of my land. She was at the hospital hushing up the assaulted fanboy. She probably checked in on him and found out I squirreled his phone."

This Town was a great spot for a motorcycle. People forget it's basically a desert. The sky half-heartedly coughs up water maybe ten days a year. Schools call a snow day if the thermostat hits forty. But the best part of having a bike is defying the traffic gods.

I slipped through the seams, riding along the dotted line in blatant violation of the time tax imposed on all commuters. Only the turns slowed me down, so I took as few as possible. Movies often cautioned people like me were followed, but I considered myself immune. Any tailers would also have to be on a bike. Or flying.

Imagine my surprise at being blindsided.

I was cruising through an intersection without a care in the world when a gray sedan in the perpendicular pole position at the intersection raced forward from a full stop. I was completely boxed in. There was a Volvo in front of me, a passenger bus walling off my left, and a delivery truck hugging my bumper.

I made the only choice available and throttled hard.

If I had been on a normal bike, they would have had to bury us together, like some kind of cyberpunk centaur. But I was on a vintage White Stag built to be the ultimate superspy ride by Ray Ford himself.

I popped a wheelie into the back bumper of the Volvo, scrambling to time the impact. Having never done it before, I vaulted from the saddle early, which was better than late, all things considered. The momentum sent me skidding off the Volvo's roof headfirst toward the pavement.

I tucked, and hit the concrete forearm first. Ray's tactical jacket saved my skin, but the limb went numb. I completed the roll with the full intention of hopping to my feet, but my legs refused to comply, so I wiped out instead.

The main benefit of expecting the worst was when it actually happened, you were ready to go. I drew the Quarreler as I flipped onto my stomach, looking for a guy in a cape. The driver of the Volvo opened his door right into my helmet.

I yelled for him to get down and spun toward the front of the car, trying to put the engine block between me and foes unknown. The gray sedan reversed in an expert V and disappeared into a lane blocked off for roadwork. Its windshield and windows were heavily tinted. There could have been a single driver or a company of clowns inside.

Figuring not much could come from shooting at a car, I held fire.

The Volvo driver, a guy my age who had made far more sensible life decisions, was inspecting the damage to his rear end. The Stag's side panels had taken the worst of it, furrowing parallel tracks into the trunk lid.

I handed over my card and let him take a photo of my insurance information without apologizing. In This Town apologies could really cost you.

"It's like that jerk was trying to kill you."

It took all the muscle I had to right the Stag back onto his wheels. "Yeah, just like that."

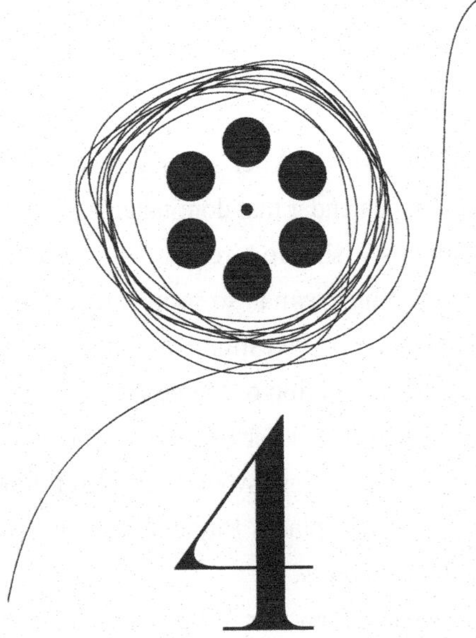

4

I WALKED THE Stag to the side of the road and waited ten minutes for both of us to level out. Ray was calling, but I didn't feel like talking. I drank some water and wondered how I had been marked as a potential problem so quickly. On the fourth try, the Stag started up.

For the remaining twenty minutes of the drive, I worked on my owl impression. My neck was going to be a day-to-day decision. The gate guard made me take off my helmet. Word was out about masked impersonators. My destination turned out to be a storage facility. Preeti was keeping our meeting discreet. The roll-up door was raised enough for me to drive under, if I ducked behind the Stag's antler bars.

The structure was earmarked for vehicle storage, stocked with police cars from every era. Considering the way the day was going, I swung around to face the Stag toward the exit, in the event a quick escape was required.

Zaina Preeti was waiting for me in the ramshackle second-story office. How she managed the steel-grated stairs in heels was a riddle my male mind couldn't solve. After sending a text, she set her phone down on the yellowing calendar that dominated a grease-streaked desk.

"Duquesne Studios wishes to hire you."

"You know, recasting Foxman so soon is really in poor taste."

Preeti didn't crack. "To investigate a pattern of suspicious incidents surrounding the production of the next Good Knights film."

My first instinct was to tell her to get lost. Ray was my priority. I was drafting my quippy response when I realized this would give me access to all the people and places Ray couldn't. When I told her my rates, Preeti raised an eyebrow.

"That's twice what we pay our in-house people."

My shrug was not an apology. "How are they doing so far?"

Preeti didn't blink. "You make a fair argument."

She reached behind the desk to retrieve a laptop bag and a contract as thick as the white pages.

"Be right back. I'm not about to autograph my way into a biopic."

I retrieved a standard agency agreement out of the White Stag's saddleboxes. Preeti reviewed it at superspeed, making amendments by pen.

"Initial these changes and I will sign this."

All her revisions were for clarity. They were so good I decided to make them permanent. When both our signatures were penned, I asked my first question.

"So, what else happened? Two incidents on rival productions doesn't make a pattern."

Preeti separated the screen from her laptop and used it to scan the agreement before answering.

"Burt Taylor suffered an acute injury as a result of a wardrobe malfunction."

"How adorable was it, exactly?"

Preeti stared until my joke was dead. "Either the script will require rewriting, or the part of Good-Man must be recast."

"What else?"

"Lidia Colby is taking time off for maternity leave."

"The Patriette is pregnant? Tell me the Straight Shooter is the father."

If Preeti had a sense of humor, it didn't keep work hours. "The identity of the father is, at this time, unknown. Her ex-husband, current boyfriend, and personal security are all possibles."

Good-Man, Foxman, and the Patriette had been printing money across mass media since Duquesne Studios bought them wholesale in the 1950s. "There's no filming around losing the three biggest heroes in the world."

Preeti studied me for a beat, recalibrating. She had been expecting an argument out of me, a protest that there was no way these unlikely events were connected. Clearly, my life story was not public knowledge.

I decided to explain myself.

"Good-Man's costume malfunction might seem random by itself, but that assault committed by the Foxman cosplayer was more that it seemed. His gear was for real and he knew how to use it. He also happened to be on set at Tachi Productions when Bill O'Wrongs died."

"What was he doing there?"

"That's on my to-do list. You should send the faulty Good-Man suit over to Ray Ford."

Preeti moved to set her hand on the dilapidated desk, then changed her mind. "It was considered, but Mr. Ford designed the costume, as well as the faulty Foxcar. We are still determining if legal avenues will be pursued."

I took a moment to survey the scene. Everything was where it should be in the garage. No drones or idling sedans detected. "If you're right and Duquesne is suffering sabotage, Ray Ford is your strongest ally. Go after him now, and you lose the one person who can prove someone has been throwing wrenches into the gears."

"I'll take it upstairs. How would you explain Ms. Colby's pregnancy?"

"Like I said, our faux-Foxman wasn't some fanboy. He gave me all I could handle. He's probably ex-military, which is a trait a lot of bodyguards share. We should take a close look at the Patriette's security team. She might have stepped into a honeypot."

It sounded like the finest of conspiracy theories, but Preeti absorbed it stoically. She wasn't the type of person who needed to take notes. "I'll get you dossiers. Any other initial thoughts?"

My reason for being here in the first place was to give Ray some peace of mind. Here was my chance. "Yeah. Ray Ford is going to need a close look at the remains of the Foxcar. He sees little details that might give us a direction. Ugandan toggle bolts, European gauge tires, that kind of stuff."

Preeti sat stock-still as she considered. "That may not be possible. The state police want to bring in a forensic engineer. If they determine negligence, Ray Ford is the prime suspect. I doubt they'll allow him access to the evidence."

"Well, they better find someone experienced with the space program. The Foxcar has more in common with a fighter plane than it does a Ferrari."

We shared a silence that signaled the end of our meeting. I tended to let other people break them. There was plenty to do with silence, like observe Preeti and decide if she knew more than she was telling me.

"I'll start taking steps immediately," Preeti said by way of a dismissal.

If she wasn't going to bother with hellos and good-byes, then neither was I. Ray waited until I was clear of the studio lot before calling. I wasn't sure if I was in for a pat on the back or a boot in the ass.

"Nice try, Ken, but they're going to wash their hands of this by hanging me out to dry."

The White Stag coughed, once and hard. Hopefully, it was temporary fallout from tipping over, but the bike was older than I was. When Ray built him, the Stag was ahead of the times. But his prime was a generation behind him.

We had a lot in common.

I felt the need to explain my actions to Ray. "Working for Duquesne Studios gives me license to poke around."

"Smart. Look, I—" Ray took two breaths from his stomach I envied. My lungs were still crackling from the gas attack. I gave him all the time he needed. He never was good with feelings.

A call alert sounded in my ear. I glanced at my watch to see who was stepping in on our moment and did a double-take. "Gotta go, Ray. You'll hear why."

When I switched over, Flint West was already talking.

". . . see what he says. Hey Ken, can you find some time for an old friend?"

Opportunity was knocking. I had gotten inside Duquesne Studios. Here was my chance at a foothold into Tachi Productions. "When can you meet?"

"How about now? I'm home."

"I'm on my way. Forty-five minutes."

A common run-of-the mill right turn felt like cresting on a roller coaster. The whole way to Flint's place, I looked over both shoulders. The drive was closer to an hour. The Stag's periodic cough developed into a chronic condition. Every time the bike lurched, I lurched with him.

When purchasing a home, A-list actors have different priorities than us little people. Who lived in the house prior isn't typically a selling point. Same for who our Neighbors, with a capital N, will be, or exactly how many vehicles will fit in the garage complex.

Keep in mind, all these considerations are for a place they sleep in maybe three months of the year.

But Flint was different. When buying a house, Flint had one main concern:

The view.

Besides being built like Thor with the charisma of Loki, Flint was also an acclaimed artist, though the world would never know.

People are most comfortable when someone is one thing, especially when that one thing brought them fame and riches. It's okay to be beautiful. The world loves beauty. But if you're beautiful and smart, it doesn't sit well.

It strikes the less blessed as unfair.

The same goes for strength. If a man is a physical specimen, that's all he's allowed to be. God already gave you height and six-pack abs. If you were also capable of advanced calculus, prepare to receive some hatred.

There's this idea that each of us only has so many points to invest in ourselves. Someone who is an average five-nine can accept it if they also have a law degree. It's okay if you have a voice for radio if your mug matches. You might never be on a magazine cover but darn it if you aren't one of the funniest people you know.

But when a perfect ten belts out the national anthem before taking the mound in the world series, a certain segment of the population is offended that demigods walk among us. That the chosen are out there, and they aren't one of them.

So, Flint West adopted a secret identity. Using the combined proceeds from professional football, box-office smashes, and auctioned art, Flint bought land in the mountains, hugged up against a national park, and built a palace worthy of Olympus. The only path in without climbing gear was through a tunnel and over drawbridge.

The tunnel always made me nervous. A million or so tons of rock hung suspended over my head. If it changed its mind, I was a goner. The lucky version was a Ken Allen pancake. The unlucky one was buried until his air ran out.

When I came out safe on the other side, I took a breath as deep as my baffled lungs would allow. The Stag did not enjoy the ascent up the mountain. The steep grade required throttle and Flint had not elected for guardrails. Being the sole resident, he also had no need to commission a second lane. Or road signs.

I'd been here plenty of times, and I'm sure the view was breathtaking, but my eyes were locked on the curve of the mountain wall. A corrugated ramp led into the garage cavern. The hollow metallic rumble signaled my arrival. I swung the Stag around and parked as level as possible, wondering if we were taking our final voyage together. Though I had only known him a few months, I loved that bike.

I chose the stairs over the freight elevator. Flint was waiting for me on the first floor, where the great room anchored the kitchen and gym. I'd never seen the levels above, which hosted the bedrooms and his studio.

Flint advanced on me with a headshake and a grin. He went right into a bear hug. "Good to see you. Real good."

I wheezed under the pressure. "You break me, you buy me, pal."

Flint's laugh was an eruption, too loud and too hard to be genuine. That's when I knew he was really hurting.

Flint had three inches on me, which automatically disqualified him from playing costar to nine out of ten leading men. And that was before accounting for his sculpted physique. Even at equal height, he made other men look small. At home, I had never seen him in a shirt. His skin was a deep umber that showed none of his fifty years. While filming, he kept his head shaved to the point it looked waxed.

He looked like a damn superhero, which made him the perfect Flying Freeman.

"Come out on the patio. I made lunch. You still off carbs?"

"On any day that isn't my birthday."

Flint nodded in full understanding. He waited for me to sit first. I angled my chair so I could watch him while also taking in the view.

"We got elk and trout, and a fall salad with walnuts. Everything is from my land, guaranteed sustainable."

We ate in silence. Flint was the most present person I had ever met. He never did two things at once. When he ate, he experienced every bite. The food was last-meal quality. I washed it down with iced green tea flavored with rose hips.

"That's one of your recipes," Flint said as I finished my glass.

"It's served you well."

"Saved my life, believe it."

When Flint hired me, he looked great, but his body was breaking down. Hard work and genetics had gotten him so far, but growing up in poverty, all he knew was fried food and processed sugar. He had been too embarrassed to ask for help, but when I shadowed him on his first location shoot, he took note of everything I ate and drank. Pretty soon, I was shopping for two.

I shrugged it off. "All I did was provide a toolbox."

Flint rolled his eyes. "If you don't take credit for your good deeds, for sure someone else will."

He cleared the table, refilled the tea, and studied the landscape. For the hundredth time, I wondered what he painted. I only knew he had a secret identity, not who that identity was. After a few minutes, Flint started to cry. He wept silently, his chin moving the bare minimum to count as a headshake.

"You want to talk about Bill O'Wrongs?"

Flint nodded.

"You didn't kill him, Flint."

"It was me." Flint picked up his tea glass. Looked at it. Set it back down. "I threw the punch. I improvised, man. It was supposed to be a straight shot, but I threw a hook instead. Thought it would show my arms better."

My head hurt. The elevation wasn't helping my breathing issues. I couldn't clear Flint's conscience without telling him what I knew.

"I keep secrets. You know that."

"Big reason I like you, Ken."

"So, you know when I say I can't talk about something, I mean it."

Flint put a little rock in his nod. "Yeah. Yeah, I do."

I walked around the table to stand in front of Flint. When he was ready, he met my eyes. I spoke firm and clear.

"You didn't kill him, Flint. There is more to this than meets the eye. That's all I can say."

The closest thing Flint had to wrinkles appeared at the corners of his eyes. He searched me out for a while, then rose to throw his arms around me, applying a squeeze I had to tap out of.

"Thank you, Ken. Thank you."

Being from a land that regularly burst into flames made a person sensitive to smoke. A thin trail wafted down from above. There was no way Flint blazed cigars. I didn't want to be intrusive, but the last time I spoke with someone who had a hidden guest, said guest turned to be the killer.

"Who's listening in on us?"

Flint looked like a kid with his hand caught in the cookie jar. "That's my girl. Hey Jaq, come meet Ken!"

Here was a new occurrence. "A girl who's allowed upstairs?"

"Oh, yeah, she's definitely an upstairs girl."

Flint didn't bother to wash away the tracks of his tears. A woman worthy of the highest levels would be well acquainted with his big emotions.

"You're going to like her, Ken. She's a princess."

A twinkle came into Flint's eyes, dispelling the sadness. He left to meet his guest halfway. I looked at the mountains and the trees and the water and worked to inhale the cleanest air I had access to since stepping back into the cloying atmosphere This Town generated.

They stopped to whisper to each other. I didn't strain to listen. Couples' conferences weren't my business. I had a critical weakness when it came to sleuthing: I wasn't much of a snoop. Eavesdropping didn't generate the thrill in me it did in others, and rifling through people's personal property only made me want to wash my hands. I kept my back to them and looked for condors.

"Ken, this is Jaq."

Talking about her, Flint sounded a little star struck, but Jaq was the opposite of what I was expecting. Light-skinned, average height and solidly built, with short, curly hair. Strong featured, Jaq looked like a Babylonian queen whose name was lost to time. Her dark eyes were piercing. She stared at me in naked evaluation.

Flint had introduced Jaq from a distance which allowed for a wave over having to decide between a hug or handshake. Jaq closed the gap, leaning forward to offer her hand. She kept her weight low, moving from her hips. The movement of a dancer. Or a fighter.

"Flint's told me so much about you."

Her husky voice embraced every syllable. Her words were less warming and more warning.

"That makes one of us," I replied.

Flint could no longer contain himself. "Jaq is Dave King's daughter."

Jaq hid her annoyance well. I suppose my reaction would be the same, if every time I was introduced it was as my famous father's child.

"Jimmy Erikson introduced us at a comic con, and since you introduced me to Jimmy, I guess you deserve credit too. It was love at first sight."

Jaq tilted her head upward at Flint. "Except you wouldn't stop talking about my dad."

"Sorry about that, babe," Flint said, wiping the heat in his cheeks away.

Jaq set a hand on Flint's chest, drawing him down with her dark eyes. "You came around, once you wore yourself out."

Flint and Jaq started kissing with building intensity. However long they had been together, they were still enjoying their honeymoon phase. The two of them forgot all about me. I wouldn't label what they were doing as inappropriate, especially in their own home, but it was my cue to make an exit.

"Have to hit the trail."

Neither of them offered a good-bye. I reached out to slap Flint on the shoulder, then changed my mind.

The Stag complained but eventually got rolling. The ride down was easier. It didn't require any acceleration and the brakes worked fine.

Dave King's daughter. What was it like to grow up the child of a legend?

Dave King was a modern mythmaker. In the sixties, he immigrated to America and took the comic world by storm, crafting a universe of heroes alongside Seth Martin, the man who invented superheroes to begin with. When Martin created Good-Man, it was in a different era. A generation later, he and Dave King made heroes who were super while also human. King's style fit the changing landscape perfectly: technicolor and pop-art heavy, infused with impressionistic emotion to match Martin's melodramatic plots.

These days they are fixtures, but at the time, heroes like the Civil Warriors were counterculture, searing social justice into the minds of young Americans and playing a significant role in the hippie revolution.

Flying Freeman was America's first Black superhero, his powers growing in times of great inequality. They toned him down in the nineties, but after 9/11 he rose to demigod status. It was Flint's dream role, playing the hero who had inspired him to strive for success. In a generation where children no longer read comic books, Flint was who they thought of when they imagined Flying Freeman. Now he was courting the royal family.

But Dave King was all but forgotten. It's lost to history, who dreamed up Hercules or Thor. Maybe people wanted to forget. Remembering where our heroes came from means acknowledging they were birthed by mortal hands. If that was true, they would belong to their creator, when in our hearts they belong to us.

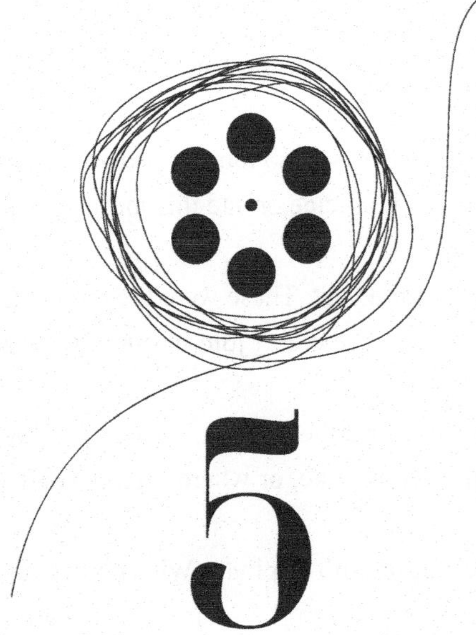

5

MY CELL SERVICE returned with seven voice mail alerts, all from Ray, all the same.

Call me. Now.

I was descending the mountain with deliberation, hand off the throttle and easing the brake. Making a call was within my degree of difficulty.

Ray didn't bother with hello. "We think you're bugged."

"Like a tracking device?" A bead of sweat tobogganed down my spine. The gray sedan that tried to take me out hadn't been tailing me. It had been hunting me.

"There's a second signal coming from your bike. Similar to the one Elaine used for your pencil cameras. Very similar."

Ray's voice drifted. His last thought had been to himself. It would do more good there anyway. Technical knowledge was not my strong suit. All my gadgets might as well have been pulled from stones or hurled from a lake for all I knew about how they worked.

"Probably why it took you so long to notice it," I said. "Someone attempted a vehicular homicide on me this morning. How do I debug myself?"

Ray went mute for a beat. These were the moments when he was consulting Elaine. Why she didn't join in our conversations was lost on me.

"You'll have to bring the Stag in," Ray said. "We don't know what the transmitter looks like, or where it is, beyond somewhere on your bike."

"Well, I guess it doesn't explode. Why bother running me over if you could just blow me up?" Voicing the question provided the answer. "Because then it wouldn't look like an accident. So far, all the acts of sabotage have built-in deniability. Our faux-Foxman was taking a risk when he made a run at me."

I brought the Stag to a halt and took in the vista. If I was bugged, then the bad guys knew where I was. Knocking me off a mountain would appear to be operator error. *Ken Allen, Past His Peak*, the headline would read. Or maybe *Ken Allen, Over the Hill.*

"You gotta bring the bike in," Ray repeated.

"Let me figure out how I'm going to get to you in one piece first."

Try as I might, I failed to devise a clever scheme. My best idea was to park the White Stag and call a cab, which didn't strike me as very heroic. If I was going to scream for help whenever there was trouble, this was the wrong line of work for me.

I had been up and down this mountain at least a hundred times while training Flint. If I was looking to run someone off the edge, where would I do it?

You'd want a sharp turn that gave you enough room to build up ramming speed without going over yourself. You'd want the drop to be sheer. You'd want to be able to wheel around. And you'd want it where no inconvenient hikers in the national park might spot it going down.

There was no such place on Flint's section of the mountain, but the fork onto his private road was the perfect runway. I parked the Stag a quarter-mile away from that junction. Whoever was tracking me knew the Stag's location. Stopping too close to the ambush point would arouse suspicion. I dismounted and closed the gap on foot. Creeping toward the turn, I saw my shadow was preceding me by a good six feet. Right now, my edge was that they didn't know I knew. I hugged the side of the mountain, plotting.

The rock wall had been carved out in strips. I climbed up to a ledge wide enough to balance on and shuffled toward the curve with my back against the wall. It was miserable. The sun beat down, scorching my already burnt skin. Ray's blazer was airtight enough to endure outer space. I used two fingers to withdraw a pencil camera. It didn't want to come out. The same tug that freed it also sent it tumbling from my sweaty fingers.

I brought my knee up to pop the camera back into play and snatched it out of the air. Sweat rolled down my forehead. Easy-peasy. I inched an arm's reach from the curve and angled the camera around the bend. Chances were low it would be spotted. The camera's tip was smaller than an eraser. The camera relayed its view to my video watch. The gray sedan was there, facing the bright blue sky, idling away the moments leading to my doom.

Though the sun was in the driver's face, the tinted windshield eliminated that possible advantage. My foes were safe inside the sedan. I needed to flush them into the open, or at the very least get to their flank.

My heart sank. I could only think of one way to do it.

I went back to the White Stag and removed anything worth saving out of the saddleboxes. For the first time, I sat sidesaddle. I gave the Stag throttle to build some momentum as we sped toward the curve. Everything in me wanted to crank the brakes. Instead, I angled him to negotiate the bend and bailed ship.

I hit the ground running to soak up the momentum. Slowing into a jog, I dispensed a green grenade into my right hand and drew the Quarreler awkwardly same-side with my left. The grenade looked and felt like a rubber ball, but its contents created a cloud of something half tear gas, half ipecac.

When the ghost-ridden Stag crested the bend, the gray sedan burst into view. The driver was a pro. They cut an angle to ensure they caught me full-on. The sedan broadsided the Stag flush. The bike was tossed into the air. I tore my eyes away and focused on my goals.

The sedan's passenger window was sunglass dark. Walking forward, I steadied the Quarreler on my right forearm and fired. The first fléchette detonated. The window spider-webbed but held. The second shot blew out a thumb-sized opening. It would have to do.

I skipped the regurgitant grenade off the ground toward the sedan. You got one good bounce out of them. That same bounce activated the agents—or maybe it was reagents, I didn't know the difference. After that, the grenade stuck where it landed. This one adhered to the door before erupting. Whatever made up the puke-juice inside wasn't inherently green, but Ray had helpfully colored the smoke so I knew what areas to avoid.

Of course, I ran right at it.

Most of the smoke was pushed downslope, but some made it into the car. If I were the driver, I would exit toward the engine block, get that solid mass between me and an attacker, while also moving away from the direction the smoke was drifting. Doing so would mean slipping around the car door, which bought me another second.

I raced toward the hood, realizing I was doing the same thing the driver had: charging forward on the gamble there would be something worth hitting when I got there. The door opened as the driver came into view.

He was wearing the Foxman costume. Rather than go around the door, he dropped back and shut it. Guess he couldn't see through the windows either. When he peeked out, he saw me leaping over the hood, feet first. He was quick. He tried to duck but something jerked him upright. I caught him square on the side of the head with a flying kick so pretty you could have put it on a poster.

He went down as I fell onto the hood. When he tried to stand, something ripped him back down to the ground. It was his cape. One of the scallops had gotten caught in the car door.

He dove backward, aiming a gauntlet toward me. The door popped open and freed his cape. I did the only thing I could and put a concussion round into his chest. The explosion sent him stumbling backward toward the edge. I scissored my legs for momentum, dropping the Quarreler as I dove to grab him.

Too late. He went over, his cape trailing behind him. I snatched it out of the air and was sent face down onto the pavement as a reward. My grip was slipping, so I added my other hand and pulled myself along the ground to get to him like I was climbing a rope. The cape's thick material had a familiar texture. It looked like a garment but felt like armor.

I was close enough to see over the edge. Faux-Foxman was trying to find a handhold, but his gauntlets were a problem. There was a reason why serious climbers didn't wear gloves. I pulled the cape tight to my body, tucking my elbows so my back muscles were doing the work of supporting his weight. He looked up at me. I stared back encouragingly but we both knew the score.

The cape ripped. It didn't go all at once. It tore smoothly, like wrapping paper being cut. Faux-Foxman clawed futility at the rockface. We spoke at the same time. The last word he said and the last word he heard were the same four-letter exclamation.

In the movies, people fell so beautifully. They faced the camera, before canting onto their back to accept the judgment of gravity with grace. Faux-Foxman slid down the cliff-face, fighting the whole way to gain purchase. He hit an outcropping that bumped him away from the mountain. He struggled to recover, to stop the spinning. His cape might have helped, but it was in my hand.

The trees did me the mercy of not having to watch his impact, but nothing I heard gave me hope. I reminded myself I had a job to do. The sedan could hold some clues. The open door gave me a preview of the interior. The windows weren't tinted. They weren't windows at all. Their backsides were solid metal. Screens mounted in the interior allowed a view out. A reusable water bottle was in the cup holder and a bag of almonds on the seat. Faux-Foxman and I had a lot in common. Our level of training took time, spoke of dedication.

What were the odds he also possessed the skills to construct his costume? That he knew how to build a vehicle that looked like a sedan but accelerated like a sports car? Slim to none.

Which meant faux-Foxman must have his own Ray Ford. And if so, did this benefactor keep a similar digital leash on him? One with a heart-rate monitor? The burning remains of the Foxcar flashed into my mind.

The closest cover was upslope. I scrambled for it. My chemically scorched lungs didn't want to cooperate. It felt like I was running in a dream. I switched to a bear crawl and dragged myself around the bend. Shrimping into a nook of shadow, I focused on obtaining oxygen.

Right around the time I started jibbing myself for being overly dramatic, the sedan exploded.

The contents of the sedan's gas tank burned as hot as those of the Foxcar but a lot longer. There had been minimal fuel in the Foxcar. At least the fumes were blown away from me. I peeked out long enough to pay respects to the White Stag on its funeral pyre. By the time I could slip past the wreckage, Ray was close enough to pick me up. He had switched back to his smaller, less obtrusive panel van.

"Elaine is in the back. We're headed to the compound."

"Aren't you needed on set?"

"Not anymore. Tachi Productions has officially severed ties with me. Call came in an hour ago. Certified paperwork is on its way to my place. Duquesne followed suit not fifteen minutes later. This is step one in gearing up to come after me."

I can't say it was unexpected, but for once, it would have been nice to be pleasantly surprised. Ray, being outside the studio system, was the obvious scapegoat. And he had no friends at the studios. He was the best but tough to work with and expensive.

"They've been wanting to stick it to me for decades, Ken. But I made them money and brought in awards. Now I have a new use. They'll crucify me to absolve themselves."

Ray stormed into the driver's cab, slamming the door behind him before I could craft any reassurances. I stumbled into the back section formerly used to park the White Stag and lay down, using my folded jacket as a pillow and covering up with the torn cape.

Had I killed faux-Foxman?

That wasn't the intent of my actions, but my shot sent him over the edge.

The moment had forced me to go all out. The man underneath the mask was too sharp for any holding back. That he was looking to kill me didn't enter my equation. What he was willing to do didn't affect what I was willing to do.

Somehow, it felt different than if my kick had snapped his neck or if I had shot him in the face instead of the chest. And I had tried to save him. Tried hard, even if it meant going over the edge after him. Breathing more easily, I closed my eyes.

The next thing I knew, six hours had passed, and Ray was shaking me awake.

"I need time to work on some stuff. The same room you used last time is ready."

I was as comfortable with hunger as any other professional in This Town, but right then and there you could have spelunked in my stomach. "Is your kitchen classified?"

Ray ground his teeth in thought. "Elaine makes sure I eat."

"Your daughter is not cooking for me, Ray."

"All right, all right. She'll have to take you there. It's not routed."

Elaine must have overheard because she was waiting at the entrance from the garage into Ray's compound. He had bought expansive warehouse space more than forty years ago in what had then been a tough area. The gentrifiers would be breathing down his neck, if they could navigate the maze of wreckage in the no man's land between the electrified fence and reinforced walls.

The few times I had been allowed access to Ray's hidden headquarters, a lighted path along the floor had laid a yellow brick road I knew better than to stray from. Elaine and I wove through a grid of hallways scavenged from former movie sets, shifting genre and time period every twenty feet. The keys to the kingdom were built into Elaine's chair. Every door opened as we approached until we hit an expansive kitchen.

As with as every other room inside Ray's fortress, the kitchen was fully custom. The walls and floor were flat-planed fieldstone. The base cabinets—there were no uppers—were reclaimed redwood. All the appliances, with the exception of the oven, were concealed inside the cabinetry. The stove was Ray's interpretation of an Aga, both gas and wood fueled, with a cheery flame greeting us. The quartz countertops had recessed sink basins.

Half of the ceiling was windowed, curving gently into a matching long wall composed entirely of glass. At the moment, the world beyond the panes was a void.

"What kind of weather are you in the mood for?" Elaine asked.

"I've met my yearly quota for sunshine."

"Only happy when it rains, Ken? That's a garbage attitude."

Elaine keyed her armrest and a clouded harvest moon glowed to life. A gentle rain fell on the conservatory-style ceiling and blew into the glass wall. I had to remind myself it was an effect. We were deep in the center of a structure which could have withstood an air raid.

"This is something else."

"It was originally for an effect Dad was working on. Next-level green-screen technology. With these as backdrops, actors could be standing anywhere, anytime with a flip of a switch. No more having to pretend that they were experiencing a world that wasn't there."

I located the concealed refrigerator. Ray and Elaine had been on set long enough that no leftovers were present. A deep freezer adjacent to the fridge conveyed its contents over to defrost via conveyor belt.

"We had some groceries delivered. Dad is smoking that brisket."

"Breakfast it is," I decided.

I browned some mushrooms and fried bacon while I located the coffee fixings. As it brewed, I assembled the scramble. A handful of glossy blackberries topped a side of fresh farmer's cheese to serve as dessert. I set Elaine's plates across from mine on the live-edge redwood table.

"Not bad," she admitted.

"The only way to know exactly what you're eating is to make it yourself."

"Dad said before you, he ate whatever was easiest so he could get back to work."

The first cup of coffee had no effect. I tried a second. "I'm sure you coming along had something to do with it."

"He didn't have me full-time until my mom passed."

"How old were you?"

"Nine."

"Tough age," I said, to say something, but the truth is any age is a tough age to lose a parent.

"I was too young to absorb it. And coming here was like stepping into Wonderland. Dad kept me distracted. One day, he walked in to find me surrounded by all the pieces of my doll's house, wrapped up in its wiring." Elaine smiled at the memory. "He was so proud of me."

"I know what it's like, growing up without friends."

"Oh, I was Miss Popular as a kid. I had the best parties. Before—" Elaine slapped the side of her chair. When she met my eye, she looked sorrier for me than herself. "Do you remember what Dad used to be like?"

I had met Ray eighteen years ago on the set of *Near Death*, my single disastrous turn as an actor. Despite being an installment of a famous franchise, it was a shoestring operation with the single goal to retain the series rights. A lot of superhero flicks worked the same way. If Tachi Productions, Flint West's current employer, didn't churn out a Civil Warriors movie every five years, the rights reverted to the estate of Seth Martin, their creator. It was a big reason why the franchise yo-yoed in quality. Their rival, Duquesne Studios, had found a way around that little problem. They bought Classic Digest, the publisher who owned Good-Man, Foxman, and the rest of the Good Knights, back in the fifties. Now they were free to take their sweet time never getting the characters right.

"Your dad wasn't on set with me long. The production couldn't afford him. He mainly broke out gadgets used in prior films and argued with the director about how I was going to get killed doing all my own stunts."

"I remember when he came back. He lost fifty pounds the year after, doing the workouts you wrote down for him in a spiral notebook. He still uses it."

"Aw shucks, you're making me blush."

Having dealt with my hunger, I was now unable to ignore how greasy I felt. "Can you ferry me to that pool your dad calls a bathtub? I could do with a wash."

"Sure thing, tough guy."

We wound our way through the labyrinth, me doing my best to keep track of the twists and turns. I stepped inside the bathroom, then put a hand over the frame to hold the sliding door open.

"Are there cameras in here?"

Elaine was good at innocent. "It's best practices to keep a life-guard on duty."

I indulged myself in the natural-esque grotto, keeping to the shadowed areas. Implied nudity was far more alluring than parading around in your birthday suit. The lighted path guided me to my usual guest room. The world was getting too heavy to hold up. The bedding was more complicated than it had any right to be. A text alert came in on my watch. It was Dean.

You okay?

I sent back a thumbs-up.

Out of town 'til tomorrow. Fish will keep.

Dean didn't reply. I could feel his disappointment through the blank screen. Two days in and I was already dropping the ball. Guess the Ken apple didn't fall far from the Allen tree. I fought to keep my eyes open long enough to reply should Dean text back, but passed out before any arrived.

Ray roused me from a dreamless slumber. He stood in the doorway, cloaked in shadow.

"Wake up. We gotta talk while Elaine's asleep."

I swung to a sitting position and squinted toward the light, waiting for Ray. He waffled long enough for my eyes to adjust.

"I don't know how to say this."

I had had enough of the coy routine. "Then I'll say it, Ray. You know who's doing this. You've known all along."

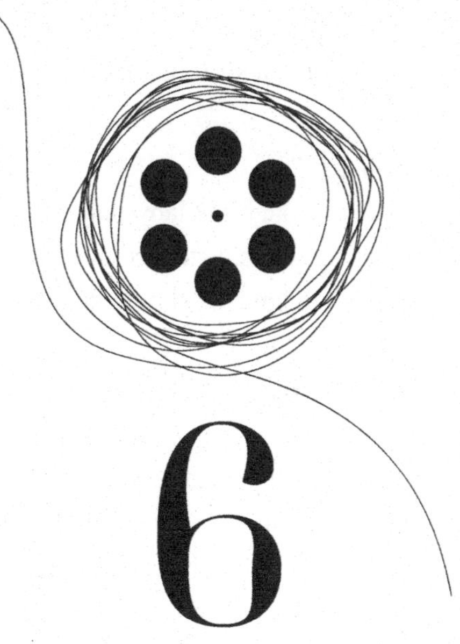

6

RAY WAS SILENT until we were standing in the armory/shooting range, where he had first presented my custom accoutrement. He shut the door and punched in some settings. Whatever he wanted to tell me, it was worth saying in a soundproof room.

"How did you figure it out?"

I wiped the crust out of my eyes. "Through the evidence. That shuriken in my jacket, it's a different shape than my fléchettes, but the firing mechanism is the same concept as the Quarreler. The smoke that almost killed me is a lot like the stuff in my grenades, and you had the antidote ready. Faux-Foxman's cape was made from the same material as my jacket, tailored into a different shape. You didn't catch that the White Stag was being bugged because the signal was too close to your own. And that gray sedan used a similar fuel as the Foxcar, which you built."

Ray nodded toward the floor and kept his eyes there.

"I've had a lot of people come to work under me through the years, but only one lasted longer than a few weeks."

"A protégé."

"Call it what you want. About fifteen years ago, a guy sought me out. Showed up on one of my sets, his bag already packed. By his size, I thought he was an adult."

Ray looked downrange.

I did my best to turn invisible.

In my limited experience, the greater space you gave people, the longer silence you provided, the more they were compelled to fill both.

"The kid was a genius. He reminded me of me. I was only twelve when I started gofering. By the time I was fourteen, I was building cars for other guys to slap their names on. The thing was, this kid was a freak. He was six-and-a-half feet tall as a teenager and only got bigger. It hurt him in the business."

I nodded.

"It screws with people's expectations."

"Right. Being Black, I knew how that felt too."

I didn't, so I kept my mouth shut. I looked like a poster boy for the master race. When I was the age Ray started assembling engines, my mom admitted she'd named me after Barbie's boyfriend.

"In the seven years he spent with me, the kid learned by leaps and bounds. He also kept growing, not just up, but out. Muscles on top of muscles. God knows there was plenty of heavy lifting to be done under my wing."

I had already figured out what happened next but waited for Ray to tell me.

"It was only natural, him and Elaine getting together. They thought it was behind my back. I was worried my approval would spoil the whole thing, so I let them keep thinking I was oblivious."

"Smart," I said to contribute.

"No, Ken, it wasn't. I gave them too much rope, and they hung themselves. One of their little side projects went wrong. He's the only person I ever trusted Elaine with, and she almost died. It was unforgivable."

"So, you dumped him."

"Worse than that." Ray's voice vibrated through his confession. "I had him blacklisted. I made it known throughout the industry that if you took him on, you could go ahead and lose my number. I got a lot of friends who did the same. And with computer graphics taking over, there weren't many practical jobs left to start with."

Talking soft kept my voice even. "Ever check in on what happened to him?"

"By the time I had cooled off, he was in the wind. But if he needed money, there was a thriving field open to him. The one I would never touch."

"Weapons."

Ray cleared his throat. "Right. Bombs. Industrial sabotage."

"Terrorism?"

"The money would be there. Three years ago, Elaine—she's better at the online stuff—she comes to me and says someone has been building drones for the private market. And not only surveillance models. Ones capable of long-range strikes."

I thought about Ray's own expansive fleet of drones. About the armored RV he used for travel work. About the compound we were hunkered down in now.

"This protégé is why you live like this. He's got you scared."

"Damn right he does," Ray admitted. "The son of a bitch forced me to build my own prison."

I sniffed hard to clear my sinuses, as if I was getting ready to step in the ring.

"What's his name?"

"Culvan Mann."

Ray granted me access to his gym and the kitchen, which was more than anyone but Elaine had earned in the last five years. I worked out primarily to test my cardio.

It was coming back slower than I liked. I texted Dean that I was stuck in the Bay Area for at least another day.

He didn't reply.

I ate alone, a double-helping of Ray's smoked brisket, which was over-the-moon good, with a spinach salad. I should have been happy, knowing who the bad guy was, but something gnawed at my gut. Culvan Mann had reason to bear a grudge, no doubt about that. But the events as detailed by Zaina Preeti spoke of a motivation beyond revenge.

My watch glowed with an alert. I was hoping for Dean, but it was Ray requesting my presence in the armory. My wardrobe had seen better days. Fortunately, I had planned ahead and had one costume change—sans jacket—salvaged from the White Stag's saddleboxes. The mourning period for the Stag was going to be prolonged. His death was on me. That forty-year-old piece of film history had lasted all of three months under my watch.

Ray was waiting for me when I got there, with a stack of cases next to him.

"I was gonna wait until your birthday, but we're going to need what's in these."

I looked down at my patched blazer, skinned and peeling from concrete surfing. "I had no idea how tough this job could be on costuming. It's no wonder detectives charge expenses."

"We'll start there then," Ray said, passing over a suit bag.

Inside was a blazer, the same color—the blue/gray of a cloudy sky—as mine, and similar cut. Except this jacket weighed maybe half as much.

"With the second-generation, I went for localized patches in the gel layer, which should help with ventilation and flexibility. I also mixed in some coolant. It will soak up the AC when indoors. At home, just toss it in the fridge."

"Ray, you are a beautiful human being."

"A guy can only stand so much whining about how the garment keeping you alive is so uncomfortable you'd rather die."

People were always perplexed how a California native could hate warm weather the way I did. "I was thinking I could use a gas mask."

"Hey me too," Ray replied. "It's collapsible and stored inside your collar. Pull the tab through and flip it up into place."

Ray pointed back to the bag I was holding. There were gloves and shoes pocketed inside.

"The gloves are a second swing at the ones I fabricated for you on the fly a few months back. The strike points firm up on impact."

"Faux-Foxman's gloves got him killed."

"These are sheer in the palm for full articulation. Just don't try to catch any bullets."

"Am I going to have to cut the laces to get these shoes off?"

Ray smiled. "Nope. Figured that out. Static charge. Just press that pump switch on the tongue. But uh . . ."

"But what, Ray?"

"You might want to shave your feet. The shoes kinda pull at the hair. Feels funky. Now on to the new stuff."

Ray passed over a sunglasses case. The frames inside were thick, curving into the peripheral.

"Good idea," I said, slipping them on. "No one will recognize me in these peepers."

Inside the glasses, the view was dark before adjusting to the ambient light.

Ray beamed. "Say hello to your new spyglasses. You can set your preferred illumination level and the lenses will dynamically adjust to the environment. I got the idea from you always having to squint and shield your eyes."

"It's the price I pay for these baby blues."

"The eyewear connects you with a new app we installed on your watch. You tell the glasses what you want to know, and you'll get an overlay. More, if Elaine is listening. Now, say a distance."

"Okay. A hundred feet."

The glasses zoomed in and autofocused.

"In addition to the zoom, there is a low-light and thermal mode. There's also a laser mic in the bridge. Tell the glasses to listen in and look toward the closest hard surface."

I smiled. "Super vision and hearing."

"The glasses are already paired to your pencil cameras." Ray's voice assumed a tone of command. "Activate hindsight."

A window opened in the corner of the left lens to display the world behind me.

"You can expand that to the whole left lens if you like. I recommend winking hard on whatever side you aren't using to avoid disorientation."

"And I'm sure you're recording."

"Always," Ray admitted. "There's going to be a time when you wished you had a second chance to look at something. Now, if you so much as glance at a screen or document, we can take our time going over the footage later."

Ray gestured for me to pull the next case onto the table. Inside were reloads for the Quarreler, or *quivers* if going by the movies which inspired the weapon. They were color coded for my convenience. In terms of restocking, I was far lower on yellow taser quivers than green concussion, and fully stocked on the red, which were the lethal rounds.

There was also a new color.

"So, what's with the blue?"

"It's a muscle relaxant, like curare. Low-dose and numbing on impact. Your target might not know they've even been hit. Once they nod off, you can take the dart and . . ."

The tip of the dart broke away from the veined tail.

". . . leave a tracker inside. The GPS portion should also separate if anyone tugs it out of their clothes or any other surface."

I liked where this was going, but the new dart had the same problem as my old standby, the shock rounds. "These are still no good against hard targets."

"Your new Quarreler has an upcast setting. More penetration but uses three times the charge. And these darts have more penetrative value."

"How low is low dose?"

"One is good for about two hundred fifty pounds. Lighter targets will go down faster and stay down longer. Under a hundred pounds, pass on these." Ray ran his hand over the blue quiver. "Three of these would be lethal at any weight."

"Two is the limit, got ya."

Ray sighed. "You keep those red quivers handy, Ken. You might find yourself in a situation where you don't have a choice."

"There's always a choice," I said. "Besides, the first time I take someone down permanently will be the last time I have this gig. Special Investigator Stern isn't about to let me play executioner."

I restocked supplies and slipped on my new jacket. It was half as difficult to bend into and four times more comfortable.

"So, what's the plan? How will you find Culvan?" Ray asked.

"I've got a couple of ideas. The first one is to figure out where Culvan is getting his help."

"His help?"

"The guys he has running around in costumes doing his legwork. If Culvan is as big a human as you say, he would stick out like a sore thumb. He'd also need a workshop, and maybe a setup like your RV for going mobile. Both those would be as close to This Town as he could manage. Someone wearing a Foxman costume would stand out in commuter traffic."

"So, back to SoCal you go. Sounds like you could use a ride."

I followed Ray into a space I had never seen before. He'd worked every aspect of the special-effects game: sets and set pieces, props, costuming. But he had made his name on custom vehicles.

Ray's private garage could have been built on an inter-dimensional wormhole. Vehicles from every era—real or imagined—ranging from long ago to far, far away waited in climate-controlled stasis. As he led me toward our destination, a spotlight flared to life to reveal his latest creation.

A White Stag, freshly born.

He was retro and modern at the same time, long and lean with a frame you could lie low on. His fully shielded front profile had a graceful slope like a stag's head and swept antler-bars anchoring a generous, wrapping windscreen. The rider's hands were fully protected without being shackled. The Stag's innards were warded by carbon-fiber panels, as was his back wheel. The flank saddle boxes were sloping and generous. All his detailing was snow white.

He took my breath away. "I'm in love."

Ray skipped forward at my approval. "All the finish panels are replaceable, for when they take impacts. The Stag is plenty heavy, which is more a help than a hindrance, in the situations you find yourself in. Don't worry, I compensated with a double measure of get-up-and-go."

As we circled the new Stag, Ray pointed out the bike's finest features. "He's a hybrid, fully compatible with that battery wall I installed in your condo."

I tore my eyes off the bike to look at Ray. "You were already working on this back then?"

"I told you as much, last time out. I wanted you off that old goat before the damn thing killed you."

"Hey, we did okay."

Ray presented me with a helmet. "The visor has the same tech as your new glasses, and the mouthpiece is a higher-rated filter than the mask built into your jacket. The app on your watch can synthesize your voice through the mouthpiece as well."

"Why would I want to disguise my voice?"

Ray shrugged. "How the hell would I know?"

I climbed into the saddle, eager to be on my way.

Ray gritted his teeth. "If we had the time, I'd run you through a course and practice all the features before I handed over the keys."

The helmet clicked on, clarifying my voice through the mouthpiece. "No test like a field test."

"If I hadn't witnessed the way you handled that old bike, I'd be more nervous," Ray replied. "We can walk you through everything on your way south."

"I've got a stop to make before I head back to This Town."

Ray, having just gifted me six-figures in goodies, swallowed hard. "Do pray tell."

"I can't imagine Culvan Mann is coming after you solely to ruin your reputation. It doesn't sit right. Think about all the time and resources you dump into me. He has to do the same for whoever he sends into the field, as well as compensate them."

"Culvan wants to run me out of town, the same way I did to him," Ray replied. "He'll do anything it takes to destroy my legacy."

"I don't doubt that. Two people dying on different sets proves you right. But the Patriette's pregnancy doesn't fit into Culvan's vendetta. It can't be pinned on you. I think there's more to the sabotages. Ruining your name might be the cherry on top of Culvan's sundae."

Ray wanted to argue but didn't have a rebuttal prepared.

"It'll take just one afternoon," I assured him. "I have a source in the Bay who can shed some light on the situation, if he can make time for me."

Having literally been built for me, the new White Stag fit like a glove. He ate up the Bay Bridge. It felt like I was flying. The drive was too short to fully savor how my new partner handled. I wasn't too concerned about having to schedule a meet but thought it polite to herald my arrival. Though his number had sat in my phone for years, I had never used it.

"Jimmy here."

Jimmy Erikson's voice was crystal clear in my new helmet. Though biologically Korean, he had been adopted by a white family from Minnesota and was a Midwesterner through and through.

"Are you holding court today? I'd like to stop by."

"You betcha. At the Palladium now."

"Still going strong. Good to hear. See you in thirty?"

"Be here or be square."

When I returned to the United States after my disastrous film shoot in Hong Kong almost twenty years ago, I was at the lowest point in my life. My dreams of stardom had ended in bloody failure, an experience to be commiserated rather than celebrated. These days, people call it a quarter-life crisis. I did the same as many others: ran back to my childhood in search of escape.

I'd always loved comic books. Maybe it was born from Saturday-morning cartoons, or that cheesy Foxman sixties spoof with all the Dutch angles. Comic books were the one possession I held on to, past the point where their covers had crumbled away. I devoured what I had in storage, then ventured into the local comic shop for more. At that time, if you walked into such a place, Jimmy Erikson's work was front and center.

When it came to comics, Jimmy was a wunderkind. Like me, he didn't bother graduating high school. He had known what he wanted to do since he was able to hold a crayon. By the time he was seventeen, he was drawing C-list heroes for Classic Digest and making them more popular than they had any right to be. At twenty, he crossed the Rubicon to pencil the Civil Warriors and became the hottest artist in the western hemisphere.

Then, in the early nineties, Jimmy did the unthinkable. While getting royalties off selling millions of books through drawing the most popular characters of the era, Jimmy walked off the line to birth his own universe. The idea that an independent publisher could somehow compete with the big two was scoffed at. But Jimmy was done with work-for-hire. The pie pan never keeps a piece. With Imagine Comics, he baked his own damn pie in whatever flavor he pleased.

The first issue of *Dragonspawn* sold 5 million copies at two bucks a hit. Jimmy pocketed half of that. This was when the publishing world thought he was insane for turning his back on fifty grand an issue. A month later, the second issue did 4 million. Second issues always sell less. The speculators punch out. Every subsequent issue, the run was lower, but Jimmy didn't care, because he owned *Dragonspawn* and every other character he created at Imagine. The merchandising, the cartoon, and the crappy low-budget movie (starring an up-and-coming Flint West)—all the points went straight to Jimmy.

In the meantime, he became a champion for creator's rights, starting a legal fund to fuel the fight for the generation who inspired him. If anyone knew why Duquesne Studios wanted to meet with Dave King, it was Jimmy. It was a pretty big coincidence, Duquesne meeting Dave King on their rival's set the day Bill O'Wrongs was killed. Especially now that I knew Duquesne had problems of their own.

I pulled into the cramped alley behind the Palladium and parked next to the rolling dumpster. Invoking Jimmy's name soothed the staff, who all belonged to the same extended family, and they started taking selfies with my new bike.

Jimmy didn't hoard all that dough. The Palladium was his gift to the next generation: An artists' co-op in the heart of the Sunset, once a

Victorian apartment building purchased in the mid-nineties before the real-estate boom. Jimmy had the first floor renovated into a cafeteria and studio space. The other two floors served as dormitories for promising up-and-comers, supported by Jimmy's patronage.

The cafeteria was medium busy. Jimmy opened it up to all comers, providing Midwestern fare at reasonable prices. It got by mostly on selling small-batch craft beer. Endless varieties of liquid bread were sold at insane prices.

Jimmy was tucked into a U-shaped booth that would have accommodated a party of six so he could layout several pages of *Dragonspawn* at once. He was bent over a sheet of bristol board, forcing perspective. He didn't look up when he sensed my presence. "One sec. Don't want to lose this. Have some fondue."

I passed on the fondue, which smelled like a Superbowl party, and snacked on the ignored celery and mushrooms. A dour woman who possibly had some German in there with the Filipino and Jamaican handed me a rundown on today's buffet.

"This sausage salad is just a bunch of sausage."

"My kind of salad." Jimmy stayed glued to his drafting. "I'm able to talk now."

I angled toward Jimmy. "What's going on with Dave King?"

Jimmy set down his pencil and took a sip of beer. It gave him time to think. "What makes you ask?"

"Some bigwigs from Duquesne Studios wanted to meet with him so bad, they crossed enemy lines to ambush him on a Tachi Studios set."

Jimmy set down his glass, picked his pencil back up. "Dave has been trying to get the rights to the characters he created for forty years."

"But Duquesne has no reason to talk to King. He didn't create any of the characters they own. Seth Martin did, twenty years before King came along."

Seth Martin was, for all intents and purposes, the god of superheroes. He created one universe before World War II, headed by Good-Man, Foxman, and the Patriette. Two decades later, he started over from scratch at Excelsior Comics. Dave King was there with Martin from day one, designing the Civil Warriors, breathing life into their stories through his art. Some fans, including me and Jimmy, believed King deserved equal credit for creating the Civil Warriors alongside Martin.

Jimmy focused on penciling. Dragonspawn was either yelling at or breathing hellfire through the fourth wall. He had turned quiet on a dime.

"So, what could Duquesne want with Dave King?"

That did it. Jimmy laid down a dark, hard line before picking up his stein. "You know, back in the day, the suits used to have a waiver printed on the endorsement line for their checks? If an artist wanted to get paid, they had to sign that month's work away."

"I did know that."

Jimmy was trying to change the subject. I read once that people unconsciously mirrored you. If you yawned, they would yawn. If you crossed your legs, they would cross their legs. If you drank, they would drink. I signaled the server what I hoped she would understand as a request for water.

Jimmy took a sip of beer without prompting. It flowed like syrup, sticking to the side of his stein. "Dave had to fight to get his art back, forty years ago, when everyone was realizing original artwork might actually be worth something."

"He won that fight."

"And it cost him every penny he had. Then, in the biggest boss move ever, he refuses to sell any of it."

The server arrived with water for me and a refill for Jimmy. I shifted it into Jimmy's eye line and took a drink. He took a drink after me. I had come on too strong. Jimmy was on guard now. It was time for a trip down memory lane. We swapped stories the both of us already knew for an hour.

In the early 2000s, my comic obsession was at its height. I scraped up what money I had earned teaching martial arts and drove to any convention within reasonable distance. I was staring longingly at a first printing of *Giant-Sized Civil Warriors #1* way out of my price range when a voice over my shoulder said, "Look at that hand. No one draws a bigger hand than Dave King. That's courage."

I had never thought about it like that before. It *was* courage: blocking the reader's view, rather than permitting it. I replied something like, *wow, yeah, you're right*, and turned around to find myself talking to a guy people stood in line for hours to meet.

We walked around, Jimmy pointing out nuances on the page I had never considered. I had never examined the craft. There was a world of process behind the medium I loved. I quit pretending not to know who Jimmy was and actually forgot. We were two guys with a shared love.

After a few hours, Jimmy dug out his badge and pinned it back on.

"Thanks, I needed that," he told me. "It's fun to be a fan for once."

Within moments he was swarmed, and I faded into the crowd.

The next year, I passed by his table and gave him a wave. To my shock, Jimmy came around to meet me, pulling his badge off.

"This is the perfect amount of famous," he said. "I take this thing off and I'm nobody. Not once have I been grocery shopping and anyone cared I drew the issue of Civil Warriors where Mongoose is forced to kill Re-Bertha."

We were walking past a display of movies bootlegged from Asia when my blood ran cold. One of the tapes was labeled LOST JOVE BRAND—HILARIOUS. The tapes were twenty bucks, or two for thirty. A middle-aged guy struggling with a crossword puzzle was behind the table.

I held up the tape. "How many copies of this do you have?"

He ducked under the table. “Including that one? Seven.”

I counted out two hundred bucks and bought the lot.

“Ha-ha, what the hell, Ken?” Jimmy asked. My arms were overflowing with video cassettes. There was no way to defend all of them. Jimmy got a glance at the fuzzy photos on the back of the box. He looked up at me, bewildered. “Holy shit.”

And so, Jimmy Erikson was the first person outside of Hong Kong to learn my secret identity.

Back in the now, Jimmy was signaling for another round.

“I can’t believe you made me sign that box.”

“I still have it.” Jimmy giggled. “So, you finally got to meet Dave King.”

“Briefly. While I was on the set, Flint West tried to hire me to work for Dave King, without King knowing. Only Flint never got around to explaining what he wanted me to do.”

Jimmy leaned close. “West is dating Dave’s daughter.”

“Yeah, he introduced me to Jaq yesterday. Then they made out until it got so awkward I left.”

Jimmy laughed. “Jaq is a badass. She’s worked pro bono for my creators legal-defense fund. Managed to get both Duquesne and Tachi to send some token suits out.”

“That’s why I’m asking about Dave King. If he really needs help, I’d love to, but I’m spinning around in the dark here.”

Jimmy was so close I was concerned about getting a contact buzz from his breath. “So, Seth Martin died last year.”

“I heard something about that.”

The All-father of superheroes passing away was no revelation. Alongside me being framed for murder, it was the biggest story of the last twelve months.

“There’s a rumor Seth left something behind. Something that would change everything.”

“Something he willed to Dave King?”

Jimmy started playing with the lid of his stein, bouncing it up and down. "Maybe Martin had a conscience after all. Tried to atone on his deathbed."

"That can happen when the pearly gates are on the horizon. But King has nothing to do with Duquesne's properties. Sol Silver was Seth Martin's artist back then."

Jimmy failed at picking up his pencil. "Martin did every artist he ever worked with dirty, Silver and King included. Silver is long gone, but he had a chance do right by Dave King before the end."

"There has to be something Duquesne wants or is worried about. Conglomerates never act out of the goodness of their hearts."

Jimmy nodded. "They only pay if the alternative costs them more."

We sat there silent while Jimmy played with negative space. Comic-book storytelling was an art unto itself. It relied on the reader to create closure. A lot went down in the gutter—the space between the panels.

"Saw a story claiming you were on set when Bill O'Wrongs died." The clipped tension in Jimmy's tone put me on defense.

"That was to meet Dave King."

"Why do you keep asking about Duquesne, Ken? If you aren't working for Flint West, who are you working for?"

"It's not like that, Jimmy."

"You're working for Duquesne, aren't you?"

The longer I went without replying, the worse it was going to get. "Ray Ford is taking the heat for accidents on both shoots, and two people are dead. I need the access Duquesne can grant me if I'm going to keep Ray out of court."

Jimmy pushed his stein away. "Yah, sure, Ken. You're not really a company man, you just cash their checks. Look, I have to get back to work here."

I sat there awkwardly while Jimmy fell into a world of his own making. All eyes in the cafeteria were on me. After a half hour of utter silence, I shuffled out of the booth with a smile. "Good seeing you, Jimmy."

Jimmy did not return the sentiment.

I cringed my way back to my bike. In the span of a single conversation, I had soured a twenty-year friendship. The cramped alley was packed with rubberneckers snapping selfies with the new White Stag. The pileup was blocking me from my own vehicle. Recent events had worn my patience thin. I flashed the strobes on the bike. The mass shirked away like Dracula from a cross.

"Show's over, folks. You don't have to go home but you can't stay here."

All but four members of the mob parted. We'd met before.

"Ken Allen, prepare yourself. Street Justice strikes back!"

Street Justice was a spin on an old classic, a neighborhood watch playing dress-up in military surplus with the addition of masks. I had run across them—over them would be less modest but more accurate—while pursuing the person who had framed me for two murders. That they would loiter around the Palladium wasn't a shocker. Wannabe superheroes needed a place to hang their capes between conventions.

I stopped seven feet away from the pose line. Interception range, if one of them jumped the gun. "Can we not do this and say we did? I'm trying to cut down on fight scenes that don't contribute to the plot."

Their leader was a double-XL corseted by a Kevlar vest. A goalie mask enameled with a silver skull saved his parents from further embarrassment. It also did a decent job muffling his lisp.

"You aren't getting away this time, Allen. We've been training for this moment."

I lifted my spyglasses to rub my eyes. Problem was, the biggest thing to ever happen to Street Justice was me roughing them up. They became a little moon orbiting my world of trouble. The video of our tussle got a hundred thousand times more hits than any of their other technically legal public harassments.

Two other members were ready to rumble. Scrawny Ninja was holding a pair of carbon fiber katanas. Steampunk Wizard had upgraded from a cane to a staff. Street Justice's only female member moved to a flanking angle for better filming. So far, this was looking like a replay of our last encounter. They didn't look any different, fitness-wise. While three months might make for a solid montage, I had been training in one discipline or another nonstop since preschool.

"So, what's my crime?"

"Huh?"

"What did I do this time? Right now, I'm just a guy trying to be on his merry way. You're the people blocking my vehicle and threatening me with weapons."

Street Justice held their poses along with their tongues. There were two dozen bystanders crowded around, waiting for something to happen. It started to get awkward. The leader turned in a circle in the quest for cause.

"You're, uh, illegally parked."

"Then scram so I can get out of here."

I came forward, hands up and empty. Street Justice didn't know what to do. Jumping a guy trying to get to his vehicle wasn't anywhere near the realm of self-defense. I squeezed sideways through the phalanx and climbed into the saddle.

Scrawny Ninja pulled his mask down. "I guess we were just mad about Jimmy. You really upset him, you know."

He voiced his feelings without pretension, one friend being honest with another. The spectators nodded in agreement. Jimmy was beloved by all those in attendance. Now it was my turn to feel awkward. The alley was packed to the point where I had to walk the bike out backward like Fred Flintstone.

I got clear and flashed a salute. "All part of a day's work."

An hour later, it was still bothering me. The kid was right. So far, playing detective was not conducive to maintaining healthy relationships. On the ride back to This Town, I tried not to think about how much my new vocation was going cost me.

7

I BURNED HALF of the six-hour drive back to This Town exploring my theory. Unable to find work in the entertainment industry, Mann had gone mercenary.

If there was more behind Culvan Mann's sabotage than ruining Ray's reputation, who had hired him, and why? Were the incidents designed to delay both productions? Or, being fresh on the job, was I comparing this case to my first one?

The sequel had that same-but-different feel so far.

I decided to play the adult and call Dean. He didn't pick up. I left a voice mail I was 99 percent sure he wouldn't listen to, informing him I would be home soon. The rest of the way was spent catching up on the Seth Martin story.

I was in the middle of his last interview when Special Investigator Stern called.

"Hey, another grown-up," I said.

"What's with this car accident, Allen?"

Seeing as there were two accidents Stern could be talking about, I kept my reply vague. “Oh, you know, one of those things. They got you working fender benders?”

“Spare me the platitudes. Anything with your name on it is flagged toward my desk. The other driver says you ran up his trunk to avoid getting T-boned.”

“Distracted drivers are a menace. I guess at the end of the day, it is what it is.”

Stern went quiet but for the clicking of her mouse. “Well, you might be in the clear on this one. The guy you hit as much as admitted you did it to save your own life, before mentioning he also has a dash cam. He emailed me the footage.”

“Some good news for once.”

I was about to ask Stern how her day was going when she broke back in.

“Apropos of nothing, yesterday the highway patrol investigated a vehicle fire up in the mountains by Angeles National Forest. Near Flint West’s place. You know him, right?” Stern’s voice was replaced by the rhythmic clicking of her scrolling through photos. “Anyway, it’s hard to tell, seeing as the explosion caused a hell of a mess, but this could be the remains of a midsize car and a motorcycle.”

And like that, a perfectly nice drive was ruined. I managed to keep my voice even. “Was anybody hurt?”

“That’s the thing, no one was on site when the authorities arrived. Now, I don’t have my Big Book of Laws handy, but not reporting a collision and ditching your vehicle at the scene might break some statute or another.”

“I guess what is meant to be is meant to be.”

When Stern was mad, she exhaled out of her nostrils like an angry bull. “You’re making my cop-sense tingle, Allen. Do me a favor and take good notes. It will give me a starting place when we find your body.”

"Quick question before you hang up."

Stern was happy to indulge my bad habit of talking to the police. "Let's hear it."

"Our last go-round, you were up on the private security outfits worth knowing in the Golden State."

"Questions have a mark at the end."

"Does that knowledge extend to mercenaries?"

Stern's voice went cold. "Why are you asking? What have you heard about mercenaries?"

Leave it to me to overstep right into it. A full five seconds passed without me coming up with a reply.

"Where are you, Allen? I'm not playing around—"

I hung up. The key word that triggered Stern had been *mercenaries*. It would be nice to be in a cat-and-mouse situation where I got to be the cat for a change. Consulting my list of people I hadn't screwed up with yet today, I remembered I had an actual paying client.

Zaina Preeti was not, however, available at my convenience. I was almost back to This Town by the time she returned my call.

"Any updates, Mr. Allen?"

"It's been less than thirty-six hours."

"I asked for updates, not excuses."

While I had my client's back, I knew better than to assume the reverse. "Let's talk about it in person. I'll be back at my office in an hour."

"You work for me, Mr. Allen."

"Do you want me to spend my time commuting or investigating?"

Preeti was the decisive type. Her pauses lasted less than a second. "I will be there in an hour."

I pushed the new Stag's pace to shave some time, savoring the way he handled. Forty-five minutes later, I parked in one of the two spots outside my office. Hooking up his charging line delayed the conversation I was dreading for a few more seconds.

Dean was waiting inside, sitting in the kitchen nook behind a huge laptop with earbuds in. He didn't acknowledge my wave, so I went over to the fridge and started assembling a salad. Like every other salad I'd ever made, it was composed of what produce was closest to going bad.

From the kitchen side, I could see Dean's screen. He was playing some video game where you fight people. I tapped his shoulder and pointed to my bowl. He shook his head at me. I topped my veg with two boiled eggs and a tablespoon of homemade Greek dressing. Then I sat down in Dean's eye line and stared at him while I ate.

The staring got to him. I meant it to be a blank stare, but the more I stared the more agitated he got, and the more agitated he got the funnier I found it. After a few minutes I was chuckling around my ruffage. It was like looking into the past. I used to handle things like Dean, simmering until my top finally blew.

Dean slammed his laptop closed. "Fine. What?"

"Can I go ahead and assume I've already apologized at the beginning of every conversation we have? Because I am sorry, but the more I say it, the less you're going to believe me."

Dean didn't know what to do with that. Chances were high every time he and his mother got into it, she overwhelmed him. Dina Calabria wasn't the type of person you could go at head on and get anywhere. She brought a ballistic missile to a gunfight.

"Okay," Dean decided.

"First things first. Yesterday was rough. A guy tried to kill me and ended up falling to his death. I played a part, and it's not sitting well. On top of that, my bike blew up."

Dean's eyes swept back and forth like he was rereading my words.

"This morning, I screwed up one of my oldest friendships in the name of justice, then rode the wave and stepped in it again by talking the cops into investigating me."

I got up and rinsed out my bowl.

Dean turned around to watch me. "Are you okay?"

I laughed so that I did not weep. "Sure. We are getting into the 'from bad to worse' portion of the case. Next visit, we need to coordinate schedules better."

Dean perked up at the suggestion there would be a next visit.

"You came at a bad time, kid, but that doesn't mean I don't want you around. Did you eat today?"

"I had some stuff out of my backpack."

"There's all kinds of places around here."

"Uh"—Dean scratched his scalp—"you didn't give me a key."

There was no stopping my groan. Father-of-the-year material right here, for sure. I keyed Dean's thumbprint into the alarm system. While we were outside, he scoped my new bike.

"When did you get that?"

"This morning with some other goodies, courtesy of Ray Ford."

"Awesome. Who's Ray Ford?"

Such was the fate of a career behind the camera. His mother helmed the most successful independent movie studio of all time that didn't have the word *star* or *wars* attached to it, and still Dean thought of movies as things actors made.

I was finishing my sigh when Preeti pulled up in a vintage two-seater convertible. The juxtaposition of the vehicle and its driver was charming. It was the first hint there might be a whole human beneath her veneer.

Dean moped back toward the kitchen nook. His mother had shunted him aside to take meetings his entire life and here I was repeating the pattern.

"Upstairs," I told Preeti, leading the way.

My office space was dominated by a three-fold desk, a piece of movie history that came with the condo. I gestured for Preeti to take a seat behind it.

"Your desk is backwards," Preeti informed me.

Which is how I wanted it. The person behind the desk gave the missions. The person facing it took them. I never wanted to be behind the desk. I slid a large drawer open and placed my watch, phone, and new spyglasses inside.

"Put any electronics you want to keep working in here."

Preeti considered me for a second and set her entire laptop bag inside. She didn't carry a purse and her pockets appeared strictly ornamental.

A tone informed us the drawer was locked. I took my seat facing the desk.

"There's a reason I wanted you to come to me. This room is a faraday cage. Nothing gets in, nothing gets out. There are no cameras or microphones. You sure you aren't stashing any electronics?"

Preeti nodded. I reached under the lip of the desk and toggled a hidden switch. If she was lying, I hoped she had shelled out for the replacement plan.

"What's with Duquesne firing Ray Ford?"

Preeti didn't blink. "It was the expedient decision. We needed to insulate ourselves from the incidents. And thus far, all evidence of negligence points toward Mr. Ford."

I didn't bother to ask who made the call. "It would be nice if you'd let me do the job you hired me for and prove it was deliberate sabotage."

"Please note you are still employed."

"And bound by confidentiality."

"You are being given every opportunity to prove your friend's innocence. How has your investigation progressed?"

"Ever hear the name Culvan Mann?"

Preeti tilted her head to think. It took her less than ten seconds to retrieve the memory. "He was once Ray Ford's apprentice. Ford had him blacklisted."

"Ray Ford believes Culvan Mann is the saboteur."

Preeti crossed her arms. "Your theory is that the incidents are due to a personal vendetta. Ray Ford's former protégé wants to ruin him at our expense."

"I'm sure that's part of it. But sabotaging two productions of this size is an expensive undertaking, in terms of both material and manpower. From what Ray Ford tells me, Mann is over seven feet tall. Which means he has to employ hired hands, like the Foxman impersonator."

"Revenge is not a rational enterprise."

It was a solid counter-argument. "Mann makes his living in corporate sabotage. If he's going to ruin Ray Ford, he might as well get paid to do it. Who profits from setting back the Good Knights expanded universe?"

Preeti engaged in another two-second deep dive. "Primarily Tachi Productions. Their next Civil Warriors installment releases opposite our Good Knights sequel."

"Seems unnecessary."

"It was their decision. When we announced, they moved up from a midsummer date to the beginning of the season."

"So, a delay would benefit Duquesne. It allows you to shift the date without it looking like you were running scared. Is your production insured against a star's death?"

The whole point of my office being a leak-proof bunker was to put clients at ease, but Preeti wasn't giving me anything. To make it as far as she had in This Town, your shields had to be perpetually raised.

"Are you accusing Duquesne Studios of sabotaging their own film? Then hiring you would be a ruse, in which case you are declaring yourself incompetent."

I didn't have to pretend amusement. Trying to target my ego was a waste of time. I'd spent almost four decades failing to locate it. "The right hand doesn't have to know what the left hand is doing. And even if it does, maybe you decided the best way to control me was to hire me."

Preeti slow blinked, a predator cat diffusing. "I understand these perspectives."

"If Mann is motivated by money, you could pay him off."

She didn't argue principal for the sake of form. In terms of budget, payoffs were just another production cost. "A possibility, if we had a back channel. You said Mann was sabotaging two productions."

Whoops.

"Bill O'Wrongs's death was his work too."

"Which means Mann's most likely employer is suffering the same issues as we are."

"Not exactly the same. As far as we know, Tachi Productions still has their heroes." I had one more shot to fire. "Why did Duquesne Studios want to meet with Dave King?"

Preeti stood up. "This has shifted from a briefing to an interrogation. I would like to retrieve my possessions now."

I came around the desk to unlock the drawer. "It's not like Seth Martin could will the Good Knights to Dave King. Martin sold them at wholesale rates to Classic Digest in the fifties, and Duquesne bought Classic Digest right after. Also, it doesn't make any sense. Dave King didn't work with Martin until the sixties, and never on those characters."

Preeti took her bag from the drawer. "I'm not at liberty to discuss Duquesne Studios' involvement with Mr. King, if any such involvement indeed exists."

I waited until Preeti got to the door. "Want to hear my theory?"

Preeti turned around.

"Martin willed the Civil Warriors to Dave King and Duquesne wants to buy them outright. Make the two universes one."

Preeti didn't blink.

"It would be the deal of the century. The crossover movie would break every box office record."

"Could you unlock this door, Mr. Allen? I delayed prior engagements to facilitate this meeting."

I tapped my watch and the door unlatched. "Am I still employed?"

"You've made notable progress," Preeti admitted. "Duquesne Studios would like these attacks on our assets to cease. Do all you can to prevent any further delays in production."

I walked Preeti out. "The Patriette's pregnancy is our outlier. How soon can you set me up with Lidia Colby?"

"Immediately." Preeti took the stairs so smooth they could have been an escalator. "She is on set today. Follow me to the studio."

"Right behind you."

I ducked my head into the kitchen. Dean was back on his laptop.

"I'm off to meet with the Patriette."

He tried to act unimpressed, but when he looked back at the screen, he was shaking his head and smiling.

It was a good thing I rode a motorcycle, because Preeti drove as if traffic violations were a business expense. I was issued another holographic bar code lanyard by the beefed-up security. With their tactical gear, the guards probably outweighed the golf carts they were paired up in.

We passed through the outer doors into a second checkpoint, where I would have been searched if it wasn't for my high-ranking patron. Preeti slipped through the magnetized curtain with minimal interference. I followed her example to be rewarded with a spectacle.

The Good Knights were the first super-team, formed by Good-Man to battle domestic threats before following America into World War II, where they faced down their Axis counterparts. In the modern day, the comic audience was predominantly grown men. But for their first forty years of existence, comics were aimed at kids. And what kid doesn't want their own secret clubhouse? Foxman's Den was the first and most famous.

But the grandest of all was where I was standing now: The Round.

There have been many versions of the Round. But whether it was located on the top of a mountain, the bottom of the sea, or in orbit around Earth, it was always anchored by its signature feature: a round table sans chairs. Because—according to Good-Man—justice never rests.

Burton Taylor and Lidia Colby were in costume as Good-Man and the Patriette, respectively. On the far side of the table, a stand-in playing Foxman was doing his best to ape Mark Caldwell's controversial take on Foxman's gravelly tone.

They got the wide shots out of the way and focused on close-ups. Burton Taylor had a rig under his cape—basically a dolly but for people—to keep him vertical. He sounded like he was speaking through a mouthful of cotton balls. Lidia Colby stayed behind her shield, which, because of the close-up, was required to be a detailed prop. As the weight of it wore out her shoulder, the shield slowly sunk out of frame to reveal traces of a baby bump. Caldwell's stand-in either faced away or kept his chin down and cape closed.

What a shit show.

The director called for dinner break. Two of the crew rushed in and converted Taylor's dolly into a gurney. The contraption was no doubt Ray's work. Two other PAs scrambled to get the stand-in out of the Foxman cowl after he started hyperventilating. Lidia Colby dropped the shield like a hot hubcap and beelined for her trailer. Preeti hustled after her with me in tow. She had to say her name three times before Colby acknowledged us.

"This is Ken Allen, a private detective. Answer all his questions frankly."

Colby laughed in our faces without slowing down.

"Might be best for me to go at her alone," I told Preeti.

Preeti spun about-face. "I wish you more success than I've experienced."

Hot on Colby's heels, I threw Preeti a thumbs-up. "This won't take long, then I'll be out of your hair."

Colby gave no indication she heard me. There was a bodyguard stationed outside her trailer. Tall and built, he was dressed like the grayscale version of me. She jerked a thumb in my general direction, and he moved to intercept. He stepped forward in the classic "not a threat" pose, both hands high, palms presented. It also happened to be the same stance Thai boxers favored. I gave him what he wanted and stepped right into the clinch.

The clinch was a smart move for a guy in his profession. You had head control, and you could scale up the severity based on how the situation developed. Elbows, knees, and sweeps were all available as needed. A layman didn't read it as a skill position, but if you didn't know what you were doing in the clinch, you were toast, and the tangle-up would be hard for witnesses to decode exactly what had happened.

The guard sucked me in and set a knee into my liver. I blocked it with a forearm, hit and inside trip, and down we went. I slipped into side mount immediately. He tried to adjust but was too many steps behind. I locked up a neck crank and whispered into his ear.

"We good?"

He had enough room left in his airway to wheeze out a "yeah."

I turned him loose but kept a stiff-arm as we untangled. The world is full of guys who will scream uncle and then sucker punch you the second you show mercy.

"I'm with the studio," I said. "This will take all of five minutes."

The guard winced as he tested out his neck. "She's been in a mood."

"I caught that," I said, before latching the trailer door behind me.

Colby was standing at the wet bar, feigning disinterest, but the trailer's window blinds were still swinging.

"Give your guy a break, he tried his best."

"Screw him. The first time he has to do his job and he bungles it. Know any virgin cocktails?"

"Yeah. I used to do this for a living. Take a seat."

Colby flopped down in a new recliner and swung her feet up. Her drink of choice must have been mojitos, because there was enough wilting mint to soothe a giant with halitosis. A handful went in a shaker with tonic, diet ginger ale, and some strawberries from an ignored edible arrangement. "How far along are you?"

She leaned over to take the glass from me. Her roots were slathered in dry shampoo. "Eight weeks."

"Early to be showing."

"That's not all kid. Can you help me out of this shit?"

"Sure."

It took me a minute to get my bearings. All the straps and buttons on her breastplate were fake. The zippers were concealed behind Velcro panels. When her ribs were finally able to expand, Colby breathed as if someone had been holding her underwater.

"I had to say good-bye to both coke and smoke," she said.

"The one-two punch of appetite suppression."

"Weren't you REDACTED's personal trainer?"

"Up until the whole false murder-accusation thing."

Colby passed her empty tumbler back to me. "Anything I can take to keep from ballooning up without my kid being born with webbed feet?"

I started assembling her refill. "Want my honest advice?"

"No."

"Make baby happy. Leak some unflattering pictures. Once you have the kid, hit it hard. Harder than ever. Your life will be hell, but when the after pictures hit the media, you'll get a mountain of press attention."

Colby leaned back and groaned at my wisdom. "I hate hard work."

"There's some questions I have to ask."

"Rub my feet and I'll tell you anything."

I pulled the stool from her makeup table over and got to work. Sports massage was part of my old gig. I decided to tear off the Band-Aid. Start with the big question, so the ones after wouldn't seem so bad.

"Who's the father?"

Colby sighed at the ceiling.

"Preeti wasn't whistling Dixie," I told her. "I signed an NDA. If a leak leads back to me, my life is over. And remember the job I had before this. Did REDACTED ever get outed?"

Colby's thoughtful grunt turned into a moan. "That's the spot. It's my ex-husband. When he finds out, he's going to bleed me dry."

"The baseball player or the guy who builds motorcycles?"

"The former."

So, her ex-ex-husband. Colby had a habit of getting married on a whim, without the benefit of a pre-nup. Her divorce settlements had been based on her income at the height of her stardom. Now she had to maintain a grueling schedule, raising tentpoles to keep up with the payments.

"Were you on birth control?"

Colby rolled her eyes. "Yes, Dad."

"What kind?"

"I had an allergic response to my new IUD. We used condoms while I got over it."

"Anyone but you have access to them?"

Colby tore her foot out of my hand as she sat up. "Shut your mouth."

"Your guy outside. Who did he replace?"

"A different new guy. My old guy had a car wreck."

Colby had been crammed into boots that would have violated the Eighth Amendment. I was dying to wash my hands but didn't want to break our vibe. "Different new guy, he have a name?"

"He wasn't around long. Studio security referred him after his own firm went bust. Cavalier or something like that."

"Chevalier?"

"Heard of them, huh?"

"We've met."

Colby's assistant provided the ex-guard's billing address, which pointed to a condo adjacent my old neighborhood. I was forced to park two blocks away in a spot sure to piss off whoever had left it vacant. The sun was fading fast, which would help with nosy neighbors. Day or night, I doubted I would catch my quarry off guard. Neil Leon, former CEO of Chevalier, was sure to have a security system.

There was no point in trying to hide from the two cameras I spotted. Even from the back, my jacket was a dead giveaway. Neil and I had parted on bad terms. Last time out, I roughed up his guys and put him in the hospital with a broken jaw. According to Lidia Colby, the fallout of going down to a rank amateur like myself had ruined his reputation. I doubted my care package of smoothie recipes and a bullet blender had been enough to heal the divide.

No one answered, so I knocked louder and dialed up the starlight vision on my spyglasses. On the far side of the bay window, a German Shepherd stumbled up to the glass and sniffed. His hipbones were prominent behind clearly defined ribs. Despite his emaciated state, the dog took his duty seriously and managed a dry bark.

That sealed it. I retrieved my multi-tool from my belt and slipped the lock-pick attachment into the deadbolt. It vibrated the tumblers. Two rotations later the door opened. The dog gave another weak *ruff* at me, still trying to do his job. I closed the door and drew my Quarreler, moving room to room. I expected a body behind every door, but the place was deserted. Neil Leon was long gone.

8

THE AUTO-FEEDER MOUNTED over the dog dish was bare. Fill lines on the side of the bin indicated it would hold out for two weeks. I dug around for anything edible. Some MREs were stacked on the shelf in a closet stocked with five gallon water jugs. Neil Leon was riding the line between earthquake ready and apocalypse prepper.

The dog jumped into a helping of military grade Beefaroni like it was his favorite meal. I was careful not to touch him while I changed his water jug in case he was food defensive. The spyglasses were handy, but lights on worked better for clue hunting. I reminded myself to thank Ray for the gloves. The last thing I needed was my fingerprints in a place they had no legal right to be. The alarm box caught my eye as I closed the blackout curtains. It read DISARMED. My lucky streak continued. One day someone was going to actually use their security system and put me in a pickle.

Normally, I used cameras mounted on the Stag to monitor my back trail, but it was blocks away, so I positioned a pencil camera on the landing facing the front door. The pet door which communicated with the dog's collar was acting up. I had to lift it manually so he could go take care of business.

I decided to start upstairs, where the private rooms were. I wanted a chance at the good stuff before the neighbors got suspicious and called the cops. The master bedroom didn't tell me a lot except Neil liked guns and made his bed, which was two marks against him in my book.

I lifted everything up, pulled everything out, and checked for loose fixtures, but nothing yielded fruit. There was a well-stocked go bag in the master closet, including two passports under different names and shrink-wrapped euros. I took pictures of the passports and left the money.

Neil used the other bedroom as a dedicated office space. Shelves on the wall facing his computer screen provided a tonal backdrop for video calls, including a greatest hits collection of military history and philosophy books, along with a series of handguns arrayed to form a timeline.

The computer was in sleep mode. Wiggling the mouse rewarded me with a log-in screen. I shut the computer down and pulled the tower out from under the desk. There were two removable hard drives. I took them both, along with a handful of flash dives scattered in the drawers. There was a leather field-notes book Velcroed to the underside of the desk. I pocketed that too.

The guns were next. Neil was a clean guy, but schmutz had built up during his time away. One of the more modern weapons had faded fingerprints under the dust. I ejected the magazine. It was normal and empty. When I eased back the slide, instead of a bullet, there was some rolled-up paper. Even though I knew the gun was empty, fishing it out of the barrel made me tense. A list of passwords was printed on the paper. Feeling like quite the super-sleuth, I started in on the bathroom. The toilet bowl was bone dry. If Neil hadn't left it up, his pooch might not have made it. I was lifting the lid on the tank when someone kicked the downstairs door in. My video watch relayed a camera feed of two guys encased in body armor with full-face masks storming toward the stairs.

The cramped bathroom was a death trap. I cracked the office door for a misdirect and slipped into the master bedroom, drawing my Quarreler. The door was situated halfway along the room's length. I moved toward the wall that put the door between them and me in case I had to use grenades.

The bad guys ignored my feint, kicked the master bedroom door completely open, and came in shooting directly at my position. Their weapons looked like old-timey blunderbusses, the kind with trumpet barrels.

Something stung my calf as I rolled over the memory-foam mattress and into the space between the bed and the wall.

Neil had elected for a metal-frame bed with plenty of storage space underneath. I turned unto my side and saw two pairs of legs. Legs weren't easy to hit, slim and always moving. I traced a line of taser darts up the closest pair from the knee to the groin. The first one stuck inside a thigh and the second one bounced off the guy's cup.

Villain #2 sprayed the wall six inches over my hair as he jumped onto the bed. I dropped the Quarreler and bench-pressed the bedframe, which sent him tumbling onto the floor. I rose with the frame under my shoulder and flipped the bed, frame and all, onto him. Villain #1 was in the middle of a herculean struggle to reach the dart in his leg. I scooped up the Quarreler and put a second dart in the other one.

Villain #2 was shoving the bed off himself. I dug a concussion grenade out of my harness and skipped it off the floor to adhere under the mattress. The grenade exploded as I was on my way out the bedroom door. The guy's mask and armor made me feel okay about maybe overdoing it.

Part of me wanted to question them but we had made quite the ruckus. I retrieved my pencil camera from the landing on the way out the door. I couldn't stop thinking about the dog.

"If anyone is listening, call 911 to this address. Be sure to mention the guys inside have assault weapons."

A text alert flashed that Elaine was indeed listening as I headed back to my bike. It was dark enough for streetlights. My spyglasses adjusted accordingly. The White Stag was parked halfway down the block. At the far end, a black sedan with a tinted windshield was hugged tight against the opposite corner.

I got low, using the wall of parked cars for cover. There was a group of porch sitters outside the fourth house. They asked each other what the hell I was doing and raised their phones to film. Behind the car adjacent to the White Stag, I keyed the auto-start from my watch. Ray possessed the foresight to skip the parking lights from flashing when the Stag was remotely commanded. Being a hybrid, the bike woke without a sound. If my watch didn't confirm it, I wouldn't have known the engine was running.

Crouched behind the back wheel of an SUV, I planned my next moves: how I would mount, the direction of my escape route. Before I could break cover, the sedan peeled away from the curb toward Neil Leon's house. My ambushers had called for an extraction.

I waited until the sedan turned the corner to leap into the saddle, unlocking my helmet and adjusting its starlight vision before giving chase. Driving at night with no lamps announcing your existence to other drivers was incredibly stupid, especially in this day and age, but I couldn't think of any other way to tail the sedan without giving myself away. The White Stag, with the one headlight, was too easy for my quarry to identify.

The sedan stopped only long enough to retrieve my ambushers. Which actually was a solid ten seconds with the way they were hobbling. I swapped quivers from yellow to blue. While the Quarreler was a miracle of modern technology, it had its limitations. One being that its effective range was only fifty feet. I would need to be close if I wanted to be sure the tracer dart stuck. But my quarry might get suspicious if a single impact echoed in their quarter panel. What I needed was a misdirect. The best thing I could come up with to fool them into thinking I had done something stupid was to actually do something stupid.

My ambushers slammed the rear doors closed as the sedan pulled away. It had to be now, before they got settled. I came up from behind, moving in the same direction as they were, and put a fléchette into the rear bumper. Good thing bumpers weren't made of metal anymore. I swerved to pass them along the driver's side. It was a tight fit, but I was hoping the driver had their hands full and the front passenger—if there was one—wouldn't shoot across the driver. I sprayed three more shots into their windows as I passed. The needle darts bounced off the impact-resistant glass.

I pulled out ahead of the sedan, the starlight vision in my helmet adjusting automatically when I flicked on my headlight. A swarm of red and blue lights buzzed in my hindsight vision, six hundred feet away and closing. The sedan accelerated in an attempt to rear-end me. They had to be kidding themselves. No way were they keeping pace with the Stag. Still, I had seen enough movies to know it was only a matter of time before someone hung their gun out the window.

It was better to overdo it than underdo it. I flicked on the rear strobe and flashed 5,000 lumens in their faces at twenty-four frames per second. At the same time, I toggled the rear grenade launcher and put two blackball grenades in their windshield. The grenades erupted, enveloping the sedan in a cloud of dark smoke they couldn't escape because it was stuck to them.

To my dismay, the cops had stopped at Neil Leon's house and missed the show. I took the first three turns that presented themselves and engaged the tracking device.

I paralleled the sedan, wondering how they were navigating. Maybe hanging their heads out the window like dogs. However they were doing it, they went close to five miles before pulling into a parking structure adjacent to a Cineplex.

The structure was too big for me to watch all the entrances. If they were swapping cars, I didn't want to miss it, so I took a gamble and went in the opposite street entrance. The tracking fléchette included elevation. They had parked on the roof. I rocketed up the lower levels, then took the final ramp slowly, cresting it only enough to peek out.

The sedan was parked by the side-by-side elevators, whose doors were closing together. I wheeled the Stag around and raced back to the bottom, but the elevator had beat me there by a wide margin. Outside the exit, a bus was sitting at the stop. I throttled toward it as it groaned away from the curb, but its dingy, fluorescent-lit interior was vacant of passengers.

I'd lost them. The possibilities were endless. They could have gone out either entrance. Or they could have gotten out on a different level and sat in their swap car to wait me out. Or they could have scattered to the winds.

Nothing outside my office/residence appeared amiss. I plugged in my bike and slipped inside. Dean was passed out on the couch, on his back, blankets half off in a scene reminiscent of a renaissance painting. I took a step forward to cover him up before changing my mind. When you're hot, you're hot.

I was too worn out to cook and didn't want to wake up the kid by running the blender, so I cut a double helping of my homemade no-bake fat-bomb protein bars. I devoured the bars in my office with thirty-two ounces of water. I didn't eat in my bedroom.

Once you got crumbs in your bed they were there forever.

I wondered how sore I would be tomorrow. Sorer than I would have been ten years ago, that's for sure. I was getting older, every day. When I was a little kid, I never dreamed I'd be as old as Foxman. I didn't want to be him anyway. I wanted to be Kid Kit. Foxman took Kit under his wing, taught him how to be a hero. Foxman was the model dad I longed for. He never ghosted a promised fish dinner. Plus, Kid Kit always got tied up with Vixen.

The protein bars imbued me with enough courage to examine my leg. My calf wasn't bleeding too bad on account of the fléchette stuck in it. Nothing fancy like the ones I used, just a good old-fashioned spike about the size of a framing nail. I searched my memory for how many fléchettes those shotguns pumped out in a single blast. From the sound of them hitting the wall, half-a-dozen. Enough where if a volley caught my legs flush, I would be out of action for a few weeks.

Around the time I dropped out of high school to train full time, I realized I was older than Kid Kit. My chances at a surrogate father swooping in to save the day were kaput. Sixteen years later, when the whole world found out my dirty secret—that I had played the part of superspy Jove Brand so poorly the movie had never been released—it hit me:

I would never be Foxman either.

Even in the most generous of timelines, Foxman was thirty-five, max. Every year—hell, every day—I was further and further from the ideal heroic age.

I disinfected my wound and hung everything up before taking a good, long shower. I tried to think about anything else, but I couldn't get the Good Knights out of my head. Humans tear their heroes from time. Their unchanging nature is part of the appeal. They will always be there, same as they ever were, trapped in the amber of our childhoods.

Heroes can't be fallible mortals. They can't have sciatica, or change diapers, or die in car wrecks. That stuff happens to ordinary people. So, wheel Burton Taylor away on a gurney and unveil the next

Good-Man. Call up a stunt guy to don Foxman's cowl the day after Mark Caldwell is immolated. I tried to reassure Lidia Colby, but she knows the score. By the time she's able to fit into the Patriette costume again, an actress fifteen years younger and twenty times cheaper will be bearing the shield.

I bandaged my calf before snuggling into bed. My thoughts were lengthening into a four-color dream space when my phone vibrated. I peeked over, deciding whoever was calling had better be pretty damn important.

The screen read KEN ALLEN. The number below the name was mine.

I slipped my Bluetooth back in and swiped the call to life. My words echoed in the serene darkness around me.

"Well hello, gorgeous."

The voice that responded reverberated, as if its owner were calling from a concert hall. Or they possessed the biggest set of lungs the English language had ever encountered.

"Hello yourself. The time has come for us to get acquainted."

I didn't bother asking who it was.

Culvan Mann had my number.

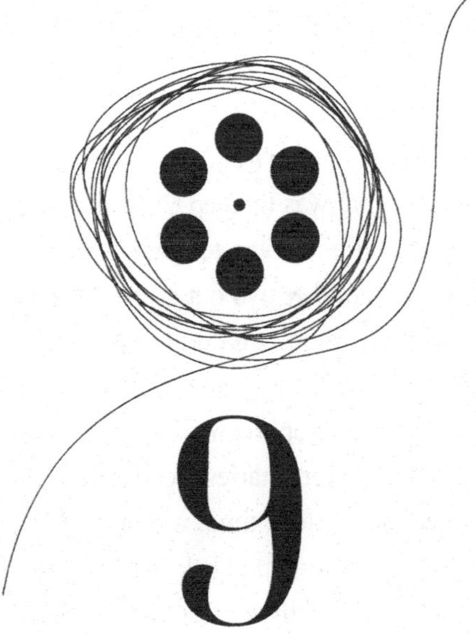

9

"I'M GOING TO kill you."

Culvan projected his voice like a factory worker on the line. Ray was the same way. Their chosen vocation wasn't easy on the eardrums.

"So far, no good," I said.

"Even if you weren't opposing my goals, Ray Ford has chosen you."

I turned on my bedside lamp. "We aren't Ray's rival sons. You need therapy, buddy."

"No further analysis is required. Ray destroyed my future. Exiled me. Now he must pay."

"Do you always talk like a supervillain?" I texted Ray:

On the phone with Culvan.

"And don't bother trying to convince me you have some lofty purpose."

"No person harms me without recompense."

"Life isn't fair. Grow up, Mann."

Either Ray or Elaine texted back:

I know. We're working on a trace.

Which meant my goal was to keep Culvan on the line for as long as possible. "You should hire some tougher henchmen. I dropped the one off a cliff and took another two out at the same time."

"Don't pretend conviction you do not possess. You attempted to save my agent from falling."

So Culvan had cameras on his mercs. Or on the sedan. Or both. He was studying me. His mercenaries were equipped the same as me. Building all that gear had to take time, which meant—

"You hired Neil Leon a while back. At least eight weeks, if you were behind the Patriette's birth-control malfunction."

"I hired Mr. Leon shortly after the Jove Brand murders were reported in the media. I recognized Ray's work, even in poor-resolution photos. Neil Leon was broken, his company's reputation shattered. He was all too happy to recall his encounters with you. To detail your methods and equipment."

I stacked my pillows into a backrest. "Five years on your own and you're still ripping off Ray Ford."

"I am besting Ray at his own game. Creators like he and I control the board. You and my agents are the pieces we employ. Ray purposefully placed you in his debt. He knew this day would come."

"All Ray had to do was ask," I replied. "You're the one who has to buy their friends."

"And your devotion comes cheap, Ken Allen. The self-imposed moral compass you follow is a fatal flaw. If you will not kill, you will be killed."

"Yeah, I'm a big softie. Neil must have written everything down, seeing as his jaw was wired shut."

Culvan paused to regroup. "I assumed Mr. Leon exaggerated his encounters with you to salve his ego, but you demonstrated expertise, escaping my trap. Your improvisational use of the environment was impressive."

Either Mann had already debriefed his mercs or—

"You hacked Leon's security. That's why his system was deactivated. To keep me there for your goons. And you were monitoring through his cameras, that's how you knew I was there in the first place. Very sneaky."

Culvan was using noise canceling. When he wasn't speaking, the line was totally silent. I imagined him crammed into a cubicle, wearing the world's largest headset.

"You are more intelligent than you affect," he said. "I had assumed Ray selected you solely based on your physical aptitude."

"Wait until I'm in touching range."

"That would be a poor tactical decision. I am your physical superior." Culvan went mute in thought. "What you say is true, I have no friends. No family. No connections to be exploited. Is the boy your son? There are physical similarities."

The blood erupted in my veins. I swallowed my first reply and reminded myself Culvan was trying to push my buttons.

"That kid is Dina Calabria's son. If you don't know the name already, look her up. I wouldn't mess with her children. She doesn't share my ethical weaknesses."

"Dina Calabria would first have to locate me. How is Elaine doing so far?"

A glance at my phone showed no new texts.

Culvan didn't wait for my retort. "I know you are listening, Ray. I want to give Elaine ample time to fail. I want you to understand how helpless you are while I ruin you, the way you ruined me."

Had Culvan Mann's surveillance gone on the entire time between my first case and this one? What locations did he have bugged, and who was he watching? How many people did he have working for him? Going by last night, at least four.

One thing was for sure: he was doing a hell of a lot to convince me this was all about him and Ray.

"No sale, Culvan. You might know gadgets, but you are terrible at social engineering. Someone is paying you to do a job and I'm going to find out who."

The line went silent. After ten minutes with no response from Ray, I went to my desk and dumped all my electronics in the faraday drawer to get some sleep.

My everyday carry now included a compression sleeve over my wounded calf. Dean was waiting at the table in the kitchen nook. I made us both an egg, cheese, and bacon scramble, topped with freshly sliced avocado. Dean inhaled the food. His plate was clear before I settled in. I ate slowly, putting off what had to be done for as long as I could keep my mouth full.

"I hate to do this, but you gotta go home, kid."

Dean's face fell. "Sorry. I tried to stay out of your way."

"That's not it. Things are heating up. The guy I'm after is bad news. He's targeting me to get at someone else. I can't keep you safe. I barely manage myself."

I rolled my pants up and the compression sleeve down to give Dean a peek at the cost of doing business. "In the past three days, I've been gassed, hit by a car, shot at, blown up, and shot at again. And I get the feeling we're only in the second act."

Dean mulled it over. I wished I could give him what he was searching for. He'd shown up with hopes over expectations, and I hadn't lived up to either.

"We'll do this again when this is all over."

"Yeah, sure," Dean replied. "Later."

His tone told me all I needed to know. Dean's mother had put him off his whole life. Here was a fresh chance at being parented, and the new prospect was pulling the same act as the old one.

"Do you have someone you can call to pick you up? Right now, I wouldn't trust a service. I'd do it myself, but all I have is the bike."

"Diana knows I'm here. She's cool with it."

"Good choice." Dean's sister had played a supporting role in my maiden voyage as a sleuth. She was cut from the same cloth as her mother.

Dean texted her while I washed our dishes and thought about my case. A minute in, I smacked myself in the forehead.

The kid was here for maybe another hour and already I was ignoring him.

"Did you see the last Unlimited Fight Challenge?"

Dean perked up. "Man, Roman Carlos is awesome."

"He's thirty-three though. He's got maybe five more years."

"What is a fighter supposed to do when he retires?" Dean asked. "I mean, there's only so many coaching spots."

"Open a school somewhere. The real money is in kids' classes. Most parents enroll their brats for the cheap childcare. Or take your nest egg, if you managed to lay one, and do something else."

Dean smirked. "Like become a detective?"

"Many are called." My leg began to ache. I sat back down, across from Dean.

"You know, when you think about it, you're sort of like a superhero," he said.

"Don't try to butter me up, kid. No way I'm buying you a puppy."

"No, really. You have a costume with a bunch of crime-fighting gear. And a lair. And a tricked-out ride."

"And a mortgage payment and five pounds I can't outrun."

Dean got up to refill his water. "So was Jove Brand always your favorite?"

"Ha. No. Your uncle casting me was a fluke. I was never much into Brand. I learned all the lore after the fact, trying to sort out what had happened to my life."

He sat back down and studied me for a minute. “Let me see . . . Foxman.”

It was the guess of someone who only knew superheroes from the screen. “Actually, Sword Saint was my favorite. He had a cool costume, and all his powers came from training instead of gadgets.”

Dean threw his hands up. “But he never drew the Lotus Blade! He had the most powerful sword ever forged and all he did was carry it around on his back.”

“That’s the whole point of the character. At any time, he could draw the sword, but it was crossing a line. His job was to guard the blade, not wield it.”

From there, the conversation flowed. Turns out the trick to family stuff was to not talk about it. Two hours later, we were taking turns showing each other videos when my watch flicked on to show Diana at the door. I unlocked it remotely and beckoned her in through the wireless doorbell. She had her hair tied back and aviators on.

“Hey, Ken. Grab your crap, Goldpecker, we take off in an hour.”

Dean turned a lovely shade of green. “We’re flying back?”

“I’ve almost logged my solo hours.” Diana clapped her hands rapidly. “Let’s go, let’s go! Bye, Ken.”

Dean scooped up his backpack and we shared an awkward silence. Diana saved us by stepping over to hug me, which gave Dean and I the cover to embrace.

“Text me when you land,” I said.

“Okay.” Dean turned away to hide his face. “Bye.”

I turned Dean around to look in his eyes. “For now.”

We smiled and nodded in concert, almost butting heads. I locked up behind them and sat down at the table with the full intention of drafting a plan of action. My condo felt empty. It had never felt empty before. I had lost count of the number of people over the years who told me a lot of men settled down later in life. That it wasn’t too late for me. Pushing forty, I had never even had a serious girlfriend.

You needed to invest in others if you wanted them to invest in you. You had to take the leap, but most of the time no one caught you. Or if they did, they dropped you on testing your weight.

My heroes, they knew better. They walked alone. Foxman didn't get stuck going to the farmer's market Sunday mornings. Sword Saint never had to negotiate where to eat dinner. My heroes were self-sufficient. They weren't burdens you dumped in a karate class after school. I got up to clean, but Dean had already straightened up. A few things were out of place. I left them that way.

Dean had been looking through my coffee-table books. *The Secret History of Superheroes* was on top. The volume was an oversized edition to accommodate reproductions of the original art from comic pages. Dean hadn't gotten far. The book was open to the first drawing of a superhero, ever.

Sol Silver was fourteen years old when he created Good-Man. Silver was a poor Jewish kid from Bed-Stuy who lived with three generations of extended family over their butcher shop. Like all the disenfranchised, Silver dreamed of possessing the power to change the world. He imagined that power in the hands of a benevolent force who could not be beaten or bought. A mythic hero for the modern age.

Silver was a born artist fortunate enough to grow up surrounded by butcher paper. Inspiration struck him like a bolt of lightning. So much so that his knife slipped. He dropped it and scooped up the shop pencil for labeling, not bothering to address his wound. The very first drawing of a superhero was anointed with the artist's blood.

He drew Good-Man in a silver bodysuit with a golden cape, intended to be evocative of a knight's armor. In later appearances, Silver streamlined the design to better display Good-Man's physique and to avoid any confusion that it was the armor that made him invulnerable. And thus, Sol Silver invented the superhero costume.

The photo of that first sketch was reproduced in my coffee-table book: Good-Man, hands on his hips, cape swept in the wind, spattered in Silver's blood. The same image had been used dozens of times, taken from a print on display in the Smithsonian. That photo was the best anyone could do. Seth Martin, Silver's creative partner, kept the original under lock and key for almost eighty years.

Now that Martin was gone, speculation abounded about what he had done with the first drawing of a superhero, ever. That piece of paper would catch eight figures at auction, easy. Surviving copies of *Best Comics #1*, Good-Man's first appearance, already had gone for several million.

Bursting with ideas and shouting into the void, young Silver showed his Good-Man sketch to anyone who would hold still. No one displayed any interest in a teenager's wild ideas. Until Silver showed it to Seth Martin.

My watch screen flashed on to show the doorbell camera. Special Investigator Ava Stern was standing with her back to the door, checking out my new bike.

"Here to ask me to the policeman's ball?"

"I'm not falling for that one, Allen. Let me in."

"Promise you aren't going to arrest me."

Stern held up three fingers. "Scout's honor."

"Show me your other hand."

Stern turned to leave. I buzzed her in.

She was dressed for action, in jeans, boots, and a short leather coat. Her hair was up in the gold coil. Nothing about its design said Stern to me. I decided it had to be a gift.

"It's time to put our cards on the table, Allen."

I started making coffee. "The cards aren't always mine. With this job, I'm holding someone else's hand."

"Fair enough. Shit, I still have your mug."

"Holding on to a reason to drop by?"

Stern took a seat in the nook booth. She shuffled around, not liking her options. Facing me put her back to the door and the table blocked her weapon. Facing how she wanted put her back to me. "Why did you ask about mercenaries, Allen?"

I decided the information wasn't privileged. "My quarry is using soldiers of fortune to do his dirty work. I was hoping to find out where he's sourcing them. Your turn."

Stern took a moment to swallow the concept of a free-and-fair exchange. "I've been working on a case. A real one. Private contractors with serious rap sheets have been traveling into the area for months now. They land at LAX and disappear. Once in a while, one of them turns up dead."

"How?"

"Choked, with a broken neck. No ligature marks. If someone is doing it without tools, they'd have to be pretty strong."

My phone started going off. I checked the screen. Ray was listening in.

I canceled the call and brought our coffee to the table.

"Scooch over."

Stern pushed herself into the spot she wanted and relaxed an inch. We sipped from our cups while I made a fateful decision.

"We might be after the same guy. His name is Culvan Mann. He's the villain version of Ray Ford, expert in technology and weapon manufacturing. He's been sabotaging productions Ray is working on. For who or why I have no idea."

Stern bit at her pinkie nail in thought. She'd traded one bad habit for another. "Any ideas where I should start looking for Mr. Mann?"

My phone turned its own ringer on and started chiming. "I haven't the foggiest. That's why I'm telling you. I assume it's a place close to the studios, where he can build and store an arsenal. He might have a vehicle, like a panel van, to act as a mobile workshop. Probably bigger, now that I think on it. Mann is supposed to be about seven feet tall and built like Schwarzenegger."

"You got a new bike. Was Mann behind the old one blowing up?"

I nodded. "His guys get around in sedans with darkened windows. The cars look stock but are anything but. And you're right about them being highly trained. They also have no compunctions about killing, so be careful out there."

We drank our coffee, thinking.

"I like this new leaf you're turning over, Allen."

"Mann is dangerous. He might get me. If he does, I'd rather the person investigating behind me didn't have to start at square one. People have died over this. In messy ways. I want it to stop more than I want to be the one who stops it."

Stern nodded like I was making sense for the first time ever. It threw me for a loop. We sipped coffee while I thought of a question.

"These mercenaries, how many are we talking?"

"At least a dozen," Stern said. "Maybe more. It's hard to tell, because former soldiers are always flowing into This Town, hiring on as private cops and consultants, maybe hoping to be discovered."

"Do you have a list of suspicious characters?"

Stern shook her head. Sharing was one thing. Me stumbling all over her investigation was another. "Try the wall at the post office. Were you in Neil Leon's condo last night?"

I wasn't about to admit to breaking and entering just yet. "Mann hired Leon right out of the hospital. Culvan knew he would have to go through me to get to Ray. He wanted a firsthand intelligence report."

"Leon's hard drives were swiped. Know anything about that?"

I finished off my coffee. "Maybe some do-gooder will turn them in, you know, anonymously."

"He better. Good Samaritan or not, he's impeding a police investigation into multiple murders." Stern pushed her mug toward me as she got up. "Anything else to offer?"

"Yeah. You should try getting your nails done. It would give you a reason not to gnaw on them."

Stern stood up. "Enough with the Shinola."

In the spirit of cooperation, I walked Stern to the door. The sunlight brought out the copper in her hair

"Stay in touch, Allen. And call me prior to doing anything especially stupid."

"If only I knew before I started doing it."

Thought I wasn't looking forward to our next conversation, putting it off wouldn't make it any better, so I called Ray right away.

"What in the hell do you think you're doing, telling her everything?"

"You wanted your name cleared, Ray. I'm clearing it."

"If the cops close in, Culvan will vanish, and I'll be looking over my shoulder until the day I die. Which will probably be the day he decides to put me out of my misery."

"See? The power of positive thinking is already yielding rewards. Are you back in This Town? I need to drop off Neil Leon's hard drives and sundry."

Ray didn't answer. The call disconnected and a minute later GPS coordinates set on my watch. I loaded a blue quiver, double-checked my gear, and got in the saddle. Ray and Elaine were back in the RV, idling outside the studio system. When I stepped close, the secret door opened. The inner door didn't unlock until I was sealed in.

The interior was sparkling like new. Ray was on a rolling stool in front of his tinker table, arms crossed. Elaine was fixated on her screens, her normally sunny disposition entirely absent. I presented Neil Leon's digital history like it was a prize bass. When no one reacted, I set it down next to Elaine.

"Sheesh. Don't everyone thank me at once."

Watching both of them in profile, they were making the same sullen face.

"You know, normally I am all for unresolved familial issues, but we're on the clock here."

The two of them clenched their teeth in synchronization. Ray leaned into the hold he had on himself. Elaine pulled a cable out of her chair so hard it reverberated and plugged in a hard drive.

"Tell you what, I'll moderate." I withdrew an imaginary coin from my pocket and flipped it. "Elaine, the opening statement is yours."

Elaine's keystrokes rang out like a machine gun. "My father might have mentioned Cul was involved at an earlier junction. Perhaps as soon as he suspected as much."

"You make a valid point. Ray, you have thirty seconds to rebut."

"I needed to be sure it was him," Ray said. "I was trying to protect you."

Elaine no longer required spurring. "I am so sick of hearing that. Five years—pardon me, I misspoke—thirty years you've been singing that tune."

"Damn straight I have. Loud and proud. And the moment I stopped, look what happened."

Ray stormed out of the room. He had always been a my-way-or-the-highway type. When he didn't want to hear something, he went deaf. When he disagreed with you, he didn't bother to argue. He wasn't interested in changing your mind and you sure as hell weren't changing his. I accepted his quirks—I wasn't about to question how my guardian angel went about his business—but I wasn't his kid.

Elaine tore the cord out of the hard drive and hooked up the other one. "Second verse, same as the first."

I pulled Ray's stool over and took a seat next to her. "How much of my conversation with Culvan did you hear?"

"All of it."

Elaine remained pointedly focused on her screen. No trace remained of the mischievous woman who enjoyed scandalizing her father at my expense.

"I don't want to pry, but it's part of the job. So is keeping my trap shut."

While I'm second rate in every other category, I'm top shelf at secret keeping. Despite what people promise, it was an extremely rare trait. I'd long ago lost track of how many people had approached me, whispering, *"Don't tell anyone else this, but . . ."*

Elaine blinked hard. "Ask what you're going to ask."

"Culvan has a weird affect. Is that real, or was he playing a character?"

"He was always like that with words." Elaine ghosted her fingers over the keys. "Crafting exactly what he was going to say before he said it. But it feels like he's gotten worse. More distant."

I could identify. "Lone wolfing it for years can do that."

"And Cul isn't one for idle conversation. He always speaks with a purpose."

"Then what was the purpose behind him calling me last night?"

Elaine stopped to glance at Neil Leon's password. It was a twenty-character jumble of letters, numbers, and symbols. She entered it faster than I could type gibberish. "I think you impressed him. Enough where he wanted more data for further testing."

"You make him sound like a robot."

"All of us wear armor to face the world. You joke. I poke. Cul speaks from behind a wall. I think . . ."

I shifted the stool into Elaine's peripheral vision to observe surreptitiously.

"It's okay to guess. Right now, I'm guessing no one knows him better than you."

"I think Cul used you to talk to me and Dad. I think he wants to be heard." She pretended to study the screen. "He disappeared after my accident. Maybe if I tried harder to find him . . . I don't know. I wish Dad could bring himself to listen."

"Say he could, what would you tell him?"

"Nothing I haven't already. That I'm my own person. That no one forced anything on me."

"To hear Ray tell it, what happened to you was all Culvan's doing."

Elaine sighed. "Because I'm forever a child."

"Leaving the nest might help that."

"I'm all Dad has. I can't abandon him too."

My watch interrupted us with a call from Flint West. I would have ignored it, but the alert also flashed on Elaine's screen and she waved me away. I headed for the airlock area in search of privacy. Here I was, boasting about my ability to keep secrets while being wiretapped. I thumbed the call on as the door closed.

"What's up Flint? Got a jar you can't get open?"

"Ken? This is Jaq, Flint's fiancé."

Either Flint had neglected that detail, or their engagement was fresh from the oven.

"Everything okay?"

"Flint is fine. I didn't intend to scare you." Jaq's smoky voice had a measured cadence. Elocution training was common in This Town. The first step in burying your past was killing your accent. "I'm calling for my dad. He wanted to meet with you. He doesn't like phones."

"I'll be right there. Where are you?" The speed of my response made me want to cringe, though Jaq had to be used to it by now.

"We're on set, in Flint's trailer. He's at a meeting concerning the future of the shoot, however long that will take."

"Are you able to get me in? Security is pretty tight."

"It's already been arranged."

"Well, see you soon then."

"Good-bye, Ken."

At least Jaq had manners. Nine out of ten people hung up on me. She was good on her word too. A badge was waiting for me. Being able to evoke Flint West's name opened doors, literally. Though his assistant was nowhere to be found, I was somehow able to find his trailer. I ducked my head inside to announce myself.

"You may enter." Jaq's voice dropped. "Are you sure you don't want me to stay, Abba?"

"Three's a crowd, kiddo."

They took their time hugging good-bye. I waited it out until Jaq pulled back the curtain.

"You could have come in, Ken."

"Better to ask permission than forgiveness."

Jaq narrowed her eyes. "I think you have that backward."

"Nah. Everyone else does."

Jaq studied me. "You mean that, don't you? I see why Flint likes you. He thinks everyone around him has the best intentions."

"Good thing you're here to set him straight."

Jaq gave a polite chuckle on her way out. "You men have fun. Good-bye, Ken."

The pneumatic door of the trailer eased shut behind her, leaving me alone with Dave King, the hand behind the heroes.

10

DAVE KING WAS sitting on the love seat with his fingers laced. I turned the desk chair so I could watch both him and the door. The curtain was open, a deliberate choice on my part. If I could eavesdrop through it, so could someone else.

King was wearing a button-down shirt with the sleeves rolled up. His forearms still showed some muscle, signs of a lifelong devotion to physical fitness.

The passage of time had eroded him, but his foundation was rock solid. Big boned, they used to say. I was willing to bet that back when King was my age, he would have been serious trouble.

"Thanks for coming, Ken."

"What can I do for you, Mr. King?"

"Glad you asked. The answer is nothing."

I leaned in. "I'm not sure what you mean."

"When we met, you mentioned you were a detective. The next day, you're at Flint's house, assuring him he didn't kill anyone. Now,

Flint's singing your praises to Jaq. Telling her you've found your true calling."

Dave King had been at Flint's, the day I visited. Upstairs, with his daughter, listening in. "Sir, I'm not sure a man your age should be smoking cigars."

"If they haven't killed me by now, they aren't going to. Flint's a decent man. I'd be proud to call him my son-in-law, maybe even see a grandchild or two before I'm gone. But I'm thinking he's trying to do more than all that. That maybe he's looking to help me get my due."

"That sounds like Flint. And for the record, he's not the only one out there who feels that way."

Dave King grunted out a sigh that told me he'd predicted my answer. "Now listen here, I've known a lot of fighting men and women in my time. People who would do whatever it took for a cause they believed in. People who would never surrender." He pointed a finger at me, his hand tremoring. "People like you."

I couldn't remember ever hearing higher praise. A rumble of emotion passed through me. I put a hand over my mouth to keep steady. Dave King stared me down. His daughter had inherited his dark, unrelenting gaze.

"You say my work meant a lot to you."

I spoke from behind my fingers. "It did."

Dave King nodded as if he had guessed correctly. "Which means you probably feel like you owe me something. You don't, but I won't bother trying to convince you of that. So instead, I'll ask: Would you do me a favor?"

A deliberate breath later, I managed a reply. It might have been *Yes, sir*.

Maybe I added an *anything*.

"Good. I'm going to say this plain: Stop trying to help me. If Flint asks you, politely decline. Or if you got it in your head all on your own, let it go. Now."

My jaw was so tight my temples throbbed. Dave King locked on to my eyes.

"No matter how many times I tell people to stay out of it, they keep trying to help me. Well, I don't want their help. And that includes you. Do you hear me?"

I examined the rug. "Yeah."

"This is my battle. I'll decide how it's fought, and I'm not looking to draft. What I want is for people to listen to me and honor my wishes. Will you do that for me, Ken?"

I moved my head the minimum amount required to qualify as a nod.

"I'd like to hear you say so."

"Yes, I will."

Dave King slapped his hands on his thighs. "Good. You're a man of your word. I've been around long enough to tell. What say we light some cigars and share a drink?"

There comes a time when a person's dedication is tested. I'd never taken so much as a puff of anything, and alcohol was sure to spike my blood sugar through the roof. And here the King of Comics himself was offering an opportunity any other fan would have killed to take.

"I'm not sure I'd survive the experience, sir."

King's laugh was deep and genuine. "That makes two of us, son."

We fell into a comfortable silence. His fingers were streaked with graphite.

"Are you still drawing?"

Dave King started massaging his digits. "I don't want to as much as I have to, if that makes any sense."

"It does. I've been training in one thing or another since I was four. If I quit—"

"Who am I?"

This time we laughed together.

"And now your daughter is in love with an artist."

Dave King looked at me in attentive confusion.

"Flint, I mean. His paintings."

"That's news to me."

Oops. I had gone and outed Flint. I assumed Dave King inhabiting the upper levels of Flint's home meant he had seen Flint's studio. Flint had a top-of-the-line trailer. It muffled conversation enough that I only heard him coming from twenty feet away.

He wasn't alone. The group's tone was one of celebration. Flint angled himself through the door. Jaq and a man I'd never met trailed in behind him.

"Hey Ken!" Flint spread his arms as he took in the scene. "Look at this, all my favorite people in the same room."

The man accompanying Flint and Jaq didn't wait to be introduced. He stepped forward and extended an arm. It was easier to pass on a handshake when it was only the two of you. As I reached out to meet him halfway, he passed me his card with a snap of the wrist as if he had them stashed in a forearm sleeve.

"Havier Cardiel, Tachi Productions."

Havier was two inches shorter than me and bordering the line between svelte and skinny. He had thick salt-and-pepper hair with a beard so well-groomed it looked like a prosthetic. His precisely creased suit was the color of aged bronze.

Flint wore a proud smile. "Havier is the go-to guy over at Tachi. Hey, you're going to need some new cards."

"Ha, guess I will," Havier said.

Jaq went to the bar. "There might be some champagne we haven't given away around here."

Flint, Havier, and I voiced a synchronized pass. The two of them laughed harder than the occurrence merited.

"What's going on?" I asked.

"What's going on is Havier here saved the day."

Havier clasped his palms together.

To anyone that didn't train, it was simply a gesture of appreciation. But his fingers fell into a gable grip—the go-to of grapplers the world around.

"It was a team effort," he said. "Anyway, we shouldn't be talking about it just yet."

Flint put his arms around me and Havier to pull us close. "Don't worry about Ken. You could sail him around the world. He's leak-proof."

"All right. It will go public in a few days anyway," Havier said. "With all the problems at the Civil Warriors shoot, we feared we might have to shut down. But I think we found a way to salvage the production."

Flint gave Havier a squeeze. "*We*, this guy says. Now that you're executive producer you're going to have to do something about all that modesty."

"Flint is the last hero standing. The Civil Warriors movie is officially shut down. Flying Freeman will soar solo."

I managed to escape Flint's trailer without ruining the celebration. Flint was ecstatic over the prospect of a Flying Freeman stand-alone film. To them, the danger was past. Flint and company thought Bill O'Wrongs's death had been due to mishap. It didn't escape me, however, that Havier had mentioned *all the problems*. As in plural. Tachi Productions was having the same issues as Duquesne.

I was dialing Zaina Preeti when my GPS threw an image onto my helmet's Head's Up Display. The sedan I had put a tracking fléchette into was moving from the parking structure. Culvan had sent his guys back for it.

I detoured toward the sedan. It came to a stop in a commercial office development. Thirty minutes later, I was on-site. I parked illegally on the far side of the next building over and walked through its lobby toward the rear entrance. The building the sedan had parked next to stood on the far side of a shared parking lot.

The structure was three stories of bland commercial space. Buildings belonging to its genus invoked bad associations. The most infamous scene of my short-lived acting career was shot in a location a lot like it, eighteen years ago and a continent away. Those modern beige labyrinths were to me what pyronite was to Good-Man. Cracks ran all along its façade. The perimeter was taped off, with signs declaring the building unsafe due to seismic activity.

I dialed Ray but didn't get an answer. I couldn't wait around all day and pondered how to handle my approach. There had to be some kind of surveillance system. I slipped my spyglasses on and let them adjust to the glare before zooming my view around. It was sunny and clear, but coming back at night might not be much better, if Culvan was as up on optics as Ray was.

A tall hedgerow ran close to the side and rear of the building, with minimal space left for delivery trucks. The row continued alongside the building I was surveying from, offering unbroken cover. A crowd of people stormed out the doors and lit cigarettes.

I went from hazy, polluted air into a full-on smoke storm inside five seconds.

"How long are we going to be down this time?" a woman with an avant-garde hairdo wondered.

"No power, no work. They might as well send us home," answered a guy who needed to be honest with himself and just shave his head.

The crowd performed a complaint chorus about how the company should move, with all the brownouts since the earthquake. Living on a fault line had finally paid off. I left back through the front doors and circled around the hedgerow to find myself in the parking strip of an apartment complex. In an attempt to not look suspicious, I jogged the length of the lot, checking my phone like I was late for something.

I reached my chosen approach vector. The hedge was dense. I buttoned my jacket and jumped the fence. My spyglasses spared my eyes, but the rest of me became one with the foliage. I leaned into the chain link and got low.

The closer to the building I got, the less coverage any surveillance cameras would have. I hoped. I broke out of the bushes, sprinting toward the corner of the building. Its rear face looked pretty much how I predicted it would.

Three sedans—including the one I'd tagged—were lined up outside of a recessed delivery dock that led to a sublevel. I took a lingering glance at the remaining two cars for future video reference as I crept along the back wall of the building.

The track of the roll-up doors was tilted, probably from the earthquake, leaving a gap of several feet between the door and concrete. I dropped over the concrete ledge and slipped a pencil camera under the door. The camera showed the interior to be an underground parking area. The space stood empty, but for the cracked support pillars, the first row of which was fifteen feet from the door. There was no time to waste. The power could come back on any minute.

I took two long strides and slid under the door headfirst. Everything above my calves made it through the opening. I broke for the pillar and put my back to it, facing the askew overhead door.

I used a second pencil camera to peek out from behind the pillar, the image windowed in my spyglasses. A sliding gate on the far wall led into the mechanical room. The elevator doors and the stair entrance were to my left. The blackout killed the fixtures, but there was enough sunlight coming through the door gap for my spyglasses to work with.

If I cut the service panel while the power was still out, Mann might assume it just never came back on. That would give me free reign from the security system. I tried to report in with Ray and Elaine, but my watch showed no service, which didn't strike me as suspicious in an underground parking garage.

The sublevel echoed with the thunderous boom as the overhead door slammed shut. Lights glared from every corner. Culvan Mann's voice boomed through a concealed PA system.

"Glad you could make it, Ken."

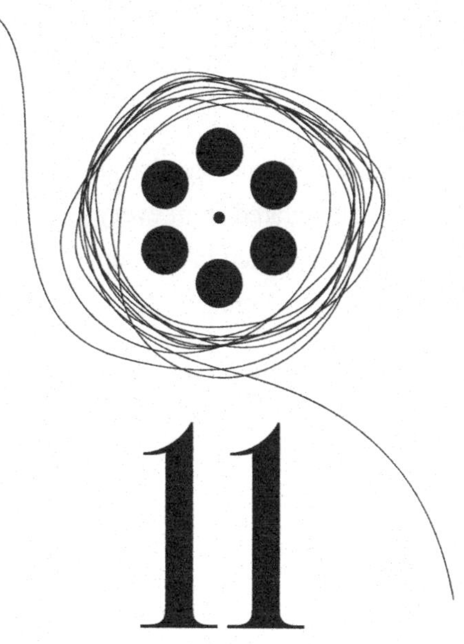

11

"YOU REACTED PRECISELY as I planned."

Culvan Mann's voice surrounded me. I broke cover toward the mechanical room. The elevator doors opened and four guys stormed out. They were identically outfitted in tactical gear and armed with fléchette shotguns.

"Like the rest of the world, like Ray Ford, you underestimated me."

I swapped quivers from tranq darts to concussive. Facing body armor, they were the best option available. I also didn't trust myself not to panic, shoot someone three times, and put them to sleep permanently. I glanced at the mechanical room. Even if the entrance led where it claimed it did, the gate might be booby-trapped.

The pencil cam showed my ambushers breaking into pairs and moving smoothly in a semi-crouch directly toward the pillar I was behind. Unseen cameras were reporting my position. Wherever he was, Culvan Mann was watching the Ken Allen show.

I fished out two smoke grenades. Aiming using my pencil camera was going to be tricky. I took a step back and whipped a grenade side-arm, skipping it off the pavement. It stuck four feet short of a pair of mercs and exploded into a black cloud. Fléchettes clattered off the pillar as I ducked back behind cover. I juked like I was coming out the other side, then went the same way as before and chucked the other smoke grenade. It bounced and stuck right at the second pair's feet before erupting.

I sprinted for the cage doors to the mechanical room, putting both teams in a line. Fléchettes rained around me as the closer pair took their best guess. The farther pair couldn't get in on the action without perforating their buddies. I stopped at the nearest pillar and angled the pencil camera. The closer pair came out of the smoke. Swarms of fléchettes skipped off both sides of the pillar. In this situation, fléchettes were a good choice over traditional firearms. The sublevel was ricochet alley. But that wasn't the point. The point was for Culvan to kill me with his take on Ray's design.

"You can't hide, Ken."

I swapped to the pencil camera positioned by the overhead door. The first pair of mercs was going wide to come at me from a right angle in order to the clear field of fire. I skipped a flash grenade hard enough that it stuck on the far wall, then spun toward the second pair of mercs and hit the deck. A hail of fléchettes went over me as I fired three times at the one on the left. All three of them hit: groin, chest, face mask.

I braced on one hand and came up from the ground, aiming an arcing high kick at the second merc. Guys were always tempted to try a sweep from my position, but sweeps were low percentage. You had to be deep enough to get both legs.

I didn't really care what my kick hit, or even if it hit anything, so long as it made the other guy defend instead of attack. I got lucky—it knocked the fléchette shotgun against the pillar. I used the momentum to stand, bracing his arm with my free hand to keep his gun out of it. Two shots went into him point-blank, ribs then head.

I was already moving as he went down, taking cover behind the next pillar over and switching back to the pencil cam stationed at the door. The remaining pair split up, each of them ducking behind a separate pillar.

Culvan Mann was issuing new instructions.

The remaining mercs and I had swapped locations. Now they were near the entrance and I the elevator. The elevator doors opened. My heart skipped as I sent my last two concussives into an empty car. Culvan screwing with me. The Quarreler snapped open. My choices were yellow or blue. I took a breath, loaded the blue, and recited a mantra:

Double tap. Two's the limit.

The elevator closed. The staircase door offered an escape. I didn't trust it. The last two guys were taking turns covering each other as they moved from pillar to pillar. There was a lag as Culvan relayed intelligence, which gave me maybe a two-second head start. They were closing in, and I was out of ideas. In my limited experience, if you didn't have a brilliant plan, the next best thing was a crazy one.

I set down the Quarreler, threw my last smoke grenade at my own feet, and pulled two flash-bangs. I tossed those close behind me, as if I were trying to flick the gloves off my hands, covered my ears and shouted. The twin booms still felt like being ear-clapped by a gorilla, but I was ready for them. Left or right. Two options, no information. My gut said left.

Enveloped in smoke, I collided with someone who wasn't me and let thirty years of training take over. At that range, being blind didn't matter—feeling was enough. He stuffed my throw attempt but fell for the inside trip. We hit the concrete with me on top.

He pulled me into the guard. Having a friend on the way, it was a smart strategy. I grabbed the Quarreler from where I had set it down, jammed it into his armpit, and pulled the trigger. His legs fell slack.

I rolled him on top of me for cover and aimed for the last man. The smoke was too thick. The guy on top of me went to sleep. I glanced at the pencil camera window in my left lens. Rather than chance the chaos, the remaining merc was backing toward the elevator. He slammed the button with the heel of his hand, his shotgun pointed toward the dark cloud concealing me.

I made my best guess using the pencil camera and shot out of the smoke. It went high and plunked into the doors. I aimed lower and the fléchette missed between his legs. He decided he had had enough and fired into the cloud. Sleepy on top me didn't react beyond a groan.

I shrimped out from underneath the deadweight to hunker down behind the pillar. We were at an impasse. It was going to boil down to who was faster on the draw. I backed toward the mechanical room, keeping the row of pillars between us. The gate's chain hung loose. Its lock had been cut. The elevator doors opened. This time there was a drone hovering in the cab.

A drone with something boxy mounted under it.

The last merc had his back to the elevator doors and didn't see the drone right off. I tumbled through the unsecured gate and slammed it shut. If the drone could work the latch I was done for. The hallway leading to the mechanical room was of block construction. I turned into a cramped space filled with commercial-sized furnaces, fuse boxes, and ductwork. I went for the ductwork.

The drone started knocking against the gate. I tore the air-exchanger access door off and crawled inside. I was pulling the panel in place behind me when the bomb went off.

It was pitch-black and utterly silent. My spyglasses were useless. Starlight technology magnified the ambient illumination and there wasn't any. All my gadgets, and I had no flashlight. I used the one on my phone and my glasses woke up. My devices were still showing no service.

The ductwork was crumpled inward. It looked like I was hiding in a punching bag. The blast had pushed the panel shut. I took a moment to savor the false security. Visions of being trapped under an office-building's worth of debris danced in my head. I filled my lungs with air, and tried, unsuccessfully, not to think about how many breaths remained in my sanctuary.

The temptation to sit there and do nothing was strong, but I hadn't packed a lunch. At least being spied on was no longer a problem, unless Culvan had built his cameras from the same alloy as the Patriette's Aegis Americanus.

I kicked the panel loose and climbed out. Besides the ductwork, the mechanical room looked pretty much the same. There was a lot of dust in the air. I adjusted my gas mask and kept the Quarreler ready. If I were a soldier of fortune, I would be none too happy my employer had blown me up. On the other hand, I also would still consider the guy I was sent to kill a threat.

The gate bordering the mechanical room had held. It took some muscle to work it open. Everything was where it had been, not that there was much in the sublevel to begin with. I didn't look too close at the bodies. Panic finally got the best of me and I ran to the overhead door. I put everything I had into it. The door didn't notice. Whatever mechanism Culvan had built to keep it down was stronger than my deadlift. My only way out was the staircase, because I sure as hell was not getting in that elevator.

The staircase door opened toward me. There was a reinforced window in the door to keep people from slamming it into each other. I shoved the remains of the window out and reached through with a pencil camera to look around.

The door was wired. There was a box like the one the drone had been carrying mounted above the exit sign. I was afraid to cut the wire. Wasn't the point for the wire to snap and set off the bomb? Or did it have to break at the contact point with the box? With no cellular reception, the option to phone a friend was off the table.

My only choice was to wiggle through the window. Going headfirst was the only option. I stretched one arm out and the other back to create as slim a profile as my shoulders would allow. Once my upper body was through, I bent toward the ground and let gravity do the work. All my weight was on the window frame. Every time the door jostled, my heart skipped.

I fell to the ground like toothpaste that missed the brush. The stairs rose above me. I took them slow, leading with my last pencil camera. When I stepped onto the landing, I finally spotted one of Culvan's cameras.

A gray blob roughly the size of a piece of chewed Hubba Bubba was stuck up in the far corner. The lens of the camera lurked inside it like an unblinking pupil. Either Culvan had taken out the building's electrical trying to kill me, or he was faking another brownout. The camera had already seen everything it was going to see. Still, I had to resist the urge to break it out of pettiness.

When I reached the door that led into the ground floor, my reception kicked back on. Either the sublevel had legitimately blocked any signal or Mann's jammers were offline.

"Can anyone hear me?"

No answer came.

"I'm not looking to chitchat. Culvan has me trapped in a building chock-full of bombs."

Again no answer.

The stairs above me went all the way up to the top floor, zigzagging at the halfway point landings. Block-and-tube stairwells summoned my aforementioned traumatic associations with office buildings. Beyond the psychological issues, physically I would be a sitting duck the entire ascent.

I didn't even know if Mann was up there somewhere. There was no indication he was even in the building. If so, he was trapped, unless he had a hang glider stashed on the roof, and cornering himself didn't seem like Culvan's style.

The view through the window mounted in the door was limited. The hall took a hard left six feet from the stairwell entrance. It would make sense to set an ambush out there, the only route of escape. I was guessing Culvan had spent all his mercs, at least in this location. It made no sense to send guys at me in waves. This wasn't a movie.

All stairwell doors opened in the direction of egress, in accordance with the fire code. Was this one wired too? Three spinning back-kicks later, the mesh window was hanging from the frame and I was scoping the scene with a pencil camera.

The door was indeed rigged.

I repeated my slug impression and dropped onto the floor. The lobby level was finished in gold trim and dark marble tile. A door labeled CUSTODIAL stood in the short hallway before the turn. Post-turn, bathroom entrances waited along the far wall. No windows were present on any of those doors. Having no way to check if any of them were wired, I ignored them.

"Ken, are you there?"

Elaine's voice in my ear made me jump.

"Yep. Still ticking."

"Tachi Productions called Dad in for a meeting. I've been listening in on that." As an afterthought, she added, "Sorry."

"Don't worry about it. We all lead full lives."

I stopped short of the corner that opened into the main lobby and scouted with the pencil camera. It was a large space with an out-of-service water feature in the center. U-shaped desks were built into each side wall.

The entrance was floor-to-ceiling glass with a revolving door. A second hallway was positioned directly across from me. A bronze plaque mounted on the wall informed me that building administration was to be found there.

Also, there was a killer robot waiting in the lobby.

It looked like a snowman with tank treads for legs. In lieu of arms, it had guns usually reserved for attack helicopters. Its head was the size and color of an eight ball. There was nothing human in its design. It had been built to suit a single purpose. It was not a protocol droid. It spoke only one, universal, language. A screen the size of a tablet was mounted on its thorax. Culvan Mann stared out of the screen at me. His broad face was contained between a shelf of brow and a cleft chin. Like Ray, his head was shaved close.

"Nice to see you, Ken."

The resolution was impressive. The screen could have been a window. Mann's voice was disturbingly clear. If the robot had been any bigger, I would have believed Culvan was inside. I took stock of my options. It wasn't looking good.

"Are you seeing what I'm seeing, Elaine?"

"Yes."

"Any ideas?"

"Working on it. We didn't plan for something like this when we designed your gear."

I was out of concussives and doubted shock or tranq rounds would do much. Grenade-wise, I had one flash-bang along with three regurgitants. Too bad my foe was immune to stomach bugs.

Culvan had murder on his mind.

"I could collapse the building on you, or bomb your condominium, or put a bullet in your head from a mile away, but it wouldn't satisfy me. I want to beat you."

"Yeah? Then why aren't you here? Scared of what's going to happen if I get my hands on you?"

Killer-bot started rolling toward me. "Be careful what you wish for, Ken."

I crept up on the corner, hoping to get the jump on it as it turned into the hallway, maybe tip it over. In response, Culvan steered wide, to maximize the distance.

Was Culvan controlling the guns, or were they motion activated? His twisted interpretation of fair play suggested he wanted to pull the trigger. Whenever the lighting conditions changed, my spyglasses took a hard blink to adjust. If Culvan was aping Ray's optics, his would take the same. I threw my last flash-bang between Killer-bot and my destination and sprinted toward the opposite hallway with my eyes closed.

Elaine chimed in too late. "Ken, don't!"

The cannon-arms blared twin eruptions. I dove into a roll, tucking my legs as marble chips sprayed around me. I scrambled behind the desk for cover, before crawling for the administrator's hallway. I didn't for one second consider bolting for the revolving door. Mama Allen didn't raise no fool.

I took a generous step past the door to the administrator's office and put thirty-five years of spinning back-kick practice next to the knob. The room didn't explode. Instead, a shotgun boomed as a dozen fléchettes peppered the wall opposite the door. With Killer-bot on my heels, there was no time to scout. I dove through the door and rolled into the front of a desk. Spinning behind it, I peeked up with the pencil camera.

There was a cannon the same as Killer-bot's arms mounted on a tripod atop the desk. It snapped around 180 degrees in my direction.

I backed under the desk to think. This wasn't a safe haven. No way could the desk withstand Killer-bot's barrage when it caught up to me. The cannon above me had to be motion based. It had turned too fast for human reflexes.

My leg was killing me. I was too scared about what I would find to investigate why. The bottom desk drawers were bigger. I pulled one out and tossed it upward, keeping my hand under the desk top.

The cannon treated the motion like a clay pigeon, obliterating the drawer and shattering the window into a million pieces. I flipped the desk over and dove through the empty window frame. My leg screaming in pain, I sprinted in the direction opposite the hedgerow, determined to put as much distance between me and the building as possible.

The main drawback of Ray's fléchette design was limited range. Personally, I didn't consider it to be a negative, because bullets kept on going past the target you missed to end up in something else. While Killer-bot probably couldn't negotiate the revolving doors, it definitely could roll though the floor-to-ceiling windows.

Smokers outside the neighboring buildings watched me flee from nothing in particular. I slowed to limp through a cluster of parked cars, adjusting my course toward the White Stag.

Life outside the death trap had continued as normal. As I entered the lot where my bike was parked, a guy waved wildly at a passenger bus as it pulled away. He threw his hands up, like he couldn't believe it was leaving him behind. I knew how he felt. This whole case had been me missing one bus after another.

The moment my butt touched the Stag's saddle, a rumbling filled the air as the vacant building collapsed in on itself.

I drove a few miles to get clear of the emergency response net. The new jacket was way more comfortable than the old one, but it was eighty degrees out and I had just sprinted a quarter mile, not to mention all the fighting for my life. I fished a sackcloth towel out of one of the saddleboxes and wiped off my face and neck.

The towel came back bloody.

"Are you there, Ken?" Elaine asked.

"Most of me."

I used the selfie camera on my phone to assess my condition. The side of my head looked like it did back in 1990 when I tried to give myself Vanilla Ice's haircut. There were a half dozen spikes lodged in my jacket and another in the center of my left thigh. Ray's ballistic blazer spared my organs, but my pants were off the rack.

On top of that, there was a parking ticket stuck on the Stag.

"Dad just got out of his meeting with Tachi Productions. They're coming after him for Bill O'Wrongs. They said since he was at the controls, he was directly responsible for the actor's death." Elaine took a trembling inhale. "Is he going to be arrested?"

"That's for the cops to decide, not Tachi Productions." I tied the towel around my head and lowered my helmet gingerly.

"I need to be with him."

"You do that." I suppressed a cry as I swung into the saddle. Ray and Elaine had enough on their minds without worrying about me. "We'll talk soon."

The drive back to my condo was absolutely brutal. The evening rush had hit. Even weaving through the lanes and cutting every corner, it took an hour to get home.

As I was plugging the Stag in to charge, a limousine pulled up outside my condo. It had been a banner day. I was in no mood to entertain visitors.

I rushed inside and slammed the door behind me.

Seven seconds later, the pounding started. After seven more seconds of ignoring it, a matriarch's voice boomed.

"Let me in, you son of a bitch."

Dean's mother wanted a word.

12

I UNLOCKED THE door via my watch while using the handrail to haul myself up the stairs. Dina was hot on my heels.

"Don't you turn your back on me! Oh my God, what's in your leg?"

My voice projected through my helmet. "It's been a long day."

I skipped my office for the bathroom. Real slow-like, I removed the helmet. The bloody towel stuck to my head.

"Jesus, Ken. You look like you got in a fight with a cactus."

I took a breath and looked in the mirror. My whole situation was worse in widescreen. I peeled the towel away to find two furrows along the back of my head.

"You should see the cactus," I said.

Up until three months ago, I went eighteen years without seeing Dina. Back then, she was an heiress who would not be denied, and I was a himbo who didn't know any better. Now she was the billionaire head of her own movie studio who would not be denied, and I was a detective who didn't know any better. She looked the same as she had last summer, when I figured out she had borne our love child, all those years back.

Which was to say gorgeous.

Dammit.

A sculptor looking to cast dramatic shadows would have chosen her features. She had predator eyes, closely spaced and intensely focused. Her olive skin absolutely refused to bow to the sun. Whatever she was taking for her hair was working wonders. It was jet-black and as wavy as an ocean storm.

Dina pulled out her phone and speed-texted. "My staff doctor is on the way."

I lay down on the bathroom floor. The tile was nice and cold. "You're too kind."

"I came to chew you out and I find you already chewed up."

"Sorry I disappointed the kid. Thanks for warning me he was coming."

Dina used a hand towel to wipe off the vanity before taking a seat. "Dean needed to see your life as it is. Any advance warning and you would have put your best foot forward instead of taking a step back."

I worked myself to a sitting position and struggled to get out of my jacket. "The art of parenting without parenting."

"Learned it from my pop."

"You and everyone else."

Dina hopped down and held my jacket long enough for me to wiggle free.

"Jesus, this thing is heavy."

Lying down in my harness was like napping on a toolbox. I shrugged out of it. "It beats the alternative."

Dina said something in Italian. It was onomatopoetic enough where I got the gist. She rubbed her eyes, then flickered her fingers like she was throwing her thoughts away.

"It's your life. That's what I said to myself when I signed the license agreement. If you want to dress up and play Jove Brand for real, who am I to judge?"

People always said that as they were judging you.

"I never wanted to be Jove Brand. It just worked out that way. 'Ken Allen, normal-guy private eye,' doesn't have the same ring to it."

Dina went back to her perch. "Yeah, well, Dean grew up hearing about Jove Brand every day of his life. What he wanted was time with plain old Ken Allen."

It was only getting darker. Dina flipped on the lights over the mirror. They had never been so bright. I put an arm over my face to shield the glare.

"Dean was never close with his pop," she said. "One look at Dean, and he knew. But being the manly man he was, he could never admit it. I'd already divorced five other husbands."

"And taken them for everything they had."

"They knew what they were getting into. Every one of them was out to conquer me. Only they got pillaged instead. Dean's father was no different. We kept up appearances, but he made himself scarce."

"Where is he now?"

Dina yawned. "Who knows, who cares? Running another art inflation scam with some new chippie he 'discovered' fresh out of school, probably. Five years ago, he came to Dean's thirteenth birthday party, saw how tall the kid was, and turned right back around."

"When did Dean start to wonder?"

Dina clicked her tongue in thought. "As a kid, he didn't suspect. None of his six sisters had present fathers, so his situation seemed normal. But after that birthday . . . like I said, Jove Brand was there, every time Dean turned around. And his sisters—"

"Gave him grief."

"Could you blame them? Dean was the chosen one, by virtue of nothing except being born with a penis."

Dina's father, "Big Don," was a legend. A sexist one. Only a male child could inherit the Calabria fortune—including their blockbuster film franchise. It took Dina seven tries to have a son. She wasn't about to take any risks with the golden goose. Dean had spent his entire life locked up in the tower his grandfather built. He was lucky to escape intact.

"Around the time *Named Brand* came out, Dean got obsessed with that piece of junk you starred in, started playing it on a loop."

"And began training martial arts."

Dina groaned. "At first, I was happy about that. Of all my kids, Dean was the only one who got pushed around. Then he asked me if he could hire a personal trainer. He tried to be coy. Your name was buried in the middle of his list."

Dean had fostered a dream about his "real" father. One who showed him love. I inhaled raggedly, suddenly glad of the distraction of pain. The kid had elevated me to hero status.

And you know what people said about meeting your heroes.

"You want to buzz my doctor in?" Dina asked.

I made Dina confirm the right guy was knocking via my video watch before popping the lock. He looked more like a television doctor than a real one, younger than me and crammed into a rash guard and basketball shorts. Then again, he was in disguise.

This Town was the last bastion of physicians who paid house calls. Per capita, you would be hard-pressed to find another place with the wealth to support such amenities. But money was only half the equation. The other half was secrecy. Celebrities had images to maintain. The threat of a HIPPA violation was paltry compared to a seven-figure payday from a tabloid. And that was just the workers bound by such practices. HIPPA didn't cover the other patients, or paparazzi pretending to be patients.

The result was first-class concierge medical care, delivered straight to your doorstep. I'm sure the doctor version of my old "Sensei to the Stars" gig paid magnitudes better. The hefty bill included all the trimmings. Your little incidents stayed secret. No candid shots of bruised faces or busted arms would appear on social media. And concierge doctors could prescribe medication to a third party, who could then fill it without being photographed by a minimum-wage worker. But above all this, only one person knew the story. If your secrets ever leaked, you knew exactly where to look.

"Doctor Don't-Tell" gave me a once over and decided to start at the top.

"Cuts on the head are superficial," he reported.

Countless rounds had internalized the instinct to keep my hands up. It had saved my life. The doctor unzipped his packed gym duffel. Inside were several smaller round cases. It reminded me of a roll of breath mints. He withdrew one to reveal everything needed to clean, dress, and bandage my cuts.

"Will I still have my looks, Doc?"

He ignored me and pressed my torso all over. The guy had huge hands. "No bruising or signs of internal bleeding."

Ray's upgraded blazer had done its job. The doctor unzipped another disc of implements and withdrew shears.

"Your pants are going to have to come off."

"They were a lost cause anyway."

In no time at all I was down to my shorts and cup. Whether it was professional or recreational, the doc was a whiz at pantsing.

"There is a four-inch long, barbed projectile in your left quadricep."

"I tripped and fell in a Lowes."

The doctor ignored my cheek and started fishing around in his surgery zip-up. "I'm going to attempt to sheathe it to ease extraction. Do you want a local?"

"What's the duration?"

"Eight to twelve hours."

In theory, I would be asleep for that long. In practice, who knew what would come up? "Is the spike in a bad spot, pain wise?"

"On the scale, I'd say we're at a six out of ten."

I laughed. According to the medical profession, being set on fire was around an eight. "Let's skip the drugs."

The doctor nodded like a man who routinely dealt with people steadfastly avoiding narcotics.

"Okay, this isn't fun to watch anymore," Dina declared. I had forgotten she was there. "I'm going to set up in your office and get some work done."

"Door is soundproofed," I told her.

"Good. I really don't want to hear you screaming."

The doctor had set up his trays and laid out his tools by the time Dina closed the door behind herself. "I'm going to stretch the wound, to keep the barbs from causing more damage during extraction."

I didn't ask if he had ever done this before. Not only because I knew that he, like me, was a person who kept secrets, but also because I was afraid he would say he hadn't.

"I'm going to go somewhere else, Doc. Back in a while."

I focused on my breathing pattern, letting everything go, leaving my body behind. Sometimes it was difficult, but not this time. I didn't want to be where I was. I drifted on waves of light, an ephemeral being instead of an animated piece of meat with a spike in it.

It wasn't dreaming, but it was dream adjacent. I let my thoughts wander wherever whim took them, which was to musing how our heroes were born.

Good-Man was the first superhero. If you ever find a reprint of *Best Comics #1*, you'll be shocked at the lack of fanfare around his introduction. On page one, Hank Heart is reading the paper and bemoaning the state of the world.

All that evil needs to triumph is for good men to do nothing! Well I will be that one good man who acts!

Hank is pretty fired up, but not enough to spit his pipe out during the declaration. Over the next six panels, we get a review of his powers. Hank can lift a tractor over his head. He can outrun a crop duster and jump up onto its wing. A charging bull bounces right off of him. Also, he can land after jumping high enough to grab a plane and not break both his legs.

Pretty tame stuff, by modern standards.

Staring at Sol Silver's prototype sketch of Good-Man woke a world of possibility in Seth Martin's brain. Martin claims the first Good-Man sketch is missing a corner because he tore it out of Silver's hands. The two of them laid out the first issue right then and there, against the meat cases with cribbed butcher paper, Martin dictating the story and dialogue while Silver feverishly drew.

Over the years, the writers who followed Martin attempted to explain where Hank Heart got his powers. One suggested the blood of Hercules ran through his veins. Another that his mother had been the subject of a eugenics experiment. There was even a period where Hank was from another world and had been beamed through the cosmos like a radio signal. I prefer the classic origin: Good-Man got his powers from nowhere. He was plain born that way. A random aberration who decided to use his fantastic abilities to "claim victory for virtue and veracity."

I have a friend who once told me you were either an Elvis person or a Beatles person, and once you knew which one someone was, you could predict a lot about them. For me, you were either a Good-Man person or a Foxman person.

A Good-Man person wanted to be inherently special. Their fantasy was they were destined for greatness: stronger, faster, and smarter than everyone around them without even trying. A Foxman person was the opposite. They believed in their hidden potential. With enough training and dedication, the hero inside would emerge.

Guess which one I was.

By the way, this whole time I was in excruciating pain. It felt like an octogenarian with arthritis was trying to finish a scarf on Christmas Eve, except, you know, inside my damn leg. Meditation has its limits, people.

The doc put stitches inside of me, applied some gooey spray stuff, put some stitches outside of me, used more of the stuff, then dressed it out. I figured I better show him my calf while I had him here. He examined my work with professional interest.

"This is really terrible first aid. Never do this again."

He repeated the process on my calf. When I stood up to test everything out, I almost slipped in the giant pool of sweat I had shed during my treatment.

The doctor nodded. "If you don't have a full leg compression sleeve, get one."

"Is this where you tell me to rest and take it easy?"

The doctor focused on packing his bag. "You're an adult. Do whatever you want."

I followed him out to my office, where Dina was behind the desk treating her phone like she had a dozen replacements lined up.

"What do I owe you, Doc?"

"Nothing," Dina interrupted. "He's my guy."

"Can I get a card?"

The doctor didn't turn around. "I don't have cards."

It was more likely he was judging my ability to pay based on my zip code. It was worse than he thought. I had made the down payment off an unforeseen windfall. Without that, I could have never afforded to live there.

Dina set her phone face down. "What are you doing?"

"I'll wear pants or not wear pants whenever I want in my own office."

"No dummy, all this. I get why you started: to clear your name. But not even a year in and you're getting operated on."

I took a seat, propping my feet on the desk to elevate my wound. "It beats telling actors to keep their elbows in and exhale during the lift."

"You haven't changed one bit. Still a people pleaser. All my brother had to do was ask, and you'd jump out of a helicopter, fifteen stories up."

"Thirteen. It was only thirteen."

"There are other ways to get by."

"Sure, I could have sold the story behind the Jove Brand Murders. The last offer was seven million bucks and a producer credit."

Dina didn't like the taste of that. I took advantage while she regrouped.

"When you have your dream job, you're never at work. Growing up, this is what I wanted to be. I just gave up on the idea it was an option."

"It's not," Dina said. "You're off in your own little world, playing pretend."

"A genius woman, whist in the act of seduction, once told me, 'The world is what you make it.'"

At hearing her own words, Dina stood up from the desk. I would have mirrored her, but the effort would have weakened my argument.

"I can't decide if you're good or bad for Dean."

"Yeah? Well, which are you?"

She stormed off, cursing in two languages. I watched her leave on my watch, in case anyone tried to slip in as the door closed. I almost fell asleep right there, but my chair started to tip when I leaned back too far.

I limped into bed and stacked my pillows. There was no comfortable position. On my back was great for my leg but miserable for my head. I was considering hanging a hammock when my body finally gave out and demanded sleep.

I woke up feeling like a million pennies. It was easier to list the things that weren't sore. Putting my bedroom on the second floor had been an enormous tactical blunder. I took my time making sure everything I needed upstairs was taken care of. Compression sleeves came first. In restocking my harness, my loadout changed based on how yesterday went. I picked up a red quiver. Ray had once called them "extremely lethal." I didn't feel any different about them today as I had yesterday and set them back on the rack.

The stairs weren't as bad as I had anticipated, which put some pep in my limp. I was hungry enough for a solid breakfast. Two days in a row wouldn't kill me, and my leg needed calories to rebuild anyway.

Sleeping had knocked some theories loose. I was getting ready to act on them when Special Investigator Stern called.

"Good day, Sunshine," I said.

"Sunshine?" Stern was in the car. The morning rush was making itself heard around her.

"Are you an Elvis or Beatles person?"

"I didn't call to chat, Allen. Neil Leon is dead."

"Let me guess: asphyxiated with a broken neck."

"No. Someone made a pin cushion out of him. His body had yellow and blue darts stuck in it. The combination stopped his heart."

13

I FELT LIKE someone had dumped a cooler over my head.

"Leon was killed with some kind of custom firearm," Stern said. "We ran into the same kind of darts a few months back, in Leon's guys. I'm on my way to your place right now."

Having been framed for murder before, I didn't say anything. Who said you couldn't teach an old dog new tricks?

"But traffic is pretty bad," Stern commented. "I picked the wrong time to hit the highway."

Maybe I was growing on Stern, for her to cut me such a big break. I wasn't so dense that I needed any more winks or nudges. I started toward the door, then stopped to take stock. I groaned an exhale from the deepest part of my being and climbed back up the stairs.

I packed for a weekend trip—the saddleboxes wouldn't hold much more—and collected my device chargers. Downstairs, I filled a bag with food and supplements. I wondered how long it would take for Neil Leon's death to hit the media. How he had died, who he'd run afoul of in the past. There were always cops looking to make a quick buck, and every entertainment outlet under the sun would eat this up.

Ken Allen, the Franchise Killer, was at it again.

I needed to stop chasing Culvan Mann around. It was a big waste of time, which was why he was working so hard to egg me on. Before I came along, no one was crying deliberate sabotage. I was also Ray's only advocate. The more Culvan was able to lead me around in circles, the less I was able to make actual headway into who had hired him and why. I set course for Duquesne Studios and dialed up Zaina Preeti. She spoke first.

"I know you are new to your chosen profession, but clients expect daily progress reports."

"I was busy getting shot at and blown up. Look, Culvan Mann didn't sabotage the Good-Man costume or Foxcar himself. He's too big not to be noticed. Someone did it for him. We need to start looking at people with access to practical effects."

Preeti muted the line. I waited for her to secure her location.

"Go on," she said.

"It's the same principle as Lidia Colby's condoms being tampered with. Someone on the inside must have swapped Good-Man's costume out. They also had enough time and access to booby-trap the Foxcar. Then there's the question of why Culvan Mann wanted a Foxman double on the Civil Warriors set."

"Maybe Mr. Mann required an emergency substitute, and Foxman was his closest available agent."

"Possible, but in my experience, Culvan Mann does everything for a reason."

Preeti didn't argue her position. Instead, she immediately acted on the new information. "Understood. I'll have jackets on the likely suspects ready in a few hours."

"We're only looking at half of the equation. Are you familiar with Havier Cariel?"

"I am."

"He let slip they had other incidents at Tachi Productions prior to Bill O'Wrongs's death."

"Mirroring our own difficulties here at Duquesne."

"If I get Havier to open up about it, maybe we can find a shared link between the studios."

"Like Ray Ford."

"Give up on Ray Ford being the guy. Your number-one proof he isn't is Culvan Mann doing everything to point at him."

Preeti didn't bite back. "And you have provided no evidence Culvan Mann is even involved. I will see if Tachi is amenable."

"Can you have someone drop a lanyard at the gate? I'm on the way over."

"It will be waiting."

I spent the rest of my commute pondering how neatly framed I was. Culvan didn't have to fake my fléchettes. He had the genuine article. Neil himself could have provided a shock dart. I put plenty of them in his guys a few months back. As for the tranq darts, Culvan had the ones I left in the sedan.

Could I account for my whereabouts at the time of Neil Leon's death? If it was recent, maybe. Some of the office workers might remember seeing me outside Culvan's death trap. Dina was with me for a few hours in the evening.

My alibi wasn't looking good. There were plenty of gaps, and Mann was smart.

"Ray, are you following along?"

Instead of Ray, Elaine broke into my Bluetooth. "He's not here. The police invited him to examine the Foxcar."

"Invited? Did he take a lawyer?"

"Do you know my father?"

"It's a trick. Get him out of there, Elaine."

"I tried. He didn't listen. He never does."

"I'm having a hard enough time clearing his name. We don't need him digging himself deeper."

Elaine's tone matched mine. "He thinks if he has access to the Foxcar, he can prove it was sabotage. He's a nuts-and-bolts person. Things are or they aren't."

On or off. Dead or alive. "He's hinting pretty heavily how I should handle Culvan."

"The situation is clear to him. Dad only sees one way out of this."

"What about you?"

Elaine typed for a moment. When she replied, her voice was distant. "There's a saying, 'past the point of no return.' I hate it. I hate the idea that we can be changed for the worse, forever. That our sins against each other are irredeemable."

I shouldered into the opening. "What was he like before? Culvan."

This time Elaine answered quickly. "A lot like Dad. Focused. Brilliant, but not as brilliant as he thinks. Unyielding. Completely oblivious to the idea that he doesn't know what he doesn't know."

"Not very self-aware?"

"Cul spends zero time considering things he doesn't value."

Culvan wasn't alone.

People ranked the qualities they possessed as the most important ones to have. If they were smart, intelligence defined being elite. Same for attractive, funny, or ambitious. The quality itself didn't matter. What mattered is that they had it.

Or thought they did, at least.

I was dying to know what had happened between Elaine and Culvan. How it started, and especially how it ended. The information was almost certainly relevant. But here I was, the detective who didn't like to pry.

"Your dad blames Culvan for what happened to you."

"Yes, he does. Completely and totally."

There was something new in Elaine's voice: scorn.

"Have you thought about why he does that?"

"Because if he does, what happened back then is not his fault, and especially not my fault. He couldn't live with either of those options."

I was thinking of an elegant way to obtain details when a call from Zaina Preeti came in. Elaine saw it too. "You're on."

"She'll leave a message."

"Your time is better spent saving Dad than examining my past."

Elaine switched my line to Preeti before I could rebut. Preeti jumped right in. "Havier Cardiel will meet you, if you agree to sign an NDA."

"Text me the address."

"I feel compelled to remind you who your current client is, Mr. Allen."

"Happy to satisfy your compulsions."

Preeti hung up on me and texted GPS coordinates, which pointed basically next door to Duquesne Studios. My route updated as I approached the studio system. Security was even beefier than before, with Hummers hunkered outside the gates and a porta potty set up for all the guards. A lanyard was presented to me after I had removed my helmet to allow facial recognition.

I swung into a guest parking spot outside the doors to Tachi Productions, the company that had acquired the rights to the most popular characters on the planet for pennies on the dollar. Back in the 1990s, Seth Martin had overextended Excelsior Comics during a collector's boom. Facing bankruptcy, Martin made it known the rights to the Civil Warriors were up for grabs.

Tachi, a Japanese keiretsu, had branched into content creation off the manufacture of home electronics. It was looking to expand internationally. Rumor has it Martin offered up the whole kit and kaboodle, but Tachi wanted to try before they bought.

In hindsight, passing on owning the Excelsior universe was a huge blunder. But at the time, it was considered the smart move by everyone on the sidelines. Tachi's production wing was in its trial stages. Films cost hundreds of millions of dollars with no guarantee of return. Tachi rented the Civil Warriors on a five-year basis for less than what they paid to use athlete likenesses in video games. Now the price increased exponentially every half decade.

Havier Cardiel was waiting for me at the building entrance. Today, his suit was the color of tarnished silver. He didn't offer his hand. He had taken note of my reaction the first go-round.

"Good to see you again so soon, Ken."

Flint's solo Flying Freeman project had the office buzzing with excitement. Everyone had something to report or request. Havier was a popular guy. He knew all his coworkers on a personal level. His energy was infectious. By the time we got to his office, I was ready to ask for an application.

Havier shut the door behind us. The slab had a seal that secured with an audible suction against a metal frame. His desk was eight feet long and chest height. There was no chair on his side. I had to climb into mine. My leg didn't love it.

The NDA was already laid out with a pen next to it. Green stickers marked all the places I needed to sign. It would have taken me all day to read and a law degree to understand. My spyglasses provided me with a record of the proceedings.

"There isn't anything in here where I would be signing away my immortal soul, is there?"

True to my prediction, Havier remained standing. "I'd never do that, Ken. Not to you, not to anyone. This is simply a confidentiality agreement."

I flipped through, a page per second, signing wherever a green sticker appeared. Green was a good choice over, say, red. Green meant go.

When I was done, Havier fed the stack into a Tachi scanner. It took a while. It jammed four times and the Wi-Fi kept going out.

"Sorry about the holdup. Tachi products aren't what they used to be." Havier smiled. "Please don't take my not sitting down as an insult or power play."

Things were adding up about Havier. His suit, his on-point grooming, the constant standing.

"You lost a bunch of weight," I said.

He smiled proudly. "A hundred pounds. I use all these little life hacks. Not sitting is one of them."

"Progress isn't a leap. It comes a step at a time."

Havier nodded, storing the quote away. "I absolutely agree."

"Did you have time to talk to Flint West?"

"Briefly." Havier rested his hands on the edge of the desk. It was bullnosed, which is a fancy word for rounded off. "He thinks highly of you."

"Flint thinks highly of everyone."

Havier laughed. "Why don't you take the lead here?"

"Duquesne's Good Knights film is being sabotaged. It started small—minor mishaps, unfortunate occurrences—but over time the incidents grew, coming to a head with the death of Mark Caldwell. Sound familiar?"

Havier braced harder against the table. "Yes, it does."

"Zaina Preeti hired me to look into it."

"I'm aware."

"I was on set when Bill O'Wrongs was killed."

"You mean died."

"No. I mean was killed."

Havier clasped his hands behind his back, elbows straight. "I must admit, I didn't expect to hear this from you. I thought you were Ray Ford's friend."

"Ray Ford isn't the one who did the killing."

Havier exhaled as if his position was taking effort. "What has your investigation uncovered?"

"Let's keep this exchange fair. I showed you mine. Now show me yours."

Havier either was thinking deeply or straining something. "Okay, but only if it's you I'm showing and not Zaina Preeti."

"You have my word."

My oath wasn't sufficient. Havier searched for an assurance he could trust. "Let me ask you a question."

"Ready."

"Who is your favorite superhero?"

"Sword Saint."

Havier raised an eyebrow in surprise. "Nice answer. The Civil Warriors shoot has had incidents similar to Good Knights. It started with Mongoose. His . . . supplemental nutrition . . . was tampered with."

It appeared Culvan Mann had a sense of irony. "Mongoose was poisoned?"

Havier locked eyes with me. "This stays between us?"

"May the Lotus Blade reflect my falsehoods."

"Someone swapped his testosterone for estrogen. It's causing physical and emotional issues. We leaked that he injured his back training. Then It-Girl broke her arm in two places after a wardrobe malfunction."

"The costume, was it a Ray Ford creation?"

Havier nodded confirmation. "Ford invented a new kind of armature. Prosthetic limbs capable of lifting hundreds of pounds while also allowing It-Girl to appear partially transformed. It was a genius solution to show the actual actress but also have her toss props around."

Havier leaned, bracing his arms against his desk.

"Are you doing isometrics?" I asked.

"Ha. You caught me. It gets to be a habit. No one has ever noticed before."

More likely they had, but Havier was beloved to the point where his quirks were endured.

"All these incidents, both here and at Duquesne, happened to heroes, with the exception of Bill O'Wrongs. The actor, was he into anything?"

Havier froze in thought. "Squeaky clean, as far as I know. And I'm the head firefighter around here. All problems are sent my way."

"Speaking of which, where does the new Flying Freeman production stand?"

"Sword Saint, huh?" Havier asked.

I nodded. "He is the Lotus Blade's guardian, not its wielder."

"We're scrambling. Rewriting during reshoots in hopes of keeping our summer release window. If we manage it, Flying Freeman wins the box-office war by default."

Havier's comment confused me. "Wait. Are you saying Duquesne Studios is delaying the Good Knights movie?"

"Zaina Preeti didn't tell you?" His eyes went wide. "They had no heroes over there left to bear the standard. I know they tried to shoot around the mess. I can only imagine what the dailies looked like."

Having been present during the recent shoot, I could confirm this was indeed the case. But Duquesne was still my client, so I kept a poker face.

Havier laughed. "I had to try. Duquesne's problem is they don't have someone like me. No one over there with any power who loves the properties. No one who understands what the fans want."

He started ramping up his routine, switching to slow-motion press-ups. "You used to train Flint, right?"

"In another life."

"Any way I can work my pecs, outside of push-ups? "

"Sure."

I ran him through a few variations. A call came in that made Havier jump. He picked up the receiver, hit a button, and the call dropped.

"See that, Ken? It's like the printer. Tachi is falling apart. It's taken me almost ten years to staff an office with competent people. The Flying Freeman movie is our big shot."

"Being the only game in town puts you in the saboteur's sights."

"So, who is this guy?"

"His name is Culvan Mann. He's Ray Ford's former protégé."

I was expecting a request to expound, but Havier just nodded. "Okay, go on."

"The guy is a giant. Seven feet tall with plenty of wide to back it up. There's no way he can sneak onto a set. Other people must toss his wrenches for him. We want to compare productions. Find crew who worked on both."

Havier pushed himself to a standing position and raised a knee into the underside of the desk. "Have Ms. Preeti send me a list."

"So you can decide a course of action when you have all the information? No good."

"But if I surrendered my own list, she would do the same thing."

I didn't have time for a corporate standoff. "How about both of you send me and your lists, I do the actual detecting, then update you at the same time?"

Havier weighed my proposal while he stretched. "I'll agree to that if you can name the wisdom inscribed on the Lotus Blade."

"That's a trick question. Only Master Monk knows. But since he had not achieved enlightenment, it drove him mad. Sword Saint refused to look. He had to defeat Master Monk blindfolded. Issue number one eighty one."

"Great story."

"A classic, but also a mistake. Before that, Sword Saint and Master Monk were a tense matchup. Once your hero beats his archvillain—who happens to be using the most powerful weapon in all the heavens and hells—while also being blindfolded, it's hard to take said foe as a serious threat."

Havier nodded sagely. "Leave your information."

I didn't have Havier's moves with a business card, but I managed to get mine on his desk. "This saboteur, he's a gun for hire. Someone with deep pockets is footing his bill. Any names come to mind?"

"Duquesne, but that doesn't make sense if they're also being sabotaged. Maybe no one is behind Culvan. He could be doing this purely out of revenge."

I could forgive Havier for believing Culvan Mann had a super-villain motivation. Our conversation on this topic was over. I shifted tacks while I had him here.

"The higher-ups giving you any grief over your new star being Dave King's future son-in-law?"

Havier stopped what he was doing. "What makes you ask about Dave King?"

I told myself I wasn't breaking my promise to Dave King and trying to help him. I was only satisfying my own curiosity. "Duquesne came to see him on the Civil Warriors set. Can't help but wonder why."

"Same here. They asked, and I figured why not? Now they owe me one." Havier looked pained, and not from a muscle cramp. "I wish I could do more for Mr. King, but that power lies above my current position. Right now, Seth Martin is the cut-and-dried owner of the Civil Warriors."

Nothing about Havier's demeanor screamed public relations. My gut told me the guy meant what he was saying. A rare thing had occurred: someone who got into the business out of love had maintained the romance. I had met another True Fan.

"Could the sabotages have something to do with the ownership of the Civil Warriors? What about Seth Martin's will?"

Havier was unable to hide his amusement. "You mean did Martin leave Excelsior Comics to Dave King?"

"It would give Duquesne a reason to come calling. They could snatch the Civil Warriors out from under Tachi."

Havier shook his head. "Martin spent fifty years defending his position as the sole creative mind behind both the Good Knights and the Civil Warriors. Hard to imagine he had a change of heart on his deathbed."

"Some of Martin's scripts have leaked online. They read more like synopses. King is at the very least a co-creator."

"Martin probably did the same thing to Sol Silver back in the forties. Except Silver never had the chance to tell his side."

Being a person who loved the stories behind the stories, I knew what Havier was talking about. Seth Martin and Sol Silver spent a year founding our modern myths. First was Good-Man, then Foxman. The Patriette and a dozen others followed, along with their requisite antagonists. In November 1941, Silver drew the first superhero team comic with the *Good Knights #1*. It was an instant classic. Martin and Silver were stars on the rise.

Then Pearl Harbor happened. Martin was drafted immediately, serving in the Signal Corps before shifting to the Training Film Division. The draft never got a chance to reach Sol Silver. Silver added three years to his age and enlisted. Full of vinegar and eager to kill Nazis, Silver forced his way to the front.

Martin returned to the States and resumed his comic career, but Sol Silver never came home. Silver was in the history books for a reason beyond drawing the Good Knights. Over the next decade, he hunted former Nazis around the world. Silver's goal was noble, but he wasn't concerned with due process. He served as judge, jury, and executioner. While considered a heroic figure by many, Silver broke dozens of international laws.

And he did it all on his own. At least on paper. Silver almost surely had support—intelligence and funding—but he was a man without a country. Movies have been made about Silver, fictional characters based on his life. Including perhaps Jove Brand, the character I had portrayed on film. Brand's official title was Royal Gamesman, but in the beginning his true role was the queen's secret assassin. It wasn't until later that Brand essentially became a superhero in a tailored suit.

It came to a head in 1954, when Silver was believed responsible for the deaths of several American rocket scientists who may or may not have been former members of the Third Reich. In the middle of the nuclear arms race with the USSR, the American government did not take it lightly. Silver became a wanted man. Pressure was applied to the international community, including a budding Israel, to capture and extradite him.

But Silver wasn't the sort of person who bowed to authority. In early 1956, cornered at a secret headquarters in Eastern Europe, Silver took his own life. Using incendiary charges, he destroyed any records of those who may have offered aid or succor. On hearing the news, Seth Martin promptly purchased the rights to their creations from Sol Silver's family and became the sole owner of Good-Man, Foxman, and the rest.

Havier again filled the silence. "Between you and me, I wish it was true. But at the moment, no one knows who inherited the Civil Warriors from Martin."

"Well, plenty of people out there think Seth Martin had an under-the-table deal with Tachi already, given the way he played hype man."

Havier laughed without amusement. "That's a fan theory. Martin's promotional work was contracted. He learned the hard way after he sold off the Good Knights. He shielded his creator's rights thoroughly. Tachi has no claim on the Civil Warriors."

After the war ended, Martin was keen to pick up where he'd left off. Sol Silver was unavailable due to aforementioned reasons, so Martin sought out the most talented artists he could afford. But without Silver, the magic was gone. The books chugged along into the 1950s, when a Red Scare crackdown on the comics industry left Martin in a financial pickle. This led to the infamous incident Havier was referencing. Classic Digest made a one-time payment to Martin for ownership of all his properties.

Classic Digest immediately turned around and sold the rights to film and radio. Television followed. They made their money back a million times over. Martin never got over it. He loudly and publicly quit comics. Then five years later, he discovered Dave King and founded Excelsior. My leg was starting to hurt, so I climbed back into the chair. Staying standing also made it easier to segue me out of the room. "But Martin was only interested in protecting himself."

Havier went back to the chest exercise I showed him, alternating hands. "Personally, I agree with you. Martin took advantage of King, but the whole thing will forever be a he-said/he-said situation. Dave King claims they had an understanding. Martin claims the sizable advance he paid King when he came to Excelsior was in exchange for sole ownership."

"I'm familiar with the case. Martin also sponsored King's immigration. That's a lot of leverage to have in a negotiation. Do you have an in with Martin's estate?"

"I do, but you can't use me as a go-between."

"Fair enough." I understood. Havier couldn't have some gumshoe burning whatever bridges he'd managed to build with Martin's potential heirs.

"The guy managing Martin's estate is a real scumbag. He has a gift for digging up dirt. We're always having to pay him off. I'd be shocked if Zaina Preeti wasn't doing the same."

Havier paused to give me room to chime in. I did my impression of paint drying.

Havier raised a hand in surrender. "Fine. The guy's name is Chuck Charles."

"Charles Charles?" I had to laugh. "That an alias?"

"Probably. He used to run a gossip site, back when people used websites: ChucksGotNews.com, before he got outed for gross behavior."

"Oh, that guy. Wonderful. What's he doing now?"

"Pretending to have a production company. He cozied up to Seth Martin, maybe three years before Martin died, and managed to squeeze everyone else out."

I had heard such rumors. "Is Charles the guy accused of elder abuse?"

"That's him."

This Town was full of remoras pretending to be sharks. "I'll figure out a clean route to Chuck Charles. Thanks."

Havier checked his watch. He was either a good actor or had run over on his next meeting. "Anything else?"

"Yeah. You have to call off the Flying Freeman solo movie. Culvan Mann isn't screwing around. He's killing people. The surefire way to halt filming would be taking out Flint West. He passed on Flying Freeman last time and went for Bill O'Wrongs instead. I doubt he'll give Flint a second pass."

Havier looked at me like I had insulted his mother. "I believe you, I really do. But the people with the power to make that happen won't take all this on faith. Bring me the kind of proof I can take upstairs."

Havier sent his list over immediately. Preeti was less forthcoming but relented when I explained Havier's caveat.

I spoke into my Bluetooth without bothering to dial. "You there, Elaine?"

"Yes. I see the lists. This won't take me long."

"How wanted am I?"

"For questioning, according to dispatch channels."

Stern needed my Quarreler, to compare the darts found in Neil Leon. If she got it, they were going to match. I dug into the Stag's saddleboxes for my water bottle. "What about your dad?"

"He won't talk to me about it."

"He needs a lawyer. A good one."

"I know. Every time I bring it up, he leaves the room."

"Maybe we can share a cell." I tried to keep my tone optimistic. "Look, I'm doing everything I can."

Elaine got the last word in. "Well, you aren't alone there."

Having no time to waste, I contacted Chuck Charles right away, punching my information into his website contact form on my phone. It was tedious, but professionals such as myself could endure any hardship.

In an exercise of irony I hid out in the garage where Preeti had hired me. Surrounded by police cars, I checked in with my nonclients. Neither Flint nor Jaq picked up his phone.

If Flint was being promoted from ensemble player to star, he was plenty busy. I decided to entice him by leaving a voice mail promising news about Dave King.

My rationalization being that it wasn't lying as long as I didn't say it was significant news.

I was in the middle of crafting a text to Dean when an unknown caller interrupted me.

"You did well, Ken. I'm impressed."

"Can it, Culvan. What's next? Forcing me to fight my way to the top of a pagoda? You have to be running low on henchmen."

"There is nothing so cheap as human life, and the mercenaries I employ have no reason to suspect their predecessors met an early demise."

"You sound like you should be petting a cat. Do you practice this whole schtick or does it come naturally?"

"It is not for your benefit. I know who is listening. Only they have the power to end this."

I decided Culvan had used up enough of my minutes. "This was fun. Have a horrible day."

"Wait. There is a purpose behind my call. I admit I did not expect Special Investigator Stern to disbelieve you were Neil Leon's killer. My plan was that she remove you, Ray's only advocate, from the board."

My throat went dry. I was tempted to threaten him, but Culvan was looking for a reaction. He filled the silence.

"My hypothesis is that she stands alone in this view. Here is my challenge, accept it or not. I am going to kill Special Investigator Stern. And I am going to do so in such a way which leaves no doubt you are her murderer."

14

I HUNG UP on someone for once. If Culvan Mann wanted me on the line, the right move was to bail. I called Stern. It took her three rings to pick up, so about a week, my time.

"Are you aware what *subtext* means, Allen?"

"Culvan Mann is gunning for you. He called me up special to let me know."

"Huh," Stern replied, to my chagrin.

"You need to take this seriously. He wants to off you and frame me for it. Which means his mercs need to put fléchettes in you."

"You mean your little dart things?"

"I hope you being reductive is a defense mechanism. Where are you?"

Stern told me. Our midpoint was maybe a half hour away. I couldn't decide if I should go to her or not. Culvan wanted me at the scene of his future crime. But how did he know Stern had given me the benefit of the doubt in the first place?

"I think Mann has you bugged."

"*You* being bugged makes more sense."

"I was, actually, but Ray Ford scrubbed me down. If I were you, I'd dump that car right now and take a close look at your everyday carry."

Stern upgraded to a considering sound. There were things I wanted to say, but Culvan Mann would hear me say them. Since he was listening, I decided to try some misdirection of my own.

"Mann is a loser. I've kicked his guys around to the point he's started throwing tantrums. Head over to Duquesne Studios. I'm there now."

I sent Stern a follow-up text with our actual meet-up location and fired up the Stag, treating the drive like I wanted to be pulled over. The more the merrier, at that point. A confirmation message from Stern hit my watch. Given the situation, I gave her a pass on texting while driving. I kept my eyes peeled for sedans. There were a lot of them, but none with tinted windows.

My GPS estimated the drive at thirty-two minutes. I arrived at my destination in twenty-five, and patrolled a perimeter for signs of ambush. Two blocks from our rally point, a sand-colored sedan was parked on a curb intersecting Stern's route. In hindsight, there were smarter ways to go about what I did next, but the situation had me boiling. I cranked the throttle and went at the sedan head on, weaving through the intersecting cars.

I was under the traffic light when the sedan roared forward to meet me. I toggled the front-facing grenade launcher. Two bombs stuck to the sedan's windshield like muffin batter. It didn't stop coming forward.

Neither did I.

The grenades detonated, spider-webbing the sedan's windshield. I rode straight up the hood, applied the brakes, and ghost-rode the Stag. It rolled on, down the back window and over the trunk. I crouched on the top of the car and waited, hoping the sound of my feet hitting the roof didn't give me away.

Two mercs exited in concert, spinning toward the back of the car with pistols which looked a lot like the Quarreler. I had a pair of problems, but it was better to go all out on one than half-assed on both. I chose the passenger. A point-blank concussive round to the head was a coin-flip between an ambulance and a hearse, so I shot the merc in the back and rolled off the roof in his direction.

He shocked me by staying on his feet. I shot him twice more as he wheeled around—one in the back and one in the chest. He took a knee but didn't tap out. His moxie was costing me too much time. I kicked him in the face and he fell onto his side.

The driver had figured out I wasn't where I was supposed to be. A shock dart missed my head by an inch as I dove into the car through the open passenger door. He beat me to the other side. A boot to my hand sent the Quarreler flying. I was prone, facedown in an enclosed space. In other words, I was as good as dead.

Fortunately, my hero had arrived to save me.

Stern's first shot hit the bulletproof window. She didn't bother with a second. I pushed myself backward as she kicked the car door into my would-be killer's pistol. The next part I missed while wiggling out of danger. The merc I kicked in the head was getting back up. I kicked him again, flush on the neck, and went over the hood to get to Stern faster.

She didn't need the assist.

Stern took hold the driver's sleeve to keep the knife he had drawn out of play and put short hooks into his nose, throat, and solar plexus. When he started to crumple, Stern cupped her hand on the back of his head and fed him knees. After the fourth one, she realized the knees were what was holding him up and dropped him on the concrete.

"Hey Allen."

"Hey yourself."

Stern produced cuffs and bent over her defeated foe. "Just the pair?"

"There are at least two more sedans out there, but this was the only one I spotted."

Rubberneckers had stopped to chronicle the events. There were so many cameras I wanted to call for Freebird. Stern surveyed the clogged intersection.

"Long time since I worked traffic."

"Is the uniform the groupie magnet I hear it is?"

"Yeah, in the sense you don't get to choose what it attracts."

The guy I put down twice was stumbling up for round three. Stern smashed an elbow into his temple. "I don't suppose you have cuffs."

"Nah."

I kept watch while Stern went to retrieve zip cuffs from her trunk. Her would-be assassins were getting some quality zzzs. To my shock, the White Stag was sitting upright with its kickstand out. The internal gyros had kept the bike level.

Stern put two sets of zip cuffs on the passenger merc—wrists and thumbs—and started gathering up weapons, which reminded me to retrieve mine. I stopped her as she went toward the sedan.

"Mann plants explosives in his vehicles to blow. If he bugged your car, he might have wired it too."

Stern called the bomb squad while we got our distance, me rolling the Stag next to us.

"So now I'm the Debra Darling to your Good-Man?" she asked.

I shook my head. "Culvan Mann thinks he's a mastermind, but he has a pattern. He always has a hidden reason behind his monologuing. For me, he wants me to believe he and I are rivals—Ray's adopted sons going head-to head—but really, it's about him trying to throw me off track. My guess is it's the same with you. You're doing something he wants to stop."

"Like getting close with my mercenary case."

"That's my guess. Culvan targeting you is a sign you're on the right track."

Stern tilted to peek into the souped-up sedan.

"What's up with the windows?"

"They're armored, I guess."

"Seems like overkill. Why not just tint them?"

Twin explosions rang out. I pulled Stern close and spun away, shielding us both behind my blazer. When I opened my eyes, Stern was staring into them.

"You okay?"

"Yeah. Let me up, Allen."

The sedan was in flames. Stern's car was less severe. The windows were blown out and interior totaled.

Stern absorbed the scene. "This might help convince my boss to clear the task force I requested. Claiming a private army is running rampant in This Town has been flirting with career suicide."

"You could always go into acting. Until you texted me back, I thought you didn't believe me."

"No thanks."

"Come on, you've got that star quality. I bet it runs in the family."

Stern stared me down. "Shutting up now would be second only to shutting up ten seconds ago, Allen."

It was good to know I was still flexible enough at my age to get my foot in my mouth. I retrieved my water bottle from the Stag's saddlebox to rinse out the taste. The travel mug Stern cribbed from me during my first case was rolling around on the pavement. She'd been using it.

Stern turned toward me. Her hair glowed in the sun. Her skin was flushed from the mutual rescue. "Hey Allen."

"Yeah?"

"You're still a murder suspect. Get out of here."

"Oh. Yeah. Roger that. Thanks for saving my life and everything."

"You're welcome." Stern waited until I was pulling away to add, "Back at you."

I was dying for a smoothie but unwilling to ingest any of the commercially available sugar bombs. The shop wasn't about to let me use their blender, which led me to ponder if there was a hole in the market for rentals. I bought a shaker bottle and a carton of almond milk to mix supplies from my saddleboxes. It was exactly as chunky as I thought it would be.

I was gargling the sediment out of my teeth when a call came in from a private number.

I answered with a smile. "That's two more goons down. Hope you got a bulk deal."

"Is this Ken Allen?"

Whoops. It wasn't Culvan, unless he was using the "nasally creep" setting on his Auto-Tune. "Ken Allen, that's me."

"Ken Allen, the detective. The Jove Brand guy."

"No, the orangutan. This is the San Diego Zoo."

The guy hung up.

I started cleaning out the blender bottle with a wet nap. If you let this stuff settle, you were in for a battle.

My phone rang again.

"Hello, this is Ken Allen, detective and Jove Brand guy."

"Okay, this is Chuck Charles."

"What's up, Chuck?"

"I got your message, and I was wondering, are you available right now? For hire?"

"Why do you ask?"

"I think someone is trying to kill me."

Chuck Charles sent over an address on the west side near Topanga. The neighborhood was too rich for Chuck's blood, but well within Seth Martin's tax bracket. I wondered how long Chuck could squat in Martin's old digs before the authorities took notice.

Five minutes into the drive the adrenaline wore off and my leg started to throb. It felt like I had a second heart in my thigh. One pulsing so hard it stretched my slacks. I fought to keep my eyes on the road.

After this was all over, I was going to treat myself to some rest. Maybe finally buy a lounge chair.

The house was built into a grade, part hobbit hole, part brutalist fortress. After a pause to verify my identity, the gates opened to admit me. I followed the winding driveway into a walk-out area sheltered by the hill. The garage door rolled up as I approached. Having recently been bushwhacked, my suspicion levels were at an all-time high. I could have been talking to the actual Chuck Charles. Or Culvan Mann had taken over Chuck's website and ordered his weaseliest-sounding mercenary to call me.

With that in mind, I swung the Stag around to face the garage doors and drew my weapon. The garage was dominated by mismatched boxes stocked with seventy-five years of memorabilia. A workbench littered with scattered tools stood against the wall adjacent the residence. There were no vehicles in- or outside. My suspicion level rose appropriately.

The door opened into a mudroom with the kitchen waiting on the far side.

"Chuck, you there? It's Ken Allen. The detective, not the ape."

"I'm back here."

I took my time heading toward the voice. Partially out of caution but also to look around. The house, which hadn't been remodeled since the 1970s, had big wood-paneled spaces and exposed beams. Someone was systematically packing up the place. Boxes were stacked in every room. The carpet was torn up and the floorboards were loose throughout.

Chuck Charles was in a big room on the mid-level. The space was a combination library and museum. Accolades were lined up under glass. I've known people with a lot of awards. The glass isn't a pretentious thing. It's way easier to clean and keeps people from goofing around with your accomplishments.

Seth Martin had gone to claim his final reward, or spiritual reassignment, or the void from whence we came, depending on what you believed. In his time on the mortal plane, the founding father of superheroes had been honored by everyone from presidents to the entertainment industry, to literary organizations, and children's networks. Martin had keys to so many different cities he'd need a Hula Hoop to hang them all.

The edges were occupied by a thicket of dreaded lifetime achievement awards. Sad to give, sad to receive, sad to watch. Whoever thought of these things needed a kick in the pants. They had somehow cast being passive-aggressive in statue form.

Chuck Charles was in the near corner of the room, rubbing his temples at the task before him. The contents of the linen closet were piled next to him like a levy of sandbags. I already didn't like the guy from what I knew about him. He'd run a sleazy gossip site for a decade before leeching off Seth Martin. My bias upgraded on seeing him. He was like anthropomorphized trypophobia. There was no one reason why he disgusted me. Everything from his face to his demeanor to his fashion choices summed up to total aversion.

He looked me up and down. "Yep, you're Ken Allen."

"Live and in person."

Chuck adjusted his latex gloves around his forearm hair. I didn't know you could feel sorry for latex gloves. He removed the glass case from the closest award, walked it over to the closet, and set it on top of the loose carpet.

"On top of being a detective, do you bodyguard?"

"What makes you think someone is trying to kill you?"

I wanted to watch Chuck and the door, so I took a few steps back. It wasn't that the guy was literally repellent.

"It was small stuff at first. I was getting terrible back pain. I couldn't figure it out. Then I bought new shoes and the pain went away. So, I inspect my old shoes. Someone had put shims in all the left ones."

I nodded. "Have you angered any elves?"

Chuck looked up from boxing a statue. "You're a real asshole, you know that?"

For years, as a personal trainer to the stars, I had to navigate a menagerie of giant, fragile egos. Lift them up, while also putting myself down. Three months away from all that and here I was, working counter to my own best interests. I took a breath and slipped on my kid gloves.

"I believe you, Chuck. I can't talk about it, but it matches up with other accounts in the case I've been working on. In fact, to prove it, I'll go next. Something around you malfunctioned. Electronics or a vehicle. You could have been seriously injured but got lucky."

Chuck's eyes went as wide as they could manage. "How'd you know?"

"It's not a magic trick." On registering my own tone, I put myself in check. "What was it?"

"My car. Well, Seth's car. The tie rods snapped. The wheel turned ninety degrees while I was doing seventy on the freeway."

"Anyone hurt?"

"Just me. My neck and back are still screwed up. I have to sleep in a recliner. And it ground everything I'm trying to get done to a halt. You know, I was the only vehicle involved and those state police pricks still wrote me a violation."

That explained the lack of vehicles on the premise. "Nothing after that, right?"

"That isn't enough?"

"What I am saying is the guy behind this uses a three-strikes system. You're on number two."

Chuck sagged. If there was one thing he was good at, it was sagging. He picked up a medal, inspected it, wrapped it in a pillowcase, and placed it in a box. The podium smashed into his shins as he hauled it into the corner. He cursed and dropped it.

In a show of good will, I moved to right the podium, but Chuck stiff-armed me.

"I don't want help."

"Well, squat instead of bending over or your back is never going to get better."

Chuck took my advice. The seam on his slacks survived and spared me from seeing more of him than I ever wanted to see. He dragged the podium where he wanted it and started in on the next glass case.

"Plus, I'm being watched," he said.

"Plain-colored sedans, right?"

Chuck turned from inspecting a statue. "You really are a detective."

"Now and then. I'm surprised you spotted the surveillance. These guys are pros."

Chuck cackled. "No one escapes the neighborhood yentas. They get on the phone tree about every car, pet, or person they don't recognize. I had a hell of a time keeping them out of Seth's business. The second I'd go out, they'd be over here, chatting Seth up."

Chuck had to wiggle the next stand back and forth to maneuver it to the wall.

"So how long have you been at this?"

Chuck didn't look up from what he was doing. "I took a break after Seth died to decompress, but my travel plans got thrown out with my back."

"You should use a dolly," I said.

"I'd have to find a place that delivers. I'm not stepping one foot outside."

I decided it was cruel and unusual punishment to tell Chuck that if Culvan Mann wanted him dead, staying indoors wasn't going to prevent it. Which meant Mann wanted Chuck under house arrest, cataloging Seth Martin's possessions.

"I could camp out here and wait for the next assault, Chuck, but my methods are more proactive. You seem safe enough staying put."

Chuck stored the next glass case. "Yeah, I'm living high on the hog. All my dreams are coming true."

"You sure you don't want any help?"

Chuck looked up from wrapping a glass monument. "Yes, I'm sure."

"Tell you what. I'll play personal shopper. Get that dolly you wanted and whatever else you're missing. Put a list together and we'll stock you up."

Chuck tilted his head, calculating. "How much?"

"Call it a personal favor."

"Thanks, I owe you one." Chuck went to fetch a notepad.

I had no illusions Chuck Charles believed in the fair exchange of favors, but that didn't matter to me. I wasn't trying to indebt him. What I wanted was for him to find what he was looking for, sooner rather than later.

"Seth leave you anything?"

Despite my best efforts, Chuck caught my tone. "I did a lot for Seth. He had no one watching out for him after his wife died."

I nodded, but not in agreement. There were clusters of pictures on the wall, various sizes arranged like comic-book panels, taking issue with Seth Martin's life story. A big photo of Sol Silver's original blood-speckled Good-Man sketch anchored photos from the 1940s. Martin and Silver only had a year before the war hit. The single photo of Silver was a grainy reproduction from a newspaper article. Despite being all of fourteen, Silver looked like a linebacker. The 1950s, being a sore spot from Seth's sale of the Good Knights to Classic Digest, was mostly ignored. The 1960s were a collage of the glory days of Excelsior and Martin's partnership with Dave King.

"What about Dave King? Was Seth watching out for him?"

Chuck made a face like he wished he could deck me but knew better. "That's between Seth and Dave King."

I tried not to make the same face back at Chuck, with mixed results. A detective in the movies would have roughed him up until he talked, but then I'd be forced to go home and wash. Anyway, there were other ways of finding out.

"What about Sol Silver? Martin ever talk about him?"

Again, Chuck looked at me like I was Svengali.

"Yeah. Jesus, Seth would never shut up about Sol Silver. I'd tell him, 'Seth, Sol Silver's been dead sixty years,' and Seth would laugh and say, 'And still I see him every day.' That's when I knew Seth was losing it. It was tough to watch."

"Bet it was." I attempted a strained expression. "Okay for me to use the bathroom before I hit the store for you?"

Chuck didn't like it, but it was a reasonable request. "There's one connected to Seth's room, two doors down."

"Thanks."

"Don't touch anything."

Chuck followed me when I elected not to answer. The furniture in Seth Martin's bedroom had been rearranged to make way for medical equipment. Chuck would have joined me in the lavatory if I hadn't blocked him at the threshold.

"I got a shy bladder."

"Don't touch anything," Chuck repeated.

I closed the door in his face and locked the knob. There were four switches on the wall. I threw them all and was rewarded with the loud buzz of a combination heater/ventilation fan. The toilet seat was up. I knocked it down and shouted over the din.

"Might be a few minutes."

Chuck cursed as Seth Martin's medical bedframe creaked in protest under his weight.

I started with the medicine cabinet. Martin had less in there than I did, which was notable for a man in his nineties. There were a handful of prescriptions, all of them routine maintenance for a nonagenarian. There were no medications even remotely related to dementia.

I turned on the faucet to further create noise while I rooted around with no results. After washing my hands out of form, I joined Chuck in the master bedroom.

"Want to do yourself a favor?"

Chuck needed the bed's guard rail to get back to his feet. "What's that?"

"If you find what you're looking for, call me right away."

"Who says I'm looking for something?"

"You're digging up the floors and shaking everything like it's a Cracker Jack box. The way I see it, there are two big prizes: Martin's will and Sol Silver's first sketch of Good-Man. If you find either of them, call me. Because that's when you're going to need protection."

I fulfilled the wishes on Chuck's list. There were no big surprises. A dolly, more boxes, tape, packing materials, a jigsaw with plenty of replacement blades, and a stud finder. His grocery list was also no shock. Chuck's diet firmly avoided the edges of the grocery store, with a medley of canned this and frozen that, along with plenty of shelf-stable carbohydrates. I threw in some anti-inflammatories and a multivitamin. I wanted him to live long enough to find what he was looking for.

After dropping off Chuck's care package, I crossed the street to a neighbor's house. I rang and took a step back as to not crowd the plate. No one answered, but a well-put-together older woman came out of the next house over.

"Were you looking for someone?"

"Yes, miss. I'm looking for whoever runs the neighborhood watch. I'm a detective."

"What kind of detective rides a motorcycle?"

Damn, she was good. "A private one. My name is Ken Allen. Google away."

The woman perked up. "Oh, I've heard of you, come on over."

Infamy had its perks.

I routed back down and up the walks as to avoid cutting across the landscaping. The woman guided me into a dining room, where her social circle was breaking bread. Six women, all of them gussied up, were mostly ignoring an impressive brunch spread. The hostess ushered me into a seat at the end of the table. All present angled to face me as if I were the guest speaker.

"So, what brings a detective to our neighborhood?"

"I've heard reports of suspicious vehicles in the area. Plain-colored sedans with tinted windows. Cars matching that description have been involved in several assaults."

The women switched languages to conference. My Hebrew was nonexistent, so I focused on their body language. They nodded a lot, as if I had confirmed their worst imaginings.

"These vehicles appear to be orbiting Seth Martin's house," I added in an attempt to get their attention.

More discussion in Hebrew. The hostess handled outreach. "We've reported such to the police, for all the good that does. Please, eat something."

While I portioned out cold cuts and a cup of cabbage soup, one of the women asked me if being a detective was like on television.

"It's basically the same, except instead of commercial breaks, there's hours of driving from place to place. I was wondering if you saw anything besides cars."

They again convened in Hebrew. Opinion levels were off the charts. I wish I knew what they were arguing about or if they were even arguing. The hostess issued a reply. "There have been those little flying things. The ones with cameras on them."

"Drones."

"Yes. Did you know they can come right up to your window and look inside, and if you shoot them down, you have to pay for them? Isn't that the most ridiculous thing you've ever heard? That can't be enough food for a man your size."

I cut a piece of asparagus quiche that looked keto kosher while a woman asked me if I was married. I held up a hand to indicate the lack of a ring.

"Oh, that doesn't mean anything. I don't let Murray wear one. Some women only go after men with a ring on. Why do you think that is?"

"Maybe they figure the guy is vetted. Anything other than drones?"

A reply came only after the requisite conference. I felt like I was playing poker against a team. "All sorts of delivery trucks, some with labels on them, some without. Cars coming and going at all hours, delivering food. Taxis and buses. I blame GPS. When traffic is bad, they route drivers through the neighborhood. These streets were not designed for commercial vehicles."

I nodded and poured a glass of cucumber water while a woman asked me how true the tabloid stories about me were.

"Not very," I lied.

It occurred to me that my seat was a place of prestige, yet no one at the brunch had given up their chair. Whoever had once occupied my spot was absent. The former neighbor across the street seemed a likely candidate. "If you see any drones flying around, or if anyone but

Chuck Charles goes in or out of Seth Martin's house, could you give me a call?"

The women paused to poll a reply. "We're not sure that's any of your business."

I rubbed my temples searching for a solution. If they had been close with Seth Martin, maybe Chuck Charles had made the same impression on them he had on me.

"Chuck Charles is across the street, digging for treasure. He lived off Seth Martin for years and now he's angling to rob his grave. I don't want that, and I don't think you do either."

My speech triggered a recount. After tallying the vote, the hostess said, "Leave your card. And consider getting a proper vehicle. You're going to kill your mother riding around on a motorcycle."

Ray broke into my Bluetooth the second I climbed into the saddle.

"I'm getting sued. From both sides. They got me on my way out of the cop shop. Contractual breech due to gross negligence causing substantial financial loss."

"Were any figures quoted?"

"Sure. Half a billion." Ray laughed without humor. "Always wanted to break into Fort Knox."

The number wasn't ridiculous. Duquesne Studios had to outright cancel their Good Knights film. Over at Tachi productions, Havier Cardiel had salvaged the Civil Warriors production by retooling it into a Flying Freeman solo film, but the budget was already eaten up. Even if Flint's vehicle carried the franchise, it would have to make double what the Civil Warriors film would have, just to equal the profit projections.

"I'm ruined. They'll keep me in court for years, bleed me before the butchering. I don't have that scratch, even if I sold everything off.

Ain't no one who will hire me after this either. That's before the cops come after me for two murders. The more I talk, the less they listen."

There was something in Ray's voice I'd never heard before. A sliver of surrender. Of desperation. I countered it with positivity.

"This all goes away when we out Culvan. Has Elaine made any progress on Neil Leon's digital history?"

Elaine, having been listening in, took center stage. "Nothing we can use. Half of it is ledgers and the other half is his memoir."

"Ledgers? Does he record being hired by Culvan Mann?"

"After Chevalier, it looks like he worked for Finger Security, but they've been around since 1940." Elaine's tone was neutral, unwilling to choose sides between my forced optimism and Ray's defeat. "Wait, I think I found the entry were Culvan paid him off. It's right after Chevalier shuttered. But there's no name, just an eighteen-digit transfer code."

"What about the crew lists from Duquesne and Tachi?"

"Another dead end," Elaine reported. "There is no overlap between productions. Not a single name appears on both lists."

15

I GOT OFF the line and called Preeti, mad enough to skip hello.

"What the hell are you doing? You know Ray Ford isn't behind this."

Preeti didn't rise to my level. "You have presented no such information. And even if that were the case, Ray Ford should have detected the sabotage. He failed in his duty to ensure the safety of the cast and crew."

I took a moment to fume. Quitting would do Ray no good. I needed the access Preeti provided. Better to take my licks until she decided to cut me loose.

"Duquesne Productions remains open to alternate explanations," Preeti continued. "Deliberate sabotage would be a peril covered by our insurers. That is a preferable outcome. It also clears Duquesne of any responsibility, while guaranteeing indemnity. Ray Ford may not possess the funds to recoup our losses. Our policy carriers do."

"Well, start working on that claim," I said, and hung up.

With the shoot canceled, the trail was cold at Duquesne. Tachi Productions was the only game left in town. What I needed was a way inside. I pulled out Havier Cardiel's card and dialed the number. To my shock his assistant put me through immediately. Havier greeted me with genuine concern.

"What's up, Ken?"

"It occurs to me if I can prove deliberate sabotage to the Civil Warriors shoot, Tachi Productions can file an insurance claim for a couple hundred million bucks. Want to help me out with that?"

"A badge will be waiting for you at the gate."

Traffic was with me, as much as This Town traffic could be, and I was at the studio gates in thirty-five minutes. The stepped-up security had done the opposite of discouraging loiterers—the block was hosting a street fair, paparazzi and fans eager for the next disaster. They parted for the White Stag, not out of courtesy, but rather to chronicle my arrival. A guard who looked like a serious veteran stepped forward to halt me. His sand-blasted skin was paler where he had shaved his beard and his sunglasses looked recovered from an archeological dig. I was again forced to remove my helmet and confirm my identity before he tendered my badge.

The route inside was easier. The "Reserved for Guests of the Studio" spots were all taken, but Preeti's roadster was petite enough where it could share with the Stag. For whatever reason, skipping was less painful than plodding long. I crossed Havier's threshold with panache.

Havier hovered next to the windows, pretending he wasn't doing a wall squat. "So, what's the plan?"

"I think Flint West is the next hero on Culvan Mann's hit list. Flint's death would be guaranteed to shut down production. Why Culvan Mann didn't target him to start with is beyond me. I need to be on set. Both for prevention and to figure out who Mann has performing the actual sabotage."

"I like it."

"It will have to be incognito. Some kind of low-skill job. One where I can wear a hat and sunglasses. Craft services, maybe."

"I've got just the thing," Havier said with a smile.

The costume was superhero meets superspy, with an armored bodysuit beneath a combination cape/trench coat. A red bull's-eye bisected by a dagger stood in in the center of the breastplate.

"You've got to be kidding me."

"Sorry Ken, but no one is going to buy you as Sword Saint's double. You're about the furthest thing from Japanese a person can get without being named Flint or West."

"But Agent Provocateur?"

"It's perfect," Havier replied. "The mask covers your whole face. You can stash your gear under the trench-cloak or in all these pouches. If you ditch the trench-cloak, the costume is fairly functional."

I circled the costume dummy. You couldn't store these costumes on a hanger. They would deform. While it looked sturdy, a hands-on check confirmed its promised protection was all for show.

"I might as well wear tights."

"We do our best to keep the costumes as light and breathable as possible. Who wants to wear a flak jacket all day?"

"Someone who gets shot at."

Havier had his hands clasped, creating his own resistance. "So, what do you think?"

"You really, really hope I won't have to do a French accent."

"You mean *you* hope."

I pulled the hood off the dummy. "No, I definitely mean you."

Since we wanted as few people as possible in on my infiltration, Havier had to play sidekick and help me into costume. He was expertly efficient.

"Did you have this job, once upon a time?"

Havier squinted as he straightened Agent Provocateur's futility belt, which contained an arsenal to counter espionage. "Started from the bottom."

"Now you're running the show."

"For now. This is a results-based industry. If the world is ready for Flint West standing alone—which I think they are—I've turned lead into gold. If not, it's back to memorizing how people take their coffee."

In the mirror, my transformation was almost complete. I slipped on the hood. There was neither hide nor hair of Ken Allen. Anyone could have been Agent Provocateur. Rumor was, Georges Roland never wore the full costume. He only showed up for the scenes where he's in civilian clothes or has the hood off. The stuntman was the real hero. Roland also literally phoned in his lines, since they had to be run through an audio mixer to get that whisper-in-stereo effect Agent Provocateur was known for anyway. The hood was two-part: visor and lower face shield. Fully masked up, all your exhales turned right back into inhales. I unsnapped the lower mask and examined my jawline.

"Can I walk around like this and not give myself away? I can't tell. I know what I'm supposed to look like."

Havier peeked over my shoulder. "You look like a generic handsome-ish white guy to me. No offense."

"Being offended by the truth is a character weakness. In case someone asks, what stunt guy am I replacing?"

"Steve Cameron, who is currently enjoying a paid vacation."

I took another look. "Yeah, I definitely could be a Steve. You walk out first, so we don't look like we're in cahoots."

"That's not too suspicious. I'm known for having personal connections with absolutely everybody."

Which wasn't necessary or common for someone in Havier's position. "Yeah, why is that?"

Havier shrugged. “I’m living the dream. And, if this isn’t too cheesy, being a good guy just feels better.”

I’m glad Havier could see me smile. “Ain’t that the truth.”

I almost asked if he wanted to hang out sometime. Then I wondered if everyone tried to buddy up to Havier, and I was fixing to steer us into an awkward moment. Making friends as a kid was so easy. Without so much as a hello, you ended up running around the playground, battling imaginary villains.

Havier slapped my shoulder. “See you in five.”

Once he was gone, I double-checked where I had stashed all my gear. Intensive training with my detective loadout had internalized where my hands should go for what, but Agent Provocateur’s setup was absolute chaos, with both a belt and a bandolier, along with arm and leg pouches. He’d be a nightmare to search if he was ever captured. Me, all you had to do was take my harness. It might be a good idea to starting stashing gadgets in my socks.

The Quarreler was in the small of my back. Grenades were distributed in the same order clockwise throughout the pouches. Pencil cameras were in one leg pocket, multi-tool in the other. Reloads for the Quarreler were the problem. Agent Provocateur’s pouches were ornamental, unless he was into Tic Tacs. And don’t get me started on his futility-belt capsules. What went in there? Toothpicks to get all the Tic Tacs out of your gums?

At least my spyglasses fit under the visor, because it was pitch-black beneath Agent Provocateur’s hood any hour of the day. The spyglasses adjusted, providing a grayscale view of the world. I tested my range of motion, slowly, in case something that looked like leather but was actually vinyl tore.

If I had to run back to emergency wardrobe, my cover was blown. Havier couldn’t find a reason to dress me himself every time I experiencing a malfunction without sparking rumors he was dating Steve Cameron’s replacement.

The double-glasses thing was screwing with my depth perception. I tumbled down the trailer steps and did a little salute to the first three people I passed, then caught myself. This was not acting like I belonged.

The problem was me acting at all. I had starred in one cosmically terrible movie. You know the expression something was so bad it was good? If you believe that, then I gave the greatest performance of all time. I have pondered long and hard what the hell my problem was when it comes to playing pretend.

If I had to boil it down, I am extremely aware when I am in the act of acting. I'm not tough, I'm acting tough. I'm not scared, I'm acting scared. I can't make my face do anything it doesn't want to do. When I deliver lines, it's a crapshoot where I'll place emphasis. A lot of people who meet me at conventions assume I'm not a native English speaker.

Maybe that's another reason why I liked Sword Saint. He was who he was, absent any secret identity. When Foxman wasn't fighting crime, he had to pretend to be billionaire bon vivant Warren Wagner. Wagner had started off as a millionaire in the 1940s, but only got richer as the decades passed, which was probably the most realistic thing about the character.

I wandered onto set, where I was bounced around like a pinball until I lucked onto my mark. The crew was working on blocking, making the present cast me and a gaggle of stand-ins. At least Agent Provocateur kept to the shadows, meaning my mark was out of direct lighting, which saved me from being souvied. He also was ever vigilant.

Scanning around wouldn't seem out of character. Havier had chosen well.

Flint West's stand-in was his physical duplicate, while lacking the electric emotional intensity that made Flint pop on-screen. His voice sounded like Flint had taken a hit from a helium tank.

“What happened to Steve?” he asked.

“Lumbago.”

“Good for him. I hear it’s nice there this time of year.”

Someone did me a favor and yelled for quiet on the set. The scene was a mirror of the disastrous Good Knights reshoot. But instead of a moon base, the Civil Warriors were assembled in the ruins of an abandoned courthouse nestled in the Catskills.

The two superhero universes had different philosophies when it came to setting. The Classic Digest heroes all hailed from imaginary cities. The Excelsior ones had actual addresses.

Same for who their heroes were. The Classic Digest roster belonged to a golden age of heroes without flaws. At the end of the Depression and beginning of a world war, fans didn’t want to read about characters who had problems putting food on the table. Golden age heroes were typically wealthy, even the reporters. As it was, the readership skewed heavily toward adolescents, who were unlikely to connect with a hero scraping to make their mortgage payment.

Twenty years later, the Excelsior heroes were defined by their problems. America was experiencing an unprecedented economic boom and could stomach some struggle in their fiction. The aged-up readership responded to adventures seasoned with a heavy dose of melodrama.

These days, neither universe gave much thought to secret identities. Being heroes made up the totality of their characters. Masks were more an accessory than disguise. An affectation over an alter ego.

In a way, Seth Martin was a product of the golden age. Over the decades his myth grew, until he’d become as much a character as the heroes he wrote about. A symbol, successful and beloved. Dave King was Excelsior all the way: a man who labored unrecognized, his heroic deeds performed without reward, scrounging to make ends meet while touching millions of lives.

The cinematographer snapped my reverie by yelling at me to stop standing like that. I tried posing how I imagined Agent Provocateur would, wary and ready to pounce. The cinematographer immediately informed me that was worse.

At the time of his creation, it was unthinkable that Agent Provocateur would become a member of the Civil Warriors. In the 1970s, he'd been a villain. Ironically, the success of the Jove Brand films was probably what led to his creation. Problem was, Agent Provocateur was just too darn cool. I was old enough to witness his hero turn in the 1980s, fueled by the ninja craze. I bought the pivotal issue off the stands by saving my lunch money. Even back then I was starving myself to achieve my goals.

The rule of cool had been invoked to transform Agent Provocateur from villain to hero. The lines were often blurred like that in the Excelsior universe. You never knew when two heroes were going to duke it out, each of them believing they were in the right.

Measured breathing had taken me as far as it could. I unbuckled my mask and drank in sweet, sweet oxygen.

The director came stomping toward me. "You, what's your name?"

"Uh," I said to buy some time. Genius undercover operative I was, I hadn't given thought one to an alias. "Rick. Rick Railsback."

"Jesus. You lunks get dumber by the day. This is a lighting test, Railsback. Keep. Your. Mask. On."

I nodded and buckled the mouth shield back into place. Taking a break had made it worse. The time had come to stop waxing poetic and start locating the saboteur. If Culvan was going after Flint, he knew exactly where Flint would be standing, which was less than ten feet from me. The set itself was supposed to be wreckage from the destroyed courthouse. The Civil Warriors were gathered around the judge's bench, mourning their dead—for now—mentor, Quinton Justice.

Nothing in the immediate vicinity spelled trouble. I risked an overhead glance while the director and cinematographer conferenced. There were no electrical cords running through the area or sandbags hanging overhead. If Culvan wanted to pin the next accident on Ray, the incident would have to be delivered in the form of an effect gone wrong. But then again, Culvan had resorted to other methods when said opportunity wasn't present.

I focused on the crew next, trying to decide who looked suspicious. Being unable to talk or access my watch robbed me of the ability to zoom in. No one jumped out. Security was tight. Anyone going in or out had their badge scanned.

Lunch break was called as the stand-ins were ushered off set to make room for their A-list counterparts. I snacked on cold cuts, cheese, almonds, and celery while being careful not to overhydrate. I'd been yelled at enough already without having to request a bathroom break.

Badge around my neck, I wandered the lot. If Culvan wasn't going to take a run at Flint on set, his trailer was the next likely location. I unsnapped the lower mask but left the hood in place to maintain my disguise, trying my best not to collide with anyone or anything with mixed results. The combination of hood and visor all but eliminated my peripheral vision.

Jaq King stormed toward Flint's trailer, phone in hand. She threw the door open as she stomped inside, disappearing through the curtain. The pneumatics caught the door as it eased shut.

I slipped off my glove to activate the laser mic on my spyglasses and looked toward the shaded window. The laser mic conveyed its signal via Bluetooth.

"Uh-huh. Uh-huh," Jaq said. They were not *uh-huhs* of belief. "If that's the case, take a picture of it and send it to me."

There was a medium-length pause as the person on the other side of the phone spoke.

"What could I do with a picture of a document? I could type up the Louisiana Purchase with my name on it, but the picture of that won't make me Mardi Gras Queen."

Another pause came as Jaq listened to the reply.

"And I think you're full of shit, Chuck. You're running a con and praying I'm naïve enough to pay you off. I'm not. Show me real proof, then we'll talk."

The next pause was brief because Jaq cut Chuck off.

"Don't bother with that routine. I have the money. Flint has an eight-figure bank account."

A short pause this time, before the sound of Jaq hanging up. My reaction was mixed. It was nice to know I wasn't the only one people cut the line on, but I also didn't want to have anything in common with Chuck Charles.

Jaq swore a few more times while punching the walls. If the clean reverberations were any indication, she knew what she was doing. From these contextual clues, I was able to deduce Flint West wasn't in the trailer. Jaq had no other reason to be wandering around set, so she must have left his side to take the call. I headed over to costuming.

Flint was standing in a T pose, the center of attention as a commercial-grade dryers shrink-wrapped his Flying Freeman costume into place. Even enduring what had to feel like the world's driest sauna, he was joking around with the crew.

I wondered if Flint knew Jaq King was consorting with Chuck Charles. Or waving his checkbook around. As a friend, was it my place to tell him?

I decided against it. First, I was undercover, and second, Flint might balk at my imposition. The guy had big emotions. If he cut me out due to overstepping, I wasn't going to be able to protect him.

I decided to shadow Flint instead. I kept near enough to intercept potential assassins while far enough away to avoid stepping on his cape. I wouldn't be needed on set until Flint arrived anyway. Flint did his best to get there in good time, but everyone and their sister was holding him up. He was too polite to refuse. It was nerve-racking. A dozen people were close enough to stuff a hand grenade down his shorts.

Then he saw me.

"Hey, Agent Provocateur! Quit creeping and get over here!"

At a loss of any way to excuse myself from the situation, I stepped over to join Flint.

"How you doing, Steve?"

I shook my head, afraid to talk. Mask or not, Flint might recognize my voice. Flint nodded like he understood if I was a little starstruck and leaned in. "New guy, huh? Don't worry, buddy. In a few days you'll be shoving me out of the way to get at the empanadas."

We posed for a few pictures before walking onto set together. The director lurched for me but withdrew on noting I was under Flint's wing. I hit my mark as Flint got situated. He was either distracted or the new rewrites were fresh off the presses, because he wasn't sure what they were shooting.

"What's on the slate?"

The schedule had gone off the rails. The director was without storyboards or scene numbers. "Exposition about the courthouse being bombed and how everyone has to go to ground."

"Man, this thing has more holes than Swiss cheese." Flint pointed to Mongoose, who was having a record easy day of shooting pretending to be in a coma. "Regeneration is this dude's whole deal. He grew back his legs last movie. How is it he's out of action?"

"Mongoose was in the courthouse with Quinton Justice when Quinton shifted to the dream realm to save himself. The psychic aftershock trapped Mongoose in a nightmare loop."

It was exactly the kind of baloney comic fans would eat up.

"There's going to be an animated movie now." Mongoose's voice was distant. They had as much of him as they could get away with buried under the rubble, but his costume was sleeveless. For the first time in fifteen years, the actor's veins were inside his body. "I can do the voice work from rehab."

Flint sighed. "Okay, what about the rest of the team?"

This one the director had to look up in the script. Every draft had different colored pages. I'd seen a narrower palette in paint stores.

"T.H.E.M. has taken over all social media. With their facial recognition algorithm, if any of the Civil Warriors are scanned, the same thermobaric missile that destroyed the courthouse will home in, killing anyone within a square mile of their location."

Flint rolled his eyes so hard his head followed along. "But somehow I'm immune?"

The director fanned through the script, gave up, and grabbed the writer who had drawn the short straw to end up on set. "Explain, egghead."

The writer scratched his head through his ballcap. "There's a story in the seventies where Flying Freeman looks different to everyone who sees him. To evildoers, he's really scary and intimidating. To kids, he's basically a cartoon. It turns out, this whole time, everyone perceives you differently, you just didn't know it. So facial recognition doesn't work on you."

I was impressed enough to nod along. It was a perfect explanation. Citing a deep cut only a serious fan would remember—*Flying Freeman #250*, by the way—to give the cop-out legitimacy via continuity.

Flint agreed. He nodded with increasing enthusiasm. "All right. Nice. Good stuff. So, we get through the setup dialogue, then what?"

The director didn't need to consult anyone this time. "Then to demonstrate the threat, there is a follow-up attack. Some minor pyrotechnics."

"Today's a boom-boom day?"

"Boom-boom," the director confirmed. "With post being rushed on this one, we have to go practical."

"Isn't practical more expensive?" Flint asked. "Havier said budget's tight."

"The pyro is repurposed from the Civil Warriors shoot."

"Reduce, reuse, recycle." Flint laughed.

"It's going to look great. You in the middle with everything exploding around you. Trailer material all the way." The director turned to signal the crew. "Ray Ford is expensive, but the man knows what he's doing."

My stomach took a dive. Culvan Mann wasn't just after Flint. He was going to take out all Civil Warriors, the crew, and me, in one fell swoop. The entire production was standing in a minefield.

16

MY FIRST INSTINCT was to yell "Bomb!" and throw Flint over my shoulders. But I didn't know if Culvan had a way of detonating the explosives himself. If I made a big scene, he might pull the trigger. I had to stall the shoot and I had to do it now. A small mess-up would only get me chewed out before the show went on. Faking a meltdown or pretending to have a beef with another player required a level of acting I was incapable of. Only one other thing came to mind.

I decided to faint.

One of the first lessons you learn in any martial art was how to properly fall down. As your skill increased, falling techniques went beyond the basic "You got me" cops-and-robbers stuff, and into *ukemi*—advanced methods for absorbing being thrown and slammed. If there was one thing I could pull off convincingly, it was falling on my face.

Flint West was halfway through a moving speech about the difference between patriotism and nationalism when I did my impression of an uprooted tree. It had to be good. Unlike the proverb, everyone was around to witness it. The full sell meant not using my hands to brace whatsoever. I hit with my chest an inch before my head, careful not to bounce my braincage off the ground.

It worked like a charm. Everyone froze, thought about helping, considered the potential lawsuit, then stepped away.

Except for Flint West.

Flint rushed over and stabilized my neck. Just like I taught him. He gently unsnapped my mask to ensure I could breathe.

"It's okay. He's new. It's probably dehydration." Flint leaned closer to check on me, got a good look at my face, and whispered, "What the hell, Ken."

Flint only had seen my nose, mouth, and jawline, but let's face it: When it comes to masks, anything less than full coverage is a fashion choice. The only people who won't recognize you are ones who don't know you in the first place.

I decided Flint's massive caped form was enough cover for me to whisper back, "Play along."

Every actor experiences the sensation of being elevated by their more talented peers. You do your best to keep up while they inject all the nuance your performance is lacking. Flint rolled me into his arms and stood tall. Cradling me like a baby, he lifted his chin, every inch the hero.

"Don't worry, I'll save him."

Flint bore me off set. When medical tried to intervene, he said, "Man needs a cool place to rest." He marched me back to his trailer, the sacred place of solitude for the A-list. I was ready to stand on my own, but Flint had me crushed in his embrace. Until he tossed me onto his couch.

"Let's hear it, Ken."

I sat up and pulled off my hood. "The set is rigged to blow. Sky high. The supposed production accidents are actually on-purposes.

Someone is framing Ray Ford. They're going to make it look like his pyro went wrong by way of mass murder."

Flint clenched his jaw. He didn't doubt me for a second. He paced around the room, shaking his head. "Why would he do that?"

"The saboteur is a mercenary named Culvan Mann. Someone is paying him to halt productions on both sides of the aisle."

Flint bowed his head for a breath. "Any idea who's paying him?"

"No."

"How about why?"

"Also no."

Flint thought about sitting down, but justice was ever vigilant. Also, there was no lounging around in that costume. "Well, what do you know?"

I paused to compose, trying to choose the right words, when Jaq King emerged from the private area of the trailer.

"Flint, what's going on?"

Flint pulled Jaq close. "Ken thinks the accidents aren't accidents."

Jaq stared at me, unblinking. "You need to take this to Havier, with any evidence you've gathered."

I got up from the couch and pulled my mask back on. "Right now, I don't have any evidence. You're going to have to trust me, Flint."

Flint was a man torn between the irresistible force and the immovable object. Retooling the Civil Warriors movie had put production in a hole millions deep. Every day, millions more were being spent, whether they were filming or not.

"That's Havier's call to make," he said.

"Then I'm going to him now. Once the tampered pyro is removed, you're in the clear. A day, at the most."

Flint nodded without looking up. He looked like a man with the weight of the world on his shoulders. Jaq King, however, never stopped staring into me, as if all of this was my fault. I didn't have to go far to find Havier. He was waiting for me back where I had taken on the guise of Agent Provocateur, using the door frame to counter his weight.

"What happened? The director called me, absolutely nuclear over the new guy."

"The set is rigged to blow."

Havier lost his grip but caught himself before he pulled a Ken Allen and fell on his face. "What makes you think that?"

"The production repurposed Ray Ford's pyro, and Culvan Mann likes explosives. Culvan's last-ditch move is to blow something up. Whenever he gets beat, he doesn't just take his ball home. He pops it."

Havier looked like he was being forced to perform advanced equations at gunpoint.

"You with me, Havier?"

"Yeah. Yes, yes. I hear you."

Now the big question. "Do you believe me?"

"Yes, I do."

Tremendous relief washed over me. "You have to clear the set. Real quiet-like. Make some excuse. Betray no indication you suspect foul play, in case Culvan installed his own plunger."

"Okay, then what?"

All of a sudden, I realized how vulnerable I was. Without Ray's gadgets, I was a mild-mannered detective. It was all I could do not to rip the Agent Provocateur costume off my body.

"I'll reach out to Ray Ford. Maybe he can work up some kind of jammer. If he can defuse the explosives, no one ever has to find out."

"Will he agree to that?"

"Ray can be stubborn, but recovering a bomb is indisputable evidence of sabotage. It would clear his name."

Havier spread his hands. "I don't know what to say. Thank you."

"Thank me by getting everyone out of here."

"On it."

Havier power walked out of wardrobe, digging out his phone. Him listening to me about Culvan Mann was half the battle. I performed a quick change while calling, then texting Ray and Elaine. Neither of them answered me. I assured myself there were plenty of reasons why that might be and dialed up Special Investigator Stern.

"Allen. Where have you been?"

"Another time. Do you have Ray Ford in custody?"

Stern took a beat to work on her gum.

"Lives are at stake here," I said.

"Ford is with our lab guys, performing an autopsy on the Foxcar."

Chances were equal: either Stern was giving Ray the benefit of the doubt or letting him dig his own grave.

"I need to see him immediately. Can you text me the address?"

She could and did. It was close. They'd taken the remains of the Foxcar to the nearest highway-patrol garage. Stern was at the gate, showing her roots in mirrored sunglasses.

"First you fill me in."

"I got a way for Ray to clear himself with Tachi, but he needs to get over there now."

It hurt to back out of our new era of sharing, but if I told her the whole truth, Stern might send the bomb squad to the studio and tip Culvan off. She stared me down, gnawing on her gum.

"There's more you're not telling me, but okay. Come on."

Ray was stationed in a taped-off space in a hangar, surrounded by technicians, forensic scientists, and enough lawyers to start an incredibly pedantic football team. While Duquesne had thrown Ray to the dogs, they still had possible exposure to criminal charges. My brain cramped attempting to calculate how many billable hours were being generated.

The Foxcar looked like a dumped-out puzzle. Ray stepped back from sorting to make room for the videographers, and I caught his eye.

"How's it going?"

"It's a mess. What the heat didn't outright destroy, it fused." Ray slipped off a glove to rub his face. "I think I'm in real trouble, Ken."

"Well, I have good news and bad news and they're the same news."

I took Ray aside and covered the bullet points. He went from out of gas to firing on all cylinders. Marching past me toward the doors, he shouted over his shoulder.

"I'm done for today. Don't anyone touch anything."

I jogged to catch Ray. He dug into his racing suit to withdraw a watch of his own.

"Elaine, break out the white-noise boxes and my EOD kit."

When no response came, I chimed in. "She didn't pick up for me either."

We started running at the same time. When Ray got close to the RV, the door opened for him. He attempted to muscle me out of the way, but I maintained point position. I was armed and armored, and he was a father who couldn't care less about his own safety.

I cleared the RV one room at a time. Nothing had been left and nothing had been taken.

But Elaine was nowhere to be found.

"He's got her, Ken. Culvan busted in and took her."

I begged to differ.

It didn't add up. There was no sign of forced entry, and as smart as Mann thought he was, I was betting Elaine had the edge when it came to technology. Like Ray, Culvan was more analog than digital.

"I'm on this, Ray. Right now, you have a bomb to disarm."

Ray fumed, stomping toward his workbench. He broke out the cases he needed, tossing everything in his way aside.

I stepped in for the heavy lifting. "You figure out how the Foxcar was tampered with?"

"Pretty much," Ray replied. "The added parts were repurposed from a diesel engine. They stood out."

Ray didn't say another word the rest of way to the studio. When we got to the door, security didn't want to let us in. Neither of us had badges. I had to call Havier, who called the security office, who called the guys blocking the door.

Ray snatched his badge from the guards and the cases from me. All these security measures hadn't prevented a damn thing. Who was in charge of hiring these guys anyway? The patches on their uniforms read FINGER SECURITY. Ray was hanging the badge around his neck when I realized who the saboteurs were. It was all I could do to stifle shouting "Eureka!" I had to play it cool. The guilty parties were watching.

"I got this," Ray said. "Go do your damn job and find my daughter."

I took his shot on the chin. What were friends for?

Back at the Stag, I checked my messages. My phone had been turned off during the shoot and since then it had been one thing after another. Seth Martin's neighbors, the ladies who brunched, had left a voice mail. I ignored it and called them back.

After exchanging salutations, the hostess issued her report.

"The drones have returned. They've been circling all morning like vultures."

"How many?"

"Two of them. One gets close the other stays far. Every two hours, replacements arrive to relieve them."

"Must be running low on batteries."

"Oh, they're leaving now. I wonder—"

The sound of a vehicle drowned out her words.

"Sorry, I didn't catch that."

"A passenger bus was cutting through the neighborhood again. I'm going to write a letter of complaint."

"What about Chuck?"

"The same. He should know better than to eat so much pizza."

"Keep an eye out. Chuck's running out of rooms. If Seth Martin buried any bombshells, he's bound to turn them up soon."

The hostess harrumphed neutrally. It was the sound of someone humoring your jibber-jabber. We said our good-byes and I took the White Stag out of the backlot, weaving through the crowd until I found a good location to wait for the saboteurs.

Havier and Preeti's crew lists hadn't lied—no one directly involved with either production was involved in the sabotage, though the sabotage was performed by insiders. And not just one insider. Many. Probably a different person every time.

These agents would have to be ubiquitous. They'd have to be experienced in the field, with practical knowledge in demolition. They'd have to be someone no one would think to question. Someone who had access to all the badges they needed. And who did the questioning? The badge checking?

The answer was security guards. Culvan's mercenaries had infiltrated the companies Duquesne and Tachi had contracted for protection. Long-established operations no one thought to question. When the incidents led to heightened security, the increased demand for manpower only made the infiltration worse.

I waited until shift change. Four guards left together, two from Finger Security and two from Sherill Protection, another stalwart of the industry. The crowd had the opposite of interest in them. They stared at guards all day. Falling unconsciously into lockstep, the guards turned right as a unit at the corner. I paralleled them from a block over. If my guess was right, there would be a bus soon.

The same that bus had been around this whole time. Shadowing me on the way to the hospital after faux-Foxman gassed me. Walling me off the first time a sedan tried to impale me. Outside the parking structure, the night I visited Neil Leon's place. Outside the vacant office building, right before it imploded. Up and down Seth Martin's street, every time the drones were patrolling.

After two blocks a passenger bus pulled up. It stopped only long enough to pick up the four guards. They disappeared inside but did not reappear through the windows. The windows displayed an entirely different interior, dingy and poorly lit. The few passengers appeared to be addicts and vagrants. Because the bus windows weren't windows at all. They were a false background, the next-level green-screen effect that Ray used in his kitchen. Screens looping out footage to discourage anyone who happened to be in the wrong place at the wrong time. The windows in the sedans were the same. They just turned them black when in action as to not give away the secret. Culvan made sure to blow them up before anyone could get a closer look.

I was kicking myself for not realizing it sooner. Culvan had to be using a big vehicle. At least as big as an RV. Not only to hold all the tools of his trade, but also as a troop transport. And it needed to be big enough for him to comfortably fit inside. Someone seven feet tall wasn't cruising around in a sedan.

Even a detective of my skill level was able to tail a full-sized passenger bus. The digital sign on the back changed from THIS TOWN to CREATIVE SOLUTIONS. Did Culvan have Elaine in there with him? With the screens it was impossible to tell.

It made its way west, me trailing behind. I kept vehicles in between us, fingers crossed no one was posting the White Stag on social media. Being high visibility was great for marketing, but it also made it tough to stay under the radar. My first case, interested parties were able to track me through tagged photos and locations.

We ended up in Silicon Beach. Birthplace and graveyard to failed start-ups, it was the perfect location for a villainous lair. The high turnover meant no one was suspicious of new neighbors, the commercial space possessed high-power-demand infrastructure, and the tech companies often bussed their workers in.

The building itself was an unexceptional two-story square cast from concrete. The windows were darkened, which was not suspicious.

Every start-up believed they had a billion-dollar secret to protect. Four sedans were parked outside, faced in alternating directions, a space left between each.

The bus pulled up to the entrance, blocking my view. I whirled the Stag around, again thankful Ray hadn't decided to add an aesthetic roar to the silent electric engine. The bus was as close to the building as it could get without rubbing the collision pylons.

The building doors swung outward remotely, shrinking my field of vision to a six-foot gap. The security guards exited first. The bus bounced as the next occupant deboarded.

Ray hadn't been kidding. Culvan was massive. Seven feet was a starting point. He skipped the steps entirely as he ducked his head through the bus doors, forced to turn sideways in order to squeeze through. I was too far away to hear the bus sigh in relief.

Culvan took one stride before my view was blocked by the tinted building doors. It wasn't much to go on, but I didn't like any of what I saw. A lot of tall people are weirdly proportioned. They had strangely long limbs or were thinner than they should be. Not Culvan; he was built like an athlete blown up 150 percent.

I read an article about monster movies once that explained you shouldn't be worried when it came to giant insects. That when certain organisms grew too big, they collapsed under their own mass.

If that was true, then Culvan Mann was defying the laws of nature.

The building doors began to close. If Culvan had Elaine, she wasn't in the bus. I raced the Stag across the parking lot as if I were aiming to collide head on with the side of the building. Sure, I would show up on the security cameras, but it would be right at the end. When people reviewed the footage, they didn't review it backward.

Overgrown spartan juniper trees lined the side of the building. I squeezed the White Stag against one and thought about maybe having a plan. I discarded that idea right away. My advantage was in acting now, while their guard was down. If Elaine was inside, every second

I waited, Culvan was one step closer to her. I sent Stern a pin to my location with the text:

Found Culvan's digs. They have a hostage. Going in.

As a law enforcer, Stern would need proof to enter the premises. Probable cause, a trip to the judge, maybe even other cops confirming through surveillance. By the time she got a warrant, Culvan would be long gone. What she could do is act under exigent circumstances. Like if some jackass detective got in over his head and called for help.

Having recently been trafficked, I was fairly certain the front entrance was not booby-trapped. I rode the Stag around toward it, staying tight to the wall. My Bluetooth signaled a call alert from Special Investigator Ava Stern. I ignored it.

I backed up against the bus, facing the doors. Laying low behind the windshield, I slammed the concussion-grenade button.

The first shot spiderwebbed the security glass. The second had them sagging in the frames. Good enough. I throttled hard through the bigger opening and fired my last grenade.

The lobby area had been converted into an armory. Costumes and tactical gear were laid out on long tables. Racks of weapons stood waiting, with bins of custom ammunition stationed next to them. Uniforms hung on rolling closet bars next to street clothes, with footwear laid out underneath.

Five seconds had passed since my first blast hit the door. All four men had hit the deck in response to the concussion grenade exploding in the center of the room. The closest of the four men was by the wardrobe. The rest were in a far corner of the room, near two doors at a right angle to each other. Culvan was nowhere to be seen. I launched regurgitants at the three and steered toward the lone man in wardrobe.

They were all pros who wasted no time standing around gaping. The closest guy jumped to his feet and sprinted for the weapons. I ghost-rode the Stag, leaving the parking to the gyros, and hit the ground running. My target wove serpentine, keeping low.

It took me three shots to get him, the third one tagging his lower back. He hit the ground sprawling as I closed on him. I put a second shot between his shoulders. By the time he had worked himself onto his knees and elbows, I was within reach. While kicking a downed opponent was considered poor form, we weren't exactly operating under Marquess of Queensbury rules.

I used a kick typically reserved for field goals, angling around his arms to catch him square in the face. In retrospect, it was probably overdoing it, but I was outnumbered and scared out of my shorts. He went down hard, his head bouncing off the tile floor.

The three guys at the far side of the room had disappeared in the direction they were headed before my intrusion. I tipped over the racks and bins, spilling their contents onto the floor. If they got past me, it would take some time to sort through the mess and match weapon to ammunition. My Bluetooth informed me Stern was calling a second time. I ignored it again.

I pulled the gas mask out of my collar and made a choice. Straight ahead was deeper into the structure. To the left was a side room. I didn't want anyone getting behind me, and therefore to the guns, so the side room was next.

The gas was lingering. I went with a patented Ken Allen move and rolled into the room. The problem with repeating a tactic is people get wise to it. What turned out to be a microwave slammed into my side. The impact shoved me into the wall, which killed my momentum and left me on my back.

The guard was equipped with his security loadout and came in leading with a stun gun. I turned onto my side and swept up with a kick to preserve space while I recovered. He saw the kick coming and trapped it between his arm and body, which gave him a clear shot at my groin with the stun gun.

I pulled in with my hostage leg while kicking his lead ankle out with my free foot. He lurched toward me enough where I could grab his wrist behind the stun gun. He pushed hard, fighting to touch a tender area. I gambled everything on taking the arm holding the stun gun, and went for the Kimura.

I locked my legs around his body and got to work. He tried to rip his arm free. I fought hard to keep it. If he got loose, the stun gun was eventually going to find an unprotected area.

I began rotating his arm the wrong way. A common mistake when applying a Kimura is forcing the arm backward instead of up. The guard turned toward the lock to alleviate the pressure. I used it to roll us over and took top position while maintaining the hold.

Here's another little secret about escaping the Kimura, also known as the double-wrist lock: If you are unable to make a tight fist, you're dead in the water. And the merc wouldn't drop the stun gun, which made him complicit in me tearing his shoulder out of the socket.

He yelped, finally giving up on the stun gun. We were in a pickle. On the mat, one guy could tap out. It was a contest. The winner released the submission and the match was over. But when someone was trying to end your life, the rules of engagement were different. If I turned him loose, he was probably going to try to kill me again.

I released his arm and dropped my forearm into his face. It worked, so I did it again. He tried to stop me, but only had the one arm. I shifted a knee to trap it and switched to punches.

The denouement wasn't pretty. I kept punching until I was sure he was out of the action. Stern was right. I needed handcuffs. Fléchettes were all I had to ensure someone wasn't getting up for another round. I was switching from concussive rounds to tranqs when the last two guys burst back through the far door.

One of them came at me, the other went for the weapons.

I didn't make the same mistake the merc I just put down had. His whole world had become the stun gun when he had three other perfectly good limbs. I dropped the empty Quarreler and got my hands up. The merc in the doorway flicked a knife open.

Military guys love knives. In the armed services, the focus is on the use of weapons. Hand-to-hand combat is mostly ignored. Given a choice of marital arts, veterans will almost always study one that includes edge play.

The merc led with the knife, his other hand high and open. I gave ground to get more information, but he didn't follow. He was going to hold the door. Keep me locked down while his comrade retrieved the hardware. Dropping the Quarreler had been a bad move. If I bent over to get it now, I was going to end up with four inches of steel in my neck. I lunged in and out with a jab I didn't really mean, drawing out a cut at my hand. My gloves and jacket protected me, but there wasn't a lot of overlap in my wrist area. I faked a second jab and put a side kick into his knee. It wasn't a fight ender, but his knife hand lowered enough for me to send a rear cross. The merc used his empty hand to parry it while I snagged his knife hand at the wrist, which left us all tangled up.

Forget the knife-fighting videos you've seen. Real knife fighting—especially when one guy didn't have a knife—was basically doing a sewing machine impression. Unleashing a high volume of stabs from varying angles to make the knife hand hard to find. A knife could cut you on the way out but also on the way back, so your withdraw should be as sharp as your thrust.

I kept one hand glued to the merc's knife arm at all times, but it wasn't always the same hand. The technique was called "Sticky Hands"—a Wing Chun principle. He pulled away, lashed around, and thrust in, but I stuck to his wrist wherever it went, trapping the hand. The hand that wasn't trapping was striking. Short, fast blows to keep him occupied while I locked my shin against his to set up a sweep.

People are always trying to shove each other into walls. The thing about walls is that they aren't as solid as they appear. Your average toddler can burst through sheetrock like the Kool-Aid Man. Rooms like this—a kitchenette in a commercial building—were worse. Often they didn't even have wood studs, only a skeletal metal framework. And modern doors were hollow. Knock hard and you were shaking hands with the person on the other side.

Door frames, however, were the exception. They were the toughest part of the wall, built to support the door and secure the lockset. Door frames were a weapon.

I hooked the merc's neck and yanked him both forward and downward. Anchored in place by my shin, he tried to adjust stance, but that only added to the momentum. His knife hand was pinned. His other hand was fumbling to get me off his neck. By the time he thought to use either to brace, it was too late.

He hit the frame full on, smashing his nose and eye sockets. Instant lights out. He slid down to rest on the threadbare carpet. I cringed with empathy while retrieving the Quarreler, before remembering these guys were willing to bomb a movie set. I put a tranq dart in each merc on the way out the door to help them sleep off the pain.

The last man was crouched on the floor, playing a game of memory with guns and ammo. The knife fight had taken too long. There was no cover between us. For reasons explained above, retreating back into the kitchenette would not provide me with viable cover, and moving deeper into the building was rushing headlong into the unknown.

All that was left was to go right at him. I dug in, sprinting as hard as my bum leg would carry me, closing the gap as I aimed. He found the ammo drum he was looking for and slapped it into place. I missed a tranq shot as he sighted from a crouch.

A double tap sounded like dry thunder. Not a fléchette weapon, but actual gunshots, deafening in the enclosed space. The merc fell on his back.

"Toss it or eat two more," Stern said.

The merc emptied his hands. Stern walked him down, smoking gun leveled.

"Answer your phone next time, Allen. I was all of five minutes away." Stern didn't take her eyes off the guy she'd dropped. "And you. I see you thinking about it. Stop while you still have brains in your head."

I scanned around to take stock. No one popped out of a trapdoor. I took the opportunity to switch back to concussives.

Stern toed the one she had downed, who let out a groan. "Quit crying and roll over, Rover."

He did as he was told, and Stern cuffed him.

"He's a security guard," I said. "Check him for keys."

Stern found a handcuff key on his ring. She shook her head, tut-tutting. "This was something a person who wanted an ambulance sooner rather than later should have disclosed."

"Four guys got out of the bus with Culvan," I told her. "I don't know what's further inside, but Culvan has set traps before."

Stern took in the scene as we made our way past the kitchenette. "These guys tick you off, Allen?"

"I wanted to catch them before they got their bearings."

"What's this about a hostage?"

I held up a pinkie to propose an oath.

"Grow up, Allen."

"Ray Ford has a secret daughter. Her and Culvan were an item. She's missing."

It was a good thing Stern didn't have laser-vision. "I thought we were sharing."

"I have a client's wishes to respect. And the hostage situation is a recent development."

When Stern reached out for the door, I stepped in front of her.

"That's pretty old-fashioned, Allen."

"Mann likes to rig doors."

I faced us away and back-kicked the door open. Nothing happened. The space beyond was another big room, a dormitory with repurposed cubicle walls to create partitions.

"I shouldn't be in here," Stern said. "If we catch Mann, I'm going to have a hell of a time making this stick."

The partitions turned the room into a labyrinth. Stern being there was a relief. I was used to trying to look around at everything all at once.

"Someone in mortal peril called in need of rescue," I said. "You had a duty to act."

"Have you ever heard of the silver platter doctrine, Allen?

"None of those for me. I grew up middle class."

An exploration of the cubicle maze yielded no results. In the center, a table was littered with pizza boxes and Chinese food containers. I counted eight beds. I'd run into nine guys. Ten, if you counted Neil Leon. I wondered how fast Culvan refilled the empty cots. Stern nudged me toward an elevator.

I shook my head. "It's a trap. No way Culvan Mann is using an elevator. He'd have to kneel."

Stern gestured toward a partition. We each took a side and walked it over to the stairwell door for cover while I worked the lever. No explosion followed. So far, so good.

"I guess it would be awkward if Mann blew up his own guys when they brought him his takeout order."

The stairs only went up. Stern pushed past me, taking the lead. I didn't like it on the basis I was more bulletproof, but she was the law-enforcement professional.

We had to take the next door on faith. Stern insisted, as I had run point on the prior two. I gritted my teeth and went down to the landing. She pulled it, backing into the wall. It didn't issue so much as a creak.

I joined Stern at the top, slipping back into pole position as she came out from behind the door.

"It feels like we're being lulled," I said.

The second floor was all Culvan's. The space was stripped to the bones. He'd taken down the interior walls and torn out the drop ceiling. Lights were mounted on armatures which could be elevated or angled, creating pools of illumination. The left wall was devoted to completed projects. Rows of drones were docked in chargers. Gadgets were stored in bins I'd need mechanical advantage to lift. Explosives were secured. The right wall was for works in progress. Culvan was tidy and methodical. Each project was laid out on its own folding table, the type people kept tucked in a corner for parties. There were no notes or labels. Either Culvan kept it all in his head or used a device for inventory management.

His living quarters were spartan. The bed was a simple frame I'd have to boost myself onto. Storage containers resembling Ray's custom cases were stacked underneath. The bedside table was bare. His clothes were crisply folded in a clear plastic dresser unit.

He had a kitchenette setup with a hot plate, microwave, blender, and six mini-fridges stacked into a rectangle. Pots and pans hung from a wire rack. Dry goods were stored in the same sort of modular unit that held his clothes. Culvan's gym space was fully analog. There were enough plates to supply a lumberjack camp. The weight on the bars was more than double any of my all-time maximums. There was a combination bench and squat rack, along with a cable system unlike any I had seen before. Mann had probably concepted it himself.

Culvan's control center stood across from that area, the last stop on his daily routine. A dozen screens were mounted on a semispherical framework which could have doubled as a jungle gym. The same number of foldable trays were attached to the superstructure, half of them deployed but vacant. A power block big enough to route a subway system squatted on the far side of the structure. Culvan's throne was welded from rebar and springs with strategically mounted foam cushions.

Elaine was there, waiting for us, next to Culvan's empty seat.

17

I STOPPED HALFWAY into my first step toward her. The relief at discovering Elaine unharmed created a false sense of security. The situation had all the makings of a trap. I waved instead of speaking, to be extra safe.

"It's okay," Elaine said. "Culvan is gone."

"Blink twice if he's making you say that."

Elaine sighed. "Get over here."

I marched over, Stern in tow, and evaluated Elaine. She looked same as always. Unmarred and clean. Her chair was free of manacles. She was wearing makeup.

Being a detective was all about asking the right questions. "What's going on?"

"Culvan is gone. He left as soon as you knocked down the doors." Elaine patted her armrest. "I disabled his security."

"Why would he bail?" Stern asked. "He had Allen outnumbered with no idea I was on the way."

Elaine studied Stern, she decided to give her the benefit of the doubt. "You don't know Culvan. He's a control freak. He would never fight on anyone else's terms."

That made sense to me. Sore losers were selective about what games they chose to play. What didn't make sense was why he left Elaine behind. Culvan could have carried her out with him, chair and all, if he wanted. Stern got on the horn to call in the cavalry.

"Did Culvan take anything?" I asked.

"His laptops and a duffel," Elaine answered. "But that doesn't mean anything. He'll have at least one other workshop with supplies cached."

With more cops on the way, there wasn't much time to poke around. I started with Culvan's bed. It was made to military standards. The memory foam mattress, though new, was depressed to the point of ending it all. His pillows were also foam, one for his head and another shaped like a capital letter *I*, the type that went between your legs. There was only the one bed. I wasn't sure how long Elaine had been gone. Maybe a few hours, maybe right after I spoke to her last.

In the kitchen, I evaluated Culvan's nutrition. To him, food was fuel. His meal plan was tailored to power lifting. He ate his oatmeal plain and took a lot of supplements. We used the same brand of protein powder, though he put frozen bananas in his shakes. He drank filtered milk and snacked on Rice Krispies Treats.

His workout gear included the wraps, belts, and braces to be found in any serious lifter's kit. All his equipment was tailored toward building functional muscle. A layer of puzzle mats acted as a barrier between the metal weights and concrete floor.

The bathroom was the only area preserved in its original location. Relocating the plumbing would have taken a lot of work. Culvan had replaced the toilet with something Mario could have taken to the Mushroom Kingdom. The tub was suitable for livestock. Fifty-pound bags of Epsom salts were stacked against the wall next to it.

I skipped the workshop areas. Time was limited and I wouldn't know what I was looking at anyway. Elaine and Stern hadn't moved. Stern was having far less success chatting Elaine up than she had with me back when I was a person of interest.

There wasn't much to gain from studying the blank monitors, so I focused in on Culvan's chair. The foam pads were precisely positioned. Two angled footplates were welded a yard apart.

Though Elaine didn't need the assist, I walked over behind her chair. "Well, this has been a gas, but we've got places to be and people to see."

Stern put her foot out to stop the chair. "Sorry, Allen, but you're my explanation as to why I'm legally allowed to be standing in this spot. You're both here for the duration."

My first instinct was to hightail it. It wouldn't have been the first time I had fled a crime scene and I doubted it would be the last. But there was Elaine to think about, in addition to destroying all the good will I had built up with Stern.

"Come on, you two," Stern said. "I'm going back downstairs to direct traffic."

I rested a hand on Elaine's chair. "I still don't trust the elevator."

Stern fumed. "Stay put and don't touch anything."

"Your wish is our command."

I waved Stern off like I would handle this, but no way I was selling Elaine out. I didn't feel too bad about lying to a cop. Stern had pretended to buddy up to me while trying to prove I was a murderer. I was only returning the favor.

I waited until Stern was on the far side of the door to talk. Even then, I kept my voice down. Big, uninsulated spaces were prone to echoes.

"Culvan didn't kidnap you, did he?"

Elaine shook her head.

"You reached out to him."

Elaine nodded.

"Want to tell me why?"

She looked away before answering. "I wanted to talk to him. Try to get through to him."

"How did that go?"

Elaine turned toward the blank monitors. "Not well. Cul was always obstinate, but he's gotten worse. He only sees in two colors now. Will you hand me one of those HD cables?"

"Like it or not, people are social animals." I passed Elaine one of the cords connected to the monitors. "Lone wolfing it for years can warp your brain."

Elaine plugged the cord into her armrest and data flooded the screen. It was not displayed in a novice-friendly format. I had no idea what any of it meant, so I stuck to the human side of things.

"Did Culvan give any hint who he's working for? What he's up to next?"

Elaine shook her head absentmindedly, fixated on the screen. "No, and asking him would have been a mistake. He brought you up more than once. I think you frustrate him."

"I have that effect on people."

"He wanted to know what you've figured out. Cul isn't half as slick as he thinks he is. How's Dad doing?"

Now wasn't the best time to tell Elaine I'd left her father to disarm a bomb. "He'll be doing better if the stuff in here ties Culvan to the sabotage. Sure he didn't reference anyone, even in pronoun form?"

"Cul only talked about people we both knew. Me, Dad, and you."

Elaine shut down the screen. When she reached over for the cord, I stopped her. She wasn't wearing gloves. It would be best if as few of her fingerprints as possible were on the evidence.

"What about anything time-line related? He say 'soon this will all be over,' or anything like that?"

This time Elaine stopped to think.

"I asked Culvan how he could enjoy living like he does. He told me to ask myself the same question. I said at least I had a home. He said having a home was foolish, because then it could be taken from you. I asked him if innocent lives were worth his revenge. He replied the fee he was paid ensures he will never again be in the position Dad left him in, destitute and desperate."

"Nice choice of words."

Elaine smirked. "Like you're never in character."

Voices echoed in the staircase.

"The cops are going to cover this place in powder. What else did you touch?"

Elaine glared at me. "I didn't sleep with him, if that's what you're asking."

"Prying is part of the job."

"We met this morning after Dad left. Culvan made us oatmeal and tea. He washed everything right after."

I was about to advise Elaine of her rights when I had the brilliant idea to call the lawyer I was working for.

Zaina Preeti sounded exactly as excited to hear from me as she had this entire case. "Hello, Mr. Allen. I've been awaiting an update."

"I found Culvan Mann's hideout, but he got away. He was using security guards to perform his handiwork. The cops are here, arresting everyone, including maybe me and a hostage. There's probably enough lying around here to prove deliberate sabotage, insurance-wise."

"Provide the address. My team and I are on the way. Inform the police I have advised you to remain silent."

She hung up before I could thank her. Stern led a troop of fellow staties into the room. I broke my silence right away. For good reason.

"I think those are bombs," I said.

That got immediate attention. Over the buzz, Stern informed everyone she had already requested the bomb squad. She separated from the pack to admonish me.

"In the future, let me do the pointing out of explosives. We have guys who can help you down the stairs. To be frank, that's about all they're good for."

Elaine exhaled hard. "We'll be fine."

I followed her down the stairs. She did all the work, tilting and braking with precision.

"Your dad did a hell of a job on the chair," I said.

Elaine shook her head. "Cul built it, before he left."

"My offer to lend an ear remains open."

"You can go ahead and stop detecting in my direction," Elaine replied.

"Ten-four."

The cops were happy to let us wait outside, but no further than that. They would not allow me near the White Stag. I was yet to be searched, but it was coming. Stern could only extend her authority so far.

Culvan's bus and all the sedans were still there. However he had bugged out, it included an unknown vehicle. I hid in the building's shadow while Elaine basked in the sun. It took all kinds.

Preeti made it to us in record time. Her legal team filled two SUVs.

"Remain here," she began. "I want you present for the absolute minimum amount of exposure. Speak only when I indicate, no matter how witty you are convinced your response will be."

"What's my cue? How about you do fingerguns at me?"

Preeti contained her reaction. "If your behavior is any indication how this will proceed, I advise you to amend your agency agreement to define bail as an expense."

Preeti and her team got as far as the door before they were rebuffed. The available angle provided them a partial view of my good deeds. Preeti glanced at me in impressed disbelief. I flashed fingerguns back. Water and some mixed nuts would have hit the spot, but refreshments were in the Stag and the Stag was off limits.

Elaine drummed her fingers on her armrest. "So, what's going to happen next?"

"You know Culvan better than I do, what's your guess?"

Elaine went silent. There's a difference between thinking about what you were going to say and thinking about how you were going to break bad news to someone. She was doing the latter.

"Cul won't take this well."

"Yeah, I really got him on the ropes."

"If there's enough inside to clear Dad, then Cul lost. He can't stand losing."

Preeti and Stern were marching their respective squads toward us. I reached into my jacket for a pen to ask who wanted an autograph first, then reminded myself to wait for an indication.

"My client witnessed the saboteurs enter the premises. He had strong cause to believe a hostage was inside, and knew if he did not act quickly, they could leverage said hostage. We have every indication that the hostage taker is skilled in explosives and has no compunction about employing them."

"Classic lack-of-compunction-clause situation. Case closed," I interjected.

I saw a video once of a lifeguard trying to save a drowning person, but the drowning person was flailing around, doing everything they could to drag them both under. Stern's expression was the same as that lifeguard's.

Preeti stayed the course. "My client is ready to detail the events leading up to the incident and how he arrived at his conclusion."

What followed was basically a Sesame Street skit about police questioning. Preeti was Bert, Stern was Ernie, and I was the producer's kid who wouldn't stop staring at the camera. Still, with enough coaching I was able to detail how I figured out about the bus and the security guards, then followed their lead in expressing my concern about a prolonged siege if the bad guys were able to entrench.

“We’re going to need your firearm, Allen.”

“Technically, it’s not a firearm.”

“We’ll decide what it is. Hand the pistol over along with whatever you used to blow the door.”

Preeti nodded at me. I reached for the Quarreler and got an idea how I could maybe get out of here with the White Stag. I unclipped my harness and handed over the whole kit and kaboodle.

“The green ones are the concussives,” I said.

Stern held a bag for me to drop the harness in and pretended not to notice that all the grenades were accounted for. “You can keep your vehicle for now.”

I kept my mouth shut and nodded.

“This is only round one,” Stern continued. “In the near future, we’ll be calling for a proper sit-down, but right now we have our hands full with this site. Get out of here, Allen.”

I turned to walk away, then promptly reversed direction, scratching at my temple. “Gotta get my bike.”

Soon enough, I was back with Elaine, somehow having resisted the urge to pop a wheelie on my way out the doors.

“I need your dad to make me a sidecar.”

“He’s on the way.”

I partook in refreshments while we waited on Ray. He pulled up in the RV and exited through an access hatch I couldn’t have located with an electron microscope. He looked concerned until he saw Elaine was safe and sound. Then his stare went cold.

“Culvan didn’t break in, did he? You left on your own.”

Elaine stared right back. “I’m not going to apologize. That’s how you know I’m your daughter.”

Ray issued a frustrated growl. “How about Culvan? He ever apologize for what he did to you?”

“Cul wasn’t the only person there that day, Dad.”

Ray turned away. “I’m done talking about this.”

Elaine headed into the RV. "Of course you are. That's how we got here in the first place."

Ray waited for Elaine to disappear inside before starting in on me. "You let him get away?"

"Culvan is a big chicken," I replied. "He bugged out the second I blew down the door."

Ray kicked his tires and swore. "Then you have to deal with him before he knows you're there."

"What do you mean by *deal with him*? I might dress up like Jove Brand, but that doesn't make me an assassin."

Ray locked on to me, unblinking. "I gave you everything you need to get it done. So, get it done."

If watching him and Elaine go at it had taught me anything, it was that butting heads with Ray would only shut him down. "About that—the cops confiscated the Quarreler."

Ray disappeared inside the RV for as long as it took to retrieve my old pistol. He threw it at me harder than a person should throw a projectile weapon.

"This is our chance to be free, Ken. You think I like living in a bunker? That I enjoy having to keep my daughter under house arrest?"

"I didn't do this to you, Ray. You did this to you."

Ray grabbed me by the lapels. He was so close I could smell the roast beef he had for lunch. "The son of a bitch crippled my daughter. And he has the nerve to bear a grudge. Where does he get off, being pissed at me?"

I let Ray tug on me all he wanted. It was his jacket any damn way.

"You gave him everything, then took it away," I said. "His family. His future."

"So, I was just supposed to let it go? Forgive and forget?"

"He thought you would. After all, you were his hero."

18

RAY LET ME loose and turned toward the RV.

"We're going home."

I stashed the old Quarreler away and got while the getting was good. No longer a wanted man, I was safe to head home. The whole drive, I fixated on Elaine's recounting of her conversation with Culvan. Particularly Culvan implying he had already been paid. If the best practices of professional sabotage followed other trades, you didn't get compensated until the job was done. Which meant whoever had hired Culvan considered his work complete.

The Good Knights film was dead in the water, all its stars out of action. The Civil Warriors movie had become a Flying Freeman solo project, but with the security infiltration outed, Culvan's access to set was blocked. There was no more framing Ray Ford. Ray was banned from set and all his effects had been either used or discarded. There had to be enough evidence in Culvan's lair to get Ray off the hook.

Which meant Culvan was out there, mad as hell at being beaten.

If you believed Elaine. Which I did.

My condo was still standing. I went right to the kitchen, made a proper smoothie, and got coffee brewing. One minute I was looking at the imprint Dean had left on my couch. Six hours later I was waking up in the exact same spot.

My bum leg was throbbing from sleeping on it. I framed it as a good thing. The pain meant it was healing. I hobbled into the kitchen and dumped out the burnt coffee to start over. On the theory you needed water in your body to make blood, I drank sixty-four ounces. Working on the same premise for muscle tissue, I devoured homemade protein bars well past their expiration date.

The only interesting article in my mail was an oversize card-stock envelope marked DO NOT BEND. The return address was a PO box. Instead of a name, someone had drawn a crown. My hands started to shake. I fished out my multi-tool and opened the envelope like I was performing surgery.

There was a sheet of bristol board inside. Withdrawing it could possibly curl the edges, so I cut the rest of the envelope away. Inside there was a note:

Thanks for all the nothing,
Dave

The only other item in the envelope was that single sheet of priceless card stock.

It was a one-page comic in four panels, written and drawn by Dave King. The main character was super-sleuth Ken Allen. The first panel was a close-up of a video-watch screen dominated by a floating crown. A jagged-edged balloon extended from the crown, denoting an electronic tone.

THE CROOKS CAME CALLING. GO GET 'EM, KEN!

The next panel was a fist slamming into an open palm so hard it thundered. A balloon extended from out of frame above the hands.

MY PLEASURE, DAVE!

The third panel was the big one. There I was, realized through Dave King's lens, in the prototypical superhero pose. Legs wide, hands on my hips, head held high in an expression of confident determination. A force for good, stalwart in the face of an unseen wind, looking toward a brighter future.

The fourth panel was a portrait of Dave King. Not the Dave King of now, but the Dave King of yesteryear, lantern-jawed with a stogie crunched in his teeth.

ATTABOY, KEN!

The page instantly became the most precious thing I owned. I set it down to get my sweaty, oily mitts off it and stared for a long time. The page was roughly penciled. Dave King had sketched it out, then gone back over it carefully. I could see the hesitation marks, the sudden darkening of a slipped line. The clean smear of a gum eraser. There were no inks. You had to be able to handle a brush for those.

My eyes started to well up. I moved away to make sure the page didn't get wet. The composition was vintage King. Energy thrived behind the lines. His anima bled into the gutters.

But King's hands refused to obey their master. The page looked like a promising adolescent's effort. A budding artist with vision and potential and passion, at the very beginning of a long career. It was something Dave King might have produced as a teenager.

. . . as a teenager.

The thought birthed a crazy theory. I studied the sketch blurred through my tears as if I were viewing it through a scrying pool. The pose was iconic for a reason. It had been there since the very beginning.

I limped to retrieve *The Secret History of Superheroes* from my coffee table. I found the image I was looking for in the first few pages. I placed Dave King's page next to the book to better compare. The lines matched exactly. The proportion, the anatomy. But also the intangibles. The style, the energy. All the details behind the lines matched as well. I got up and did a crooked lap around my condo, talking to myself.

"No way. No way. It can't be. But it is. It is."

I went back and looked again. Side by side, the similarities were undeniable. You could have laid one over the other. I pinched myself to make sure I was awake. That didn't convince me, so I knocked myself in my injured thigh. It hurt like hell, but I couldn't stop laughing.

Once again, I had gone and solved a mystery that had nothing to do with the murders. Or did it?

Here was where it would have been good to a have an established crime-fighting process, but I had only ever solved the two cases. I didn't have anyone I could talk it through with. Ray had acted as my sounding board the first time around. Since he was listening in all the time anyway, I didn't feel bad about spilling anyone's beans.

Why disrupt two separate superhero productions? In my first case, the killer believed if they sabotaged the Jove Brand franchise, they would inherit several billion dollars in film rights. But in this case, delaying the productions didn't have any effect on who owned the characters. Seth Martin had sold the Good Knights more than fifty years ago, after paying off Sol Silver's estate. Meanwhile, on the other side of the fence, until someone came forward with Martin's will, ownership of the Civil Warriors was up in the air.

So, who had hired Culvan Mann?

I leaned on what I had learned from watching too much true crime, and asked myself: Right now, who was benefiting from the sabotage?

I didn't like the answer, but no second option presented itself.

I worked backward from the suspect. Scientifically, it's the wrong direction to work. It creates confirmation bias. The things that fit your hypothesis will jump to the fore, the things that don't get ignored.

I reminded myself of that phenomenon again and again, because everything pointed at the same person. What I didn't have was any proof, and I could only think of one place to get some.

I flipped open my old Quarreler and found a red cartridge staring back at me. Once again, Ray had elected for the lethal option. It hadn't escaped me the new tranq darts also had lethal potential. And that Ray had been sure to tell me the magic number. I swapped to taser rounds and restocked the rest of my gear for a possible life-or-death showdown. I sent Dean a text.

You're a good kid. It's everyone around you dropping the ball. Myself included. Hope to see you again soon.

I shut everything off, locked everything up, and deleted my internet histories. If things went south, the last thing I needed was a tabloid article about how deceased wannabee detective Ken Allen had to Google if there was a *Criminal Justice for Dummies* book.

My first stop was Seth Martin's former abode. I didn't call ahead in order to catch Chuck Charles flat-footed. Or tilted-footed, depending on what shoes he was wearing. The brunch crowd flagged me down on spotting me. They were kind enough to let me park around back, out of sight of Seth Martin's house. The hostess opened the conversation after I resumed my spot at the foot of the table.

"Everything stopped yesterday. The cars, the drones."

Someone chimed in out of turn. "Even the terrible buses."

There was literally a quiche with my name on it. I set the toothpick flag out on the plate. "It should stay that way. Is this tea unsweetened?"

"Yes, it is. So why are you here?"

"One reason was to talk to you, actually."

The hostess looked surprised. People usually were when they realized I had figured something out. "Oh?"

"Chuck Charles is across the street, tearing Seth Martin's house apart in search of buried treasure. But I don't think he's going to turn up anything." I stopped to take a sip. "Because his treasures aren't over there. They're over here."

The table went completely quiet. No clinking of silverware or cup against saucer. No whispered conversation. Only the collective holding of breath.

"My guess is Seth Martin used to sit in the seat I'm currently occupying. Chuck Charles said whenever he'd leave, one of you would be over at Seth's. I'm betting you brought some things back with you at his behest. For safekeeping."

I had to hand it to them. They only paused for a beat. But a brunch full of people all of a sudden not eating, drinking, or talking was a dead giveaway.

The hostess smiled. "That's quite a bit of thinking, guessing, and betting."

"What I don't get is what you're waiting for."

"Assuming you are correct, we would be doing a service for a dear friend. Honoring that friend's dying wishes."

Seth Martin was already dead. Why would he delay his final testament? Only one reason came to mind.

"Did Martin tell you to hold out until Dave King joined him in the ever after?"

Everyone fixated on their plates. Guilt emanated off them in waves. "You can rest easy. Seth's last wish may seem petty on the surface, but he had a good reason. Martin was honoring Dave King's wishes."

That got their attention.

"The first drawing of Good-Man, do you have it? I'd like to see it."

The hostess shook her head.

"I'm not going to snatch it out of your hands."

"You seem like a nice person, Ken. Seem."

I couldn't fault their caution. "I am. A bad guy would already be twisting your arms."

They huddled to discuss in Hebrew. The debate included several rounds of rebuttals. It was hard to tell who was in what camp. The ladies of brunch switched sides on a dime. The deliberation paused for the hostess to address me. "You won't try anything?"

"May God strike my mother dead."

It was the right thing to say. The hostess left the room. I ate a handful of mixed nuts for dessert and finished my tea. She returned in time to interrupt my crushing defeat in a dispute over motorcycle use. She had taken the time to don latex gloves.

If I was handling a piece of paper worth billions of dollars, I would have done the same.

"Can you see it from there?" the hostess said by way of a warning.

"Yes. Yes, I can."

All the touches we accept as rote in the genre were present from the start. The stylized G inside an equilateral diamond. The golden cape, flapping like a flag in the wind. The classic hero stance: Good-Man's fists against his hips, elbows out, as if he were offering to escort us into a new age. The paper was the same as in all the pictures: yellowed, battered, and speckled with blood.

I stared at the blood for a long time. There was enough of it.

"All done. Thank you."

I waited until the hostess returned from stashing the drawing to get up from the table to prevent alarming the assemblage with any sudden moves.

"Stay the course. It might not feel like it, but you're fighting the good fight."

I wished them a lovely day and took the Stag across the street. Chuck Charles didn't reply to my text, but he did let me in. He was still pushing the boulder that was Seth Martin's trophy room up the hill. There were enough statues left to start a museum.

"You're a free man, Chuck."

He squeezed at his lower back, squinting at me. "What are you talking about?"

"Take a gander out the window. I chased the bad guys off. You aren't going to find what you're looking for anyway. Martin made sure of that."

"Screw you."

I looked around for the perfect decoy to bait the killer with. "Consider me screwed. Which makes you and me a matching pair, because Martin wasn't about to leave the golden ticket anywhere you could find it."

"What do you know about it?"

"Nothing I'm telling you."

I found something dreams could be made of on the shelf with the least amount of dust: a lifetime achievement award shaped like the Empire State building. Its dimensions could accommodate a rolled-up document. As a booby prize, it didn't merit a glass case. I scooped it up.

"Hey! You can't take that."

Chuck was incensed enough to step toward me but smart enough to keep his hands off. I turned my back on him without fear.

"Get some sun, Chuck. Take those vitamins I bought you."

I wrapped the award in the towel I kept in the Stag's saddleboxes like it was precious cargo and headed toward the mountains. It hadn't rained since my last visit. The wreckage of the sedan and the vintage White Stag were gone, an oil stain marking the site of their demise. Stern never did find faux-Foxman's body. Culvan Mann couldn't have the cops discovering a corpse in a costume and ruining his frame job.

Of course, no one nearby reported it anyway.

Now that I was sure I would beat anyone racing home, I called Flint West. It went to voice mail.

"I found something in Seth Martin's house. I can't say what but it's a big deal. Too big to bring to the studio. I'm headed to your place. Could you kill the alarm? I don't want to be loitering around with this thing."

Jaq King took all of thirty seconds to get back to me. "Security is disabled. If you get there first, go on in. We're on the way."

The way clear, I called my friendly neighborhood law-enforcement agent.

"What is it this time, Allen?"

"Get to Flint West's place. I'm going to leave this line open."

I cruised through the tunnel. The drawbridge-style ramp into Flint West's getaway mansion was still descending from its upright position. Once inside, I positioned the Stag so its cameras could cover the maximum area and retrieved my towel-wrapped decoy. I set two pencil cameras on the ground floor to overlap coverage and went upstairs. Keeping the mountain view in mind, I found Flint's studio on the first try. The outer walls were floor-to-ceiling glass, with skylights above. The copious natural light gave me an excuse to leave my spy-glasses on. I didn't want to be, but I was right about what was in the room. And what wasn't.

Every last piece of Flint West's art was gone. All the evidence of his secret identity erased. Empty nails dotted the walls. Easels, stands, and racks stood bare. Paint speckled the wood floor like blood at a crime scene. Brushes, and other supplies were boxed up in the converted closet nook.

A drawing table and battered chair, the only furniture left, stood in a windowed corner. Dave King was next to them, looking over the mountains.

"Now these. These are big enough," he said. "These will be here forever."

I came to join him at the window, hating myself for finding the right angle to catch his reflection in the glass. "So will your creations."

Dave King didn't react. He'd long since purged any tells. Bristol board was matted on the drawing table. Despite his hands, he was still trying. The hero on the page looked like something he would have drawn as a child. It was all I could do then to keep it together. Dave King gave no indication he noticed me cracking. The man was a mountain in his own right. I took in the view, regulating my heart rate through measured breathing. I was always okay during the event, but time before was unbearable. The anticipation being worse than the thing itself was true for me.

The cameras on the Stag activated from the motion of the garage door opening. They came in separate cars: Flint and Jaq in one and Havier Cardiel in the other. Flint was wearing sweats and a hoodie, which was probably what he wore into costuming that morning. Jaq wore leggings and a tee with extra short sleeves. Havier had his jacket laid out on the backseat. His pale gold suit was crisp to the point of being origami. No one snuck in behind them or climbed out of the trunk. None of them appeared to be armed.

Why would they be? They thought I came bearing good news. That Ken Allen had saved the day.

Flint's voice echoed through the open floor plan. "Ken?"

"Up here. In the studio." My response felt small in comparison. I cleared my throat and got into character.

Flint busted into the room with Havier and Jaq close behind. All three of them were athletes, but Jaq was the one to watch.

I swept the hand that didn't hold the award through the empty space. "Figured you wouldn't mind. It's not like I'm seeing anything I'm not supposed to, right?"

Flint switched from urgency to confusion. And people said he had limited range.

"What did you find?" Jaq asked.

"You know what." Keeping it vague let Jaq fill in the blanks. I pulled the towel off to reveal Seth Martin's lifetime achievement award. I tried not to let on how much it weighed. It was cast solid, a lump of lead under a gold veneer. "Martin stashed it in here."

Jaq had good eyes. She read the inscription without getting any closer. "That son a bitch hid his will in there of all places?"

"Martin was bitter to the end," I replied.

Still taking in the view, Dave King laughed without mirth.

Jaq decided to go with honey over vinegar. She stepped forward and put her hand out. "Thank you, Ken. This means so much to my dad."

"Not so fast." I tucked the award under my arm. "We have to talk about Culvan Mann."

Havier spoke for the first time. He was the troubleshooter; here was trouble. "What about him?"

"Culvan Mann is my price for forking this over. You give me Culvan, you get this."

Flint squinted like he wasn't sure what he was hearing. Jaq dug the balls of her feet into the floor.

Havier stayed the course. "What are you talking about?"

"Don't insult my intelligence. You hired him. You have to have a way of contacting him, even if it's only to tender payment."

Havier tried looking concerned while also shaking his head. Choosing one or the other would have been more convincing, but acting wasn't part of his skill set. He was a behind-the-camera guy. "Where did you get that idea?"

"Give it up, Havier. For the first time since I met you, you aren't shoving a wall."

No one broke. This wasn't going to be easy. There was a reason why police isolated their suspects.

"You're going to make me monologue? Fine. But since you know what I'm about to say, I'll keep it brief." In truth, I was guessing big time. The more I said, the greater the chance they'd realize it. "It took me a while to figure out, I think because I didn't want to be right.

When you don't want to be right, you'll dig deep for any other explanation."

Flint put his hand over his mouth, listening. Havier crept closer under the guise of being interested in what I had to say. Happy with her distance, Jaq stayed put.

"The big question was, who is profiting from the sabotage? It doesn't matter if this new crop of movies comes out or not. The companies can delay production as long as they want. They control the rights, until someone else proves different." I held up the statue as if said proof was inside. "The answer is you, Havier. And you, Flint."

No one offered a reply, so I was forced to continue.

"The only way for Havier to move up the ladder was for someone above him to get the chute. Havier needed a cataclysmic situation for him to swoop in and solve. The best way to have a solution ready is to create the problem."

Havier had his response prepared. "Nice theory. But it's flawed. It doesn't explain the incidents at Duquesne."

"But it does muddle the field by making the sabotage look nonpartisan. It also clears the release slate. Instead of head-to-head against a Good Knights movie, your Flying Freeman solo project stands alone. And who knows, maybe you get a chance to play the two studios off each other. Write your own ticket."

Havier made the same mistake as before, shaking his head while also throwing his hands up. "Come on."

"I had the same reaction at first. I didn't have you or Flint down as people ambitious enough to resort to murder. But Jaq's a different story."

That was enough to get Dave King to turn around. His face could have been carved from stone. I couldn't decide if the revelation helped or hurt Jaq in her father's eyes. It could have been either, now that I knew what Dave King was capable of.

Jaq brought her hands up, palms out.

She looked from me, to Flint, to her father. "Ambition? You think this is about ambition?"

Havier pushed a palm toward Jaq. "Shut up."

"No Jaq, talk," I said. "I want to hear how you convinced Flint to sell off his art for the money to hire Culvan Mann."

Flint's face screwed up like he'd kicked a boulder barefoot. He was a big man, with big emotions. A strength, but also a weakness. He never learned to reel them in. Why regulate what brought you success?

Flint looked to Dave King, then back at Jaq. His hero and the love of his life. "I didn't do this for me, Ken. You know me. I'm not that guy."

He backed up a step, to block the door. Jaq and Havier moved to flank me.

"Havier is like you and me," Flint went on. "A true believer. After this, he'll be in a position to make real changes. He's going to give creators their fair share, starting with Dave and my Flying Freeman movie. It was part of my new contract."

Havier reached into his jacket. I dropped the statue and drew in one motion. We were close enough where aiming was secondary to speed. My shock dart hit him center of mass before he could get his weapon clear. He went down, muscles locked, experiencing next-level isometrics.

Jaq was on top of me before I could pivot. Her disarm technique allowed me the choice of keeping my pistol or my fingers. She followed it with an uppercut that left me admiring the light fixture and kept up the pressure on a flurry of punches. I tried to angle away, but she cut me off, steering us toward Flint. If he got ahold of me, Jaq was going to treat me like a heavy bag. Stern kicked the door into Flint and circled hard to train her service weapon on Jaq.

"Pump the brakes, lady."

Jaq twitched toward Stern, then glanced behind her. Stern had put her in a straight line with Flint. If Jaq slipped Stern's shot, it would go on into him. I kicked Havier's pistol into the far corner. It looked a lot like mine. A knock-off produced by the student instead of the master. "Pretty good workout, isn't it, Havier? Send me the bill to press that suit."

Gloves on, I patted Havier down, not stopping when I found the first cell phone, a company-issued Tachi product. He had a second one in his opposite breast pocket. It looked like something you'd find in a convenience store. I slid them across the floor toward Stern.

"Culvan left his laptops behind. Wonder if anything on them—messages, transfers—matches up with what's on one of these phones."

Flint put his palms up, as if I were the one who needed to dial it down. "It wasn't supposed to go this way, Ken. The agreement was only for minor mishaps. But the studios wouldn't give up. They just kept pushing production forward."

"So Culvan turned up the heat."

Flint nodded. "Havier tried to call him off, but Culvan refused. 'I will complete our contract. Renege, and I will forward proof of your involvement to the authorities.' Who the hell says *renege*?"

"You almost told me, didn't you? When you invited me out here, the day after Bill O'Wrongs died,"

Flint stood stock-still.

"But I talked you out of it. I convinced you it wasn't your fault." If I had stuck to my rules and kept my mouth shut, Flint might have confessed right then and there. But I broke my code and discussed the case. I put friendship first, and here we were.

"You seemed to know so much already," Flint replied.

"Yeah, I'm a real Columbo. The biggest clue was staring me in the face on day one. Every other victim was a hero. Bill O'Wrongs was the only villain targeted, and you were right there, hooked up to the same wires as he was. Why not go for you?"

Flint looked away. "I was hoping you could stop Culvan, and you did. He's gone now, it's over."

Containing my anger wasn't easy. "You left me to fumble around in the dark, clueless, with Culvan's goons all over me. They tried to kill me, right outside your front door."

Jaq looked at the award on the floor. "I don't care what happens to me, but please give that to my father. I beg you."

"There's nothing in there. I'm sorry, Jaq. It's as worthless as any other award."

Jaq locked eyes with me. "You're a cruel person."

I was in no position to disagree with her.

"We didn't mean for anyone to die," Flint repeated.

"People are dead." Stern's eyes and aim were steady. "Someone has to answer for that. How have you been contacting Culvan Mann?"

Flint gestured to Havier, who was still tap-dancing lying down. "It's all through him. I don't know anything about the dark web."

I tugged the fléchette out of Havier. "Let's hear it."

Havier needed a minute for his jaw to unlock. "It doesn't matter. Even if you were able to prove it, Culvan's long gone."

I stood up, nodding. If I couldn't save the day, at least I could foil the villains. "Your big plan amounts to nothing anyway. Because of Sol Silver."

That got Dave King's attention. He turned toward me, which is all the reaction he betrayed.

Havier thought about sitting up but abandoned the plan halfway through. "Sol Silver has been dead for seventy years."

"You sure about that?" I asked. "They never recovered his body."

"In seventy years, someone would have seen him," Havier countered.

"I agree with you, but let's start at the beginning. Sol Silver was a kid in the forties. He had this big idea, but no one thinks a kid is going to change the world. Except another visionary. The second Seth Martin saw Sol's sketch, he knew Silver had struck gold."

Flint West squinted, trying to make sense of my weird tangent. Jaq listened, fascinated, but not on a personal level.

"For a year, Seth Martin and Sol Silver created a better world. One packed with heroes. Then they went to war. Martin kept away from the action, but Silver wanted the opposite. He lied about his age and did everything he could to get to the front lines. It might seem crazy to us, but he was a Jewish kid who wanted to kill Nazis. A big kid, too. One who grew up with a bloody knife in his hand."

Dave King looked back out over the mountains, uninterested in my story. I continued.

"What Sol Silver did after the war wasn't legal, but it was right. In hunting down war criminals, Silver probably broke a hundred international laws, if that wasn't the irony of ironies. After ten years, he found his fill. Maybe he had seen enough darkness and started thinking what the world needed was more heroes. But Sol Silver was a marked man. He needed an alter ego. And thus, Dave King was born."

All heads turned toward Dave King.

Jaq's hands dropped. Flint studied him in a new light. I went to join Dave King at the window. Whatever he was thinking, I didn't want to know.

"He contacted his old friend Seth Martin. Together, they worked out a plan. Martin would sponsor the newly minted Dave King, citizen of Israel, for American citizenship, and set him up in the States. But everything they created had to be in Seth's name. Dave King couldn't afford people poking around in his past. King was going to have to trust his friend to do right by him."

Dave King spoke for the first time. "I told you. I told all of you, a hundred times, to stay out of it. That I didn't want your help. But not a one of you would listen."

Jaq ignored the gun on her and approached her father. She took his face in her hands, forced him to look at her. "Abba, why didn't you tell me?"

Dave King barely shook his head. "Sol wasn't anyone I wanted you to know. You deserved a better father."

"Martin respected your wishes, right to the end," I said. "But on his deathbed, he had a change of heart."

The blood drained out of Dave King's face. "The hell he did."

"Don't worry, Seth has it all worked out. None of this goes public until you're gone. Then everything goes to your heirs."

Jaq tore her eyes from her father. "Seth left the Civil Warriors to Dad?"

"Not just the Civil Warriors. He left the Good Knights too. In a way. See, when Martin sold them off, Sol Silver was believed dead. But if Sol is still out there, he has a claim on his creations."

Dave King shook his head. "Not going to happen. Anyone who knew Sol Silver is gone. Whatever claims Seth may have made, there's no way to prove what you're saying."

"Sure there is. The proof is all over the first drawing of Good-Man. Maybe in the forties a little blood was nothing. But today we have DNA testing."

Dave King's hand went over his eyes, his mouth trembling.

Jaq started to cry, shaking her head at the tragedy of it all. "I don't want it. I didn't do it for me."

Flint took her in his arms. "I know baby. We couldn't just stand by."

Dave King took them under his wing. "You were trying to do me justice. Now shush, the cops are listening."

Stern reached for her cuffs. "Thanks for the mess, Allen. Now I get to be the bad guy."

I should have felt better than I did. But Culvan Mann had gotten away. He was probably halfway home by now. *Home.*

Culvan had slipped up, talking to Elaine. Said something he actually meant. Told her, if you had a home, it could be taken away from you. Culvan wasn't running. He was going back to the only home he'd ever known. He was going to Ray's.

19

I LEFT STERN to wrangle the chaos and made for the garage, cursing whoever invented riser-less stairs. Navigating the mountain was easier when I was worried about someone else's skin. Ray didn't pick up when I called. If the Fords headed north straight from Culvan's secret lair, they would have gotten home hours ago. Just behind Culvan. Maybe I was wrong. Maybe Ray and Elaine were having a heart-to-heart. Or maybe they were crashed out, dead to the world.

Or maybe they were just plain dead.

When someone you cared about was hurt, a twenty-minute drive was excruciating. A six-hour drive becomes an episode of the *Twilight Zone* where you're locked in a room for a hundred years, then a guy in a suit opens the door and tells you that was the end of the first day.

I called every fifteen minutes and shouted Ray's name into the air every five, but no one answered. I vacillated on bringing Stern into it. But by the time her plate was free, she would be hours behind me, which meant whatever troopers were local to the Bay would be facing

Culvan and a hit squad inside Ray's booby-trapped fortress. Police procedure leaned toward siege tactics. By the time they resolved to brave the labyrinth, it would be all over.

Four hours in, the Stag switched to its backup tank. I forged ahead, praying I wouldn't end up on the side of the road with my thumb out. Five hours in, I couldn't stand it anymore and stopped to use the restroom. My stress level almost convinced me chocolate-covered almonds were mostly almond. I narrowly made it out intact.

I took sixty precious seconds to shake out the stiffness and got back on the road. For the hundredth time, I shifted polarity, this time back to positive. Ray had been hardening his defenses for years. His compound was both a digital and analog fortress, with him handling the practical aspects, while Elaine erected firewalls. No way Culvan was storming the ramparts. Unless he had an ulterior motive for agreeing to meet with Elaine.

I gunned the throttle, praying the demand for extra juice didn't leave me on the side of the road. The Stag didn't drink anything sold at a run-of-the-mill has station. My heart jumped every time the Stag burped. Less than a mile off the freeway, the bike ignored my requests to mush.

The White Stag coasted to a halt as Ray's compound came into view. Pushing it by hand wouldn't do any good—its arsenal was offline without the battery to fuel it. I tucked the bike in between two parked cars, a horrendous traffic violation sure to get me towed at the least.

Even from a distance I knew something was wrong. The fleet of drones which usually patrolled the air space over Ray's compound were absent. The twelve-foot-high fence surrounding the compound normally sparked with the threat of electrocution. Now it stood silent, the double-gate thrown wide open.

I moved to draw the Quarreler to discover it was already in my hand. I buttoned my jacket as high as it would go. My spyglasses were on, and I had one good leg. The area between the gate and the compound proper was a graveyard of junked vehicles spanning Ray's sixty-year career. Their remains had been ruthlessly plundered for parts, creating a thicket of jagged, rusty edges. That I couldn't remember my last tetanus shot meant it had been too long.

I didn't want to hug up to the wrecks and risk injury, but also didn't want to be out in the open, so I split the difference. There was no telling how many guys Culvan had brought with him. Inert drones littered the ground like turtles trapped on their backs.

I wove through the aisles, turning to try to keep out of sight of the expansive warehouse network Ray called home in case Culvan had set up surveillance. There was a small lot on the west side of the building where I usually parked. I figured if Culvan posted a human sentry, they would be stationed there, which was a glaring rookie mistake.

A blast caught me three-quarters from shoulder to hip. I rolled over the wreckage of a riding lawnmower, catching some more fléchettes on the way, to land stuffed between it and a rusting vintage tractor. I crouched behind a flat tire. My ambusher tried to skip a volley of fléchettes off the crumbling concrete, but the mower was sitting too low.

I ducked around the tractor behind me in an attempt to level the playing field. Another blast of fléchettes impacted close, splashing my arm. Now I knew what fighter pilots felt like when a bogey was on their tail.

A vehicle a magnitude larger in size squatted behind the tractor. A combine, I think it's called. Though what it was a combination of, I had no idea. A tractor and a battleship? I slipped underneath whatever it was called and propped the Quarreler up on the tire. Then I took a gamble and stayed right where I was, behind that same tire.

In fighting, feinting only works against the competent. There's no point in faking an attack against an opponent you can just punch. Then there was the double bluff—when a feint was designed to be detected as false, to draw out the expert's reaction, which you were ready for. I was betting my ambusher was an expert. A pro who thought he was dealing with an amateur. If he wasn't, my double bluff was going to end in a dead Ken Allen.

A set of boots that tickled my memory appeared around the corner. They paused between the tires, analyzing. I crept around from behind my tire to the side they had come from, thankful it was wide enough to hide behind.

I saw my ambusher for the first time. His back was to me, but there was no mistaking his getup. He fell onto his side, facing the tire without the Quarreler sitting on it, where he presumed I was hiding, and blasted into empty space. He was rolling in my direction when I got to him. I round kicked his weapon out of line, transitioning into a side kick to the neck.

It was a low move, but I didn't have many options, considering what he was wearing. Elaine was right in guessing Culvan had gear cached. The pickings must have been slim, however, because my ambusher was in a fully functional Pulp Hero costume.

Pulp Hero was one of the Good Knights. Costume-wise, he was a mummy wrapped in newsprint instead of bandages, the headlines shifting to match his mood. The movie version was far less visually interesting, with tactical armor emblazoned with pop art. The fandom was forever petitioning for a faithful interpretation, but the studios were afraid a general audience would find it too corny.

Which was good for the mercenary I was currently stomping on. His torso and legs were armored but his hip wasn't. My heel connected solidly on the ball joint. He grunted loudly and tried to bring his gun back into it. My foot was busy, so I did the first thing that came to mind and dropped a knee into his groin. The shock sat him up enough for me to get ahold of his neck.

He tried everything he could, bucking and twisting, to no avail. The fourth time I felt something jab into my side I realized he was trying to knife me but the stabs weren't making it through my blazer. Two seconds later, he went limp. It was a blood choke, so I couldn't wait to find out if he was bluffing. I released with my hands ready, in case the knife was on its way.

He was dead asleep. I retrieved the Quarreler, swapped cylinders, and put a tranq dart in him. His Pulp Hero costume disguised him from head to toe, which caused me to ponder a wardrobe change.

I decided it was a bad idea. There was a chance I would literally get caught with my pants down. Worse than that would be if the Fords mistook me for a henchman and sent a missile my way. Better to take my chances as Ken Allen.

I didn't feel any new injuries and was too afraid to check and discover different. After gathering myself, I took a more methodical approach toward the warehouse entrance. The exterior door was portal style, the kind normally found on submarines. Or on submarines in movies, at least. It was hanging wide open. I approached it from the blind spot, ready to perform emergency gymnastics at a moment's notice.

The foyer beyond served as an airlock area. The outside door normally closed before the inside unlocked. Both were thrown open. The hallway beyond was also familiar, salvaged from the set of a spaceship exploring new frontiers.

All the sliding doors in the hallway were retracted. I had no idea where I was going. During my past visits, Ray had employed track lighting to guide the way, opening only the doors he wanted me through. Unless Ray had dramatically altered the layout in the past five years, Culvan knew this place intimately. I didn't know where the Fords might hole up or how to get there.

There was enough light for my spyglasses to work with, though I doubted they were any advantage. Culvan's mercs weren't sporting masks on a lark. I used a pencil camera to scout the rooms branching off the hallway. One was a half bath and the other a mudroom loaded with cabinets, shelves, and hooks. If I lived in a sprawling complex, I'd want to keep my wallet and keys next to the door too.

The next pair of rooms were for temporary storage, one of them for outgoing packages and the other for incoming. I had been through the following door on the left. It led to a cozy den where Ray met with visitors. The right door went nowhere. Someone had pried open the façade to confirm plywood wall sheathing behind the false portal.

The den stood empty. I took three steps down the hallway, remembered the last time I was in that room, and turned back around. The space had not changed, with dark-stained wood-paneling and a natural stone floor. Trophy heads were displayed on the walls—the remains of creatures-who-never-were, designed by Ray for one film or another, with the fictional weapon that dealt the fatal blow mounted beneath them. Two leather recliners which looked vintage but were anything but sat in front of a hearth you could have parked a golf cart in. I went for the hearth.

During my inaugural case, Ray had made a grand entrance, striding through the blazing fire into the den. Which meant there was a passage secreted in the hearth. I rooted for a hidden switch but came up empty. The mechanism might have been electronic, like his RV door, keyed to open when Ray got close enough. But the room felt older than such technologies. Of course, that was how it was supposed to feel.

I stepped back out of the hearth, ready to give up, when I remembered the masonry concealed a coffee station. I opened it and pushed every button inside. None of them worked. There was a second compartment, mirroring the first, on the opposite side of the hearth.

Two levers were secreted inside. Analog construction. They should still work, power or not. Which meant whatever pulling the wrong lever did was also still operational.

Left or right? Which one would Ray have chosen? They were close together. You could bang your knuckles on the right lever while pulling the left. Inconvenient for Ray, but it also made the right lever the easy choice. And most people were right-handed. Or was Ray going for a bluff, fooling an intruder into pulling the left lever? Feints only worked on experts, and only an expert would have found the levers to start with.

I tilted my head, trying to think like Ray. At heart, he loved smoke and mirrors. Ray was always up to something behind the scenes. Like everything else, Culvan Mann had emulated the behavior of his mentor, presenting an illusion while concealing the truth.

I pulled both levers together.

If I wasn't listening for a sound, I wouldn't have heard it—the whisper of a click.

The door was positioned on the corner in two panels, barely wide enough for a slender person to slip through. No way Culvan Mann had gone this way. I squeezed through the opening and latched the door behind me. The passage was a glorified gap between two walls, the wood framing protruding on both sides. Unable to negotiate the space forward-facing, I worked out a shimmy, tilting my shoulders one way, then the other. It felt faster than turning sideways but probably wasn't. At least the cameras were off, because my little dance was definitely blooper-reel material.

The passage ended in a T-junction, forcing a choice. I headed toward the center of the structure. Thirty shoulder wags later, the passage dead-ended. The door switch was easier to find from the inside. Not knowing where I was going to come out, I eased it open and worked a pencil camera through the gap.

The room was dark. Too dark for optics. I stepped into the room and switched on my camera flashlight. Once my spyglasses had something to work with, they adjusted to provide a view.

The space was the refined version of Culvan's battle station: a combination security epicenter and editing booth, with multiple monitors stationed on adjustable arms. There wasn't much to be done here without power. I had the exit door handle halfway down when I remembered to shut my camera light off.

A peek with a pencil camera revealed a bad guy dressed as Good-Man stationed at the end of the hallway. Since Good-Man didn't wear a mask, the merc had gone with off-the-shelf night-vision goggles. We were around twenty feet apart. And Bad Good-Man wasn't slacking. He was in a semi-crouch, weapon leveled in my direction.

I took a moment to visualize my plan of attack. Swapping the Quarreler to my left hand, I dispensed a flash-bang grenade into my right.

I swept the door inward with my foot and whipped the grenade sidearm. As soon as my hand was exposed, a blast of fléchettes filled the hallway. My forearm was okay, but my right hand felt like I punched a beehive.

The flash-bang went off behind him, maybe close enough to cause him issues, maybe not. The angle was all wrong for shooting left-handed, and my right wasn't able. I tossed a pencil camera into the hallway to gather intelligence.

Bad Good-Man shed his goggles and switched on the tactical light mounted under his fléchette shotgun. He was eight feet from my door, tucked against the far wall for maximum angle. He blinked hard, trying to clear his vision.

All Bad Good-Man had to do was camp out at a lethal distance. Either I would show myself or he would run out the clock while Mann did what he came to do. Retreating back through the passage would only leave me farther down the same path. The only way forward involved taking a hit.

I pulled my gas mask into place and chucked a puke grenade into the hallway. Bad Good-Man withdrew, retching. He tried to keep his gun online, but that's hard to do while you're emptying your guts. I barreled in to spend as little time as possible in the smoke. He tried to line up a shot, bent over and gun sideways. It wasn't ideal but I was at point-blank range. I vaulted toward the far wall in an attempt to get clear. The shot went wide. I kicked off the wall, twisting toward him. On the way down, my knee caught him square on temple.

Bad Good-Man crumpled, his wires clipped. I was hot enough to give him one for good measure, but my better angels intervened. Swapping to tranq darts was tougher left-handed. After putting one in Bad Good-Man to keep him in dreamland, I decided to leave them loaded. I had no idea how Culvan was dressed, but I doubted a concussive fléchette would faze him even if I caught him fresh from the shower.

I couldn't help but look at my right hand. The glove had done as much as could be expected. There was one fléchette in my palm and another in the heel of my hand. I guessed I wasn't supposed to pull these things out. Professionals would do it at whatever hospital I should have been on my way to. But I had miles to go before I slept, and the spikes were in the way.

The first instinct was to yank, but I calmed down. Was I supposed to stretch my hand out or close it as I did this? Closing it sure felt better, but weirder. I worked the spike in the heel of my hand around a little. Fireworks of pain exploded while phrases like *nerve damage* danced in my head.

Flattening the spike flush against the flesh worked best and I eased it free. The fléchette in my palm was deep. I wanted to give up, but if a bad guy grabbed it when we were scrapping, I was going to scream loud enough to audition for a Led Zeppelin cover band.

I worked the fléchette back and forth like a metronome until it wiggled loose. I wasn't proud of the noises I made during the journey but reminded myself society permitted tears shed for manly reasons. I scooped up the Quarreler left-handed.

A trio bad guys were down. So far Culvan had rented them in fours. Maybe mercenary outfits had some kind of buy three, get one free deal going.

Making a fist felt amazing but releasing it was agony. Not having a first-aid kit as part of my everyday carry was a glaring oversight. Ray's kitchen was on the other side of the door. I thought about cleaning my hand in the sink but really didn't want to take my glove off. What if I couldn't get it back on? I compromised by wrapping a flour-sack towel around my palm, tightening the knot with my teeth.

I halfway knew where I was going from the kitchen. I passed the guest room where Ray put me up, and the grotto-style bathroom, ignoring their siren promises of relief. The entrance to the armory, where Ray had presented me with my crime-fighting gear, was open. A safe room was built into the wall. If the vault door hadn't been popped, I never would have noticed it. An empty spot on the wall had recently accommodated something bazooka sized.

Past that point was the great unknown.

I listened for sounds of an argument or struggle. The rooms close to the center of Ray's labyrinth were more opulent, and themed. Each door served as a portal into another reality, some long ago, others far away.

The hall ended with an expansive chamber in a celebration of Ray.

Like Seth Martin, Ray had been at the top of his game for decades, continually raising the bar every other effects expert strove to reach. The bigger the star, the greater their gravity. Ray had attracted every industry award ten times over. But unlike Seth Martin, Ray hadn't placed them under glass.

Each award was displayed with the creation which had earned it. Monsters bore golden cups. Medals hung from alien necks, or the closest thing they had to necks. Art deco statues posed against dioramas. A constellation of globes hung from the ceiling, suspended over a cityscape of glass accolades of every imaginable geometric shape.

Foxman was waiting for me, standing next to a one-sixth miniature of the car that had sealed his fate.

"Pretty cool, huh?"

A different man was inside the fully functional Foxman costume. His jawline was paler than his sun-scarred mouth and nose. Masks didn't work when you knew the person beneath them. It was the security chief. Turned out, he hadn't shaved the beard to look more professional. When you cast a hero, it was all about the jawline.

"Culvan has been killing off his henchmen. You're no exception."

Foxman shrugged. "He's welcome to try."

I flicked the Quarreler open, swapped from tranq darts back to concussives. There was no way he didn't notice my awkward left-handed draw. "It'll be easier for Culvan when I'm done with you."

"I don't think so." Foxman stood pat while I got my ducks in a row. "See, I've figured out your weakness: you can't pull the trigger. That's a real handicap in a fight to the death."

I stayed outside of fifty feet. Foxman's gauntlets were a knock-off of the Quarreler, making his range the same as mine. Time to put *Criminal Justice for Dummies* to use. "Out in the world, I don't have an excuse. But you're breaking into a private residence with a deadly weapon. I'm in reasonable defense territory."

Foxman shook his head as much as the costume allowed. "Nah. I served with guys like you. The shit goes down, and they either freeze or shoot anywhere the enemy isn't." He threw his cape over his shoulder, keeping his gauntleted hand down at his side. "Let's do this."

Neither of us moved. He knew the range too. I needed to get close to him. He was more dangerous at a distance. Where my Quarreler was designed for versatility, his gauntlets were engineered for maximum lethality. Foxman's gas capsules were also deadly, but using smoke on me at close range was as good as using it on himself.

I rushed forward, angling right, so he would have to aim away from his centerline. Cowls were terrible for peripheral vision. There was a reason Foxman had to turn at the shoulders when he went to talk to anybody. I fired off a fléchette as Foxman launched a shuriken. Mine went into the Foxcar and his sunk into a werewolf holding an

Academy Award. I reversed direction, slipping like I was trying to avoid a punch.

It was a good guess. Leading his aim, Foxman's next shot went wide. He was already moving. My return fléchette wasn't even close. I ducked behind a hunter from another galaxy and peeked out between his leg and his spear.

Foxman's cape was poking out from behind a one thirty-second scale space battle. There was no angle for a shot. I broke cover toward a robot frozen in transition between truck and man.

Foxman sent some gas my way. I pulled the mask from my collar and snapped it into place. The capsule impacted behind me, the gas expanding to flush me toward him. Foxman had made an error assessing the risk. No power meant no ventilation. I needed to get closer, because if he kept it up with the gas attacks, he was going to kill us both.

I made for an enormous tree with nine animals hanging from it, including the strangest fruit. Foxman popped up and sent off a shuriken. I dropped into a slide and fired back. It was a crappy shot, but it forced him to adjust. His next shuriken skipped off the tile in front of me. As I was circling the tree, Foxman slammed into the trunk on the far side.

"Man, this is cool," Foxman said.

"Yeah, what a gas."

He was right-handed, and I was left, which meant the safest angle for each of us to shoot would put us face-to-face. I decided to go the counter-intuitive direction, maybe catch him off guard, and we ran straight into each other.

I dropped the Quarreler to tug his arm out of the way and make room for a straight right. He slipped toward me to avoid the punch. I helped him on his way, pulling his head into my knee. He interposed a forearm and threw a body shot my jacket soaked. Before I could riposte, he drove a knee into my wounded right leg.

A sound halfway between a scream and a whimper escaped my lips. Neither of which are great noises to make during a fight. Either

Culvan had footage of my injuries or Foxman caught something in how I was moving. But how he knew was immaterial. What mattered was that my weakness was exposed.

The instinct to retreat was strong, but distance was not my friend. My weapon was on the ground and Foxman's was undroppable. He flicked out a jab and I knew what was coming next. I forced my knee up to check the blast-off kick aimed at my bum leg. I got there too late to make him regret throwing it but in time to keep me bipedal. He stepped through the kick and shoved his gauntlet point-blank into my face.

If I needed to consider a response, I would have been a dead man. Fortunately, my instincts were thirty-five years in the making. I slipped and drove a right hand into his liver. His body was armored, and my right hand was injured. My punch hurt me more than it did him. I grunted, half in frustration, half in pain.

He tried an elbow. Elbows are devastating at the proper range. They are also easy to avoid. I slipped behind it and rocked his chin upward with an uppercut. We were too close for a kick, so instead he used a Wing Chun-style stomp on my wounded leg.

Pain exploded, radiating out. Desperation came with it. Since I was going down anyway, I dragged Foxman with me. We fell in a pile, and I started scrambling like my life depended on it, ending up on top.

Foxman knew what he was doing. He locked down on my bad leg while working to get his gauntlet arm free in order to pump me full of shuriken. I stayed tight to avoid becoming a pincushion and thought about my life choices while slamming a knee into his crotch to hinge my posture. Though his protective cup kept his sensitive places safe, it also provided a fulcrum. I drew his arm close, locking up behind the fluted lip of his gauntlet.

Foxman struggled to rip his arm from my grasp. While he was occupied, I used my free hand to hammer him in the temple. It got results so I did it again. He started pounding a fist of his own into my injured leg, which only made me madder. We abandoned smart tactics for stupid brutality.

I rained down hammer fists and he kept on punching. I aimed for that perfect jawline, trying to slam his brain against his skull. Foxman started to lose the race. He gave up hitting back to try to guard his chin. I adjusted my hook on his arm and sunk into the crouching arm bar.

Arm bars were generally applied incrementally, increasing pressure until your opponent surrendered. But generally you weren't in a death match. I torqued my hips. He made the wrong decision and tried to yank his arm out. Arm bars were like dog bites. The deeper you shoved, the safer you were. Foxman's gauntlet became the fulcrum. Instead of a dislocated elbow, he got a broken forearm.

It was Foxman's turn to yell. I kept my knee braced against his short ribs and hammered until he went quiet. The Quarreler was resting against the hanging tree. I switched to tranq darts and sent him off to dreamland. Four were left in the quiver. I used a branch for support and tried out my leg.

It hurt to the point where the bone felt cracked. It wasn't. That was all in my head. It was only muscle pain. Muscle pain didn't affect performance. All it did was hurt. I jogged toward the far door to prove it, looking like a marathoner who was going to finish if it killed them.

The double doors were sealed. They had been plundered from a comic-book adaptation that never was—the gates of horn and ivory bordering the dream world. I worked my fingers into the seam and applied the barest pressure to make space for a pencil camera. Turned out, the doors were spring-loaded.

The gates burst open, and I became the fourth person alive to see inside the magician's workshop.

20

THE BALANCE OF Ray's compound was a fantasy land, each room a façade themed to enhance your entertainment experience. But the center of the labyrinth was a factory—all practical, no aesthetics. Workstations for every project in production stood apart, cordoned off by floor tape. Adjustable light fixtures loomed overhead like some mad scientist's operating room. A blue blazer was hanging piecemeal from a fitting dummy. On the table next to it, prototype trousers were in the planning stage.

So close, but yet so far.

Ray, Elaine, and Culvan were waiting in the center of the room. Ray was slumped on a low-backed stool that belonged on a galaxy cruiser. Elaine was in her usual chair, looking at none of us, as if she were thinking about something else entirely.

Culvan was dressed in racing coveralls like Ray's, but red instead of blue. From what I could tell, he wasn't armed. The components of a firearm normally reserved for helicopters was strewn at his feet.

Culvan's family-sized lungs pushed out a surround-sound voice. "Finally, we meet face-to-face."

I closed the distance, trying my best to appear confident. "You knew where to find me at. You also knew what would happen if you came calling."

Culvan held up a lighter-sized remote. Two of his murder-bots, one left and one right, came out from their hiding places in the shadows behind Ray's works in progress.

"Disarm yourself, Ken. Remove your jacket and harness, along with those glasses."

I complied lackadaisically, buying time to figure out how the hell I was going to get out of this one. I piled everything up, ending with the Quarreler on top.

"Now move forward six paces."

I wasn't sure what a pace was, so I came toward him until Culvan raised a palm to indicate I should halt.

"Okay, what happens now?"

Culvan turned to Ray. "You hoped this man would come to your rescue, but there is no escape from the consequences of your actions."

Mann tucked the remote into his breast pocket and faced me, his fists balled.

I rolled my neck around and loosened my shoulders. "All right. Let's do this."

Culvan shook his head. "You misunderstand. We aren't fighting. If you strike back, I will activate my sentries. You, Ray, and Elaine will be instantly killed."

Culvan faltered on the last clause. There was something in his voice I'd never heard before. A lack of conviction. It gave me an inkling what this was all about. What Culvan Mann really wanted from the start. Now if I could just live long enough to exploit it.

Culvan stepped toward me, away from Ray and Elaine. I had caught a glimpse of him from a distance. Close up, it was worse.

Physically, he shouldn't have existed. Seven and a half feet tall with ten percent body fat, Mann was a walking special effect. His arms were longer than my legs, which meant anytime I was close enough to kick him, I was also in hugging range.

Culvan had his hands down, and why not? It wasn't like he had to defend himself. He started with a slap. Casual as it was, it carried enough force to brain me. Instinct took over and I slid away, pushing off my good leg to create distance.

Culvan took a step forward to reset the range. "Now Ken, have you already forgotten the conditions of this encounter?"

Over Culvan's shoulder, Elaine gestured for me to run. No way that was going to happen.

"What, don't you want to work for it, even a little? You can't be that afraid of getting hit."

"What you're talking about, Ken, is finding out which of us is the better man. There is no point to performing an experiment where I already have the answer."

Elaine was shooing me away with both hands now. A lightbulb went off over my head. I withdrew into the largest unoccupied space. Culvan followed, twenty feet from Elaine now. He retrieved the remote from his breast pocket.

"One more step, Ken, and I activate my sentries."

Before I could reply, Elaine interrupted our man talk.

"Cul, you aren't going anywhere."

Elaine had her armrest open. She keyed in a code and the workshop powered up. All the lights flared on as the ventilation rumbled alive. At the same time, Culvan's sentries fell limp, their cords cut.

"Always so sure you're the smartest person in the room," Elaine said. "I knew what you were up to when you agreed to meet me. I rode the little Trojan horse you planted in my chair right back into its stable."

Culvan turned, taking in the room section by section, reformulating. Elaine managed to look down on Culvan from her seat.

"Oh, you're trapped now, Cul. Trapped where you've been dreaming of being for the last five years. Welcome home."

Elaine's plan took nerves of steel to execute. She had to be patient. Play the helpless victim. She had to hope I could handle the mercs. Wait for Culvan to be out of reach of stopping her. The only flaw in her plan was my part. Unless Elaine had weapons systems built into her chair, how it played out was down to me and Culvan.

Culvan took a step toward Elaine. She typed out a sequence and her chair's suspension settled. "Don't bother. It's bricked. No going back now, Cul."

Culvan paused to analyze his situation. He was closer to Ray or Elaine. He could get to them before me. Threaten them to make me comply. If I was right about him, he wouldn't.

Culvan nodded at Elaine, then turned his attention back on me. I had been training martial arts for thirty-five years. In comparison, Culvan lifted weights. Normal people were like children to him. If he got ahold of me, he could tear me limb from limb without having ever taken so much as a karate class. It was patently unfair.

Culvan raised his hands into a boxing position. His giant lats kept him from tucking his elbows. He looked like he was trying to eat a pizza without cutting it first. Point one for Ken Allen: there was a ton of real estate to choose from. Mosquitos had an easier time getting inside your guard than middleweights.

There are two basic stances in fighting. The first stance was for power, with your dominant hand to over your back foot. Boxers called this orthodox. Culvan was in that stance. The other was dominant hand forward, like a fencer. I took that approach. I had to fence Culvan. Trying to match him power for power would end up with someone reading my eulogy.

Culvan jabbed out. He was quick, despite all that muscle. I slipped it and put a lead hand into his liver, then I got the hell out of there as fast I could, using my uninjured leg for propulsion. He turned with a sweeping backfist, a giant trying to swat a fly. The blow passed over my head as I sent a lead hand into his solar plexus. His chest muscles contracted in reflex, clamping down on my hand. I tore free of his cleavage as a left hook crashed into my guard. I flowed with rather than fought against the impact, surfing on the force to end up on my butt ten feet away.

Culvan pursued me with a measured stride. That he didn't pounce while I was down supported my theory as to his possible weakness. I wiggled my eyebrows at him as I worked to my feet. He threw a jab followed by a rear hook to my ribs I had to do a matador impression to avoid. I set a hook of my own into his kidney and broke off before I got greedy. One punch too many was a curtain call for Ken Allen.

Culvan stopped to calculate, his chest beginning to heave. I took the opportunity to make conversation.

"I know what you want, Culvan. You need to accept that you are never going to get it."

Culvan decided to try volume punching. He stepped in and threw a classic four-piece combination: jab, cross, left hook, right hook. I avoided them, slipping and circling out.

"This whole time, you've been an empty shirt. You aren't going to hurt Ray or Elaine. You can't bring yourself to do that."

Culvan surged forward. He tried to corral me with body hooks. I faded away, timing each one as it came. It wasn't that he was a complete novice. He knew how to throw punches. But he threw them like he'd learned how watching a video tutorial.

I whipped a backhand at Culvan's left eye, keeping my fingers loose to brush his cornea. Tears immediately started to roll down his face, his eyelid pinching shut in reflex.

"What you really wanted was for Ray to admit he was wrong."

Culvan growled, winging punch after punch. It was the offense of a person who owned a heavy bag but never actually fought. But no number of rounds on the heavy bag could ever equal in-ring experience. Without a live opponent, Culvan never learned to vary the cadence of his attacks. He was fast, but him having only one gear made him easy to time.

I stayed out of reach as Culvan beat the air around me. When his flurry came to a halt, I poked him in the other eye. I used my middle finger, slightly curved and braced against the pointer finger as if intended to break a promise. Fast and loose. It went deep. I felt the side of Culvan's eye socket.

Culvan's hand flew to his eye in reflex.

"That's all you wanted. For Ray to say he was sorry. To admit he wronged you. But he just can't do it." I looked to Ray. "Can you?"

Ray shook his head at the ground.

"Do you know why, Culvan? I do."

That got Culvan's attention. He forced one of his eyes open to look at me.

"It's because he's not sorry. And he's never going to be."

That did it.

Culvan loosed a roar and charged me, arms wide. He was willing to take some hits if it meant getting his hands on me. I did the smart thing and ran. He kept after me, all thought of preserving energy abandoned. Hope blossomed that I had a chance of surviving this. I had noted an oversight in Culvan's gym setup. He had everything a powerlifter needed: a squat rack, a bench, wraps and belts.

But he didn't own a single cardio machine.

No bike, or elliptical, or rower. No treadmill. They probably didn't manufacture equipment in Culvan's size. It was a pretty niche market, though Culvan could have built one for himself if he wanted to. He spent his waking hours indoors, at a worktable or keyboard. As much as going on a walk was a risk he'd be spotted.

Then there was his bathtub. And all that salt.

Culvan came to a halt, panting. His hands fell to his waist. I lunged in and crushed his nose. He didn't react, so I did it again. It started to bleed. By the time it occurred to Culvan he should probably punch back I was long gone.

Culvan had built a suit of armor around himself. As much muscle as his body could support. But it came at a cost. That big tub Culvan owned wasn't for lounging. He didn't have bath bombs and body oils lined up. It was to take the weight off. That's why he had bags and bags of Epsom salts stockpiled. The high salt ratio helped him float in such a small relative space. His chair told the story. The position of the pads. The foot rests. Our bodies are a burden we are forced to bear our entire lives. You didn't see big men like Culvan in retirement homes. The brightest of candles burned twice as hot.

"You want closure, but there's none to be found here, Mann. Sometimes the people we love just plain fail us. We discover they aren't who we made them out to be."

"Shut up!"

Culvan sent another salvo at me, every blow a bomb capable of ending my world. But launching rockets required a lot of oxygen. He was starting to turn purple.

He had slowed down to the point where I was able to circle behind him. I jumped, coming down on the back of his leg with a stomp, as if I were trying to break a tree branch. Culvan dropped, his knee slamming into the concrete. He put his hands down to catch himself, so I round kicked him in the face.

He did his best to ignore me and worked at standing up. I side kicked his jaw. He rocked back to the ground and restarted the standing process. This was the moment where the music swelled. Where the hero hit the villain with everything in the book, showing off his best moves. But I wasn't feeling like a hero. What I was feeling was done with this whole ugly mess.

I stumbled over to my piled gear and retrieved the Quarreler. Careful to keep out of arm's reach, I put a dart in Culvan's neck. He didn't seem to notice. I sighed and put a second one next to it.

"Go ahead, tell him, Ray. Culvan's waiting. Tell him you regret ruining his life. Tell him you're sorry."

Ray stared at Culvan. Culvan, tears rolling down his face, fought to keep his eyes open, trying to read Ray's expression. But Ray's face was vacant. He didn't say anything. His chin moved an inch in either direction, the barest a head shake could be. He'd made up his mind, five years ago, and nothing was going to change it.

Culvan stayed on his knees and elbows, head bowed, and started to crumble.

I dug out my phone.

"What are you doing?" Ray asked.

"Calling the cops. Do you have a pallet jack or something? No way I'm dragging him out of here."

Ray shook his head. "This isn't over yet."

Special Investigator Stern was in my phone under "Cutie Pie," in preparation for the inevitable day when she seized my devices.

"Elaine, can you block his phone?" Ray asked.

"No, Dad."

I couldn't tell if Elaine was saying her systems were down, or that she didn't approve. Former or latter, both made sense.

Ray pointed to my hand, at the Quarreler he had built.

"You're a dart short of getting the job done, Ken."

Stern picked up first ring. "Good news or bad news?"

"Good news. I'm at Ray Ford's compound." I gave Stern the address. "Mann and four of his guys are here. Bring your livestock-grade paddy wagon. Mann is huge."

"I'm hours away. Sending troopers over now."

"No rush. The bad guys will keep." I hung up and addressed Ray. "Culvan will love prison. They have shop class and weight rooms."

Ray used the table to get to his feet. "You can't be this stupid. Either he'll break out, or they'll cut him a deal. He's too useful. In a few years he'll be back after us again. You have to finish this."

I stared at Ray. Everything in his demeanor signaled complete conviction. Next to him, Elaine shook her head as if she had predicted this. Culvan, laid out flat now, was still fighting to find his feet.

"I'm going to go wait for the cops. They'll need a guide."

I turned my back on Ray and headed toward the exit. Around that time, the adrenaline faded and my body reminded me of its various woes. It was all I could do to not lie down next to Culvan.

Ray yelled at my back. "You walk out now and we're done, Ken. When you needed help, I gave with both hands, and this is how you repay me? We're done. You hear me? Done."

I stopped at the pile of my gear. Ray's gadgets had turned me from mild-mannered Ken Allen into superspy Jove Brand. But Jove Brand was something I could never be:

A killer.

I set the Quarreler down on top of the bulletproof blazer.

"Good-bye, Ray."

Getting out was easy. Once you knew where you were headed, the path leading to the light was as simple as trusting your gut. In time, Elaine came out to meet me.

"Did he do it?" I asked.

"No."

"Good."

"Yes," Elaine agreed. "Good for him."

I sat in the shade of a salvaged Huey. "So why not let me in on the plan?"

Elaine smiled. "I've seen the movie you were in. The less you need to pretend, the better."

I nodded. "You know, you got the best parts of Ray."

"But they're still his parts," she replied. "Dad will come around. Eventually."

"No, I don't think he will." Lying on my back felt way better than sitting up. "Are you ready to talk about it?"

Elaine thought for a moment. "I guess you've earned it."

"This isn't a thing to be earned, Elaine. But you know who I am by now. Anything you tell me stays here. And I think you need to tell someone."

Elaine turned her chair away from me, to make it easier. I closed my eyes, partly to help and partly because keeping them open was a lot of effort.

"We were building a jetpack," Elaine said. "Culvan and me. A real jetpack. Not the lame ones that run for two minutes or can only be used over water."

I kept quiet and still.

"It had to be me. To test it, I mean. Culvan was just too heavy." Elaine paused. "But that's not the whole truth. It was my design. I wanted to be the one. It took a while, but I wore Culvan down."

Elaine started to cry. Silent tears that brought me right along with her.

"I was still conscious when Dad got there. That was part of my punishment, I think. To bear witness. We tried to explain, but Dad didn't want to hear it. He said he treated Culvan like a son and he'd broken that trust, plain and simple."

The best thing to say was nothing, so I stuck with that. Elaine looked up at the clear sky and bright sun.

"I wanted to fly, Ken. Now I'll never feel the ground under my feet again."

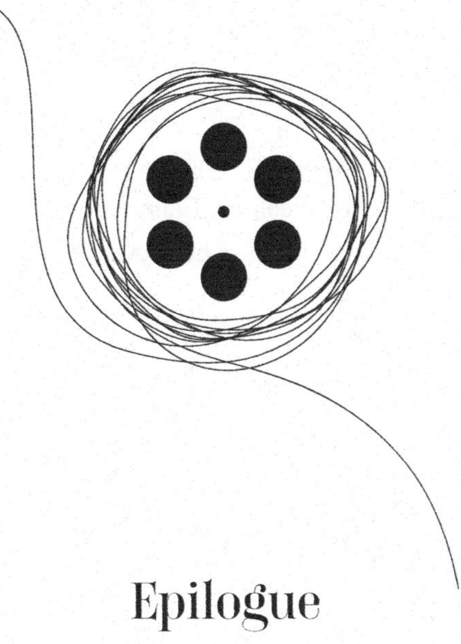

Epilogue

WE DECIDED TO start at the northern end. That way we were moving steadily toward home.

My leg was better, if a little tight. I didn't want to wait so long, but Dean talked me into putting it off until the heart of autumn. Turns out he didn't enjoy the heat either.

Dean smiled at me, a little nervous, a little excited. "Ready for this?"

I smiled back, feeling the same. "More than ready."

I was wearing what the internet said to wear. My backpack and everything inside it was new. Newer than Dean's gear, even. But it was all camping supplies. No armor, no gadgets, not even a watch.

We took the first step together. The trail was well-worn but unknown to us. Comforting and daunting at the same time.

"I've never done anything like this," I admitted. "Outdoors stuff, I mean."

"Me either." Dean laughed.

We took in the sights.

It felt good, not having to think about anything beyond my five senses. Dean waited until we had settled in to broach what was on his mind.

"I know you can't give details, but how did it turn out?"

I had to smile. Dean must have noticed the weight I was carrying, beyond my pack. He was asking for me, not for him.

"The stuff on Culvan's laptops lined up with the contents of Havier's phone. It's clear Culvan was the one who put murder on the menu. Nonetheless, Havier is ruined and facing prison. Neither Jaq nor Flint are mentioned in any of the correspondence, and so far, Havier hasn't rolled."

"Why not?"

"Everyone has their own code. Havier included."

Dehydration set in before you felt thirsty. I stopped for a sip. Dean drank with me.

"As far as the rest . . . after Dave King passes, the world will learn who was really behind their heroes. Jaq inherits the Civil Warriors and the footing to fight for the Good Knights. Meanwhile Stern tries to make a case against her. Maybe Jaq gets away, maybe she doesn't."

Dean squinted in calculation. "So, the good guys kind of won and the bad guys kind of lost?"

"Yep. A lot like last time, and I'm starting to think like always. What is right isn't always what is legal."

Dean dug out some trail mix. "How do you handle that?"

I waved off Dean's offer to share. His had dried fruit in it. And M&M's. "I do what I can. I don't do what I can't."

"Wow. Super-deep, dude."

I thought about it around some salted, toasted almonds. "What really hurts us, as people I mean, is when we act out of character. When we betray who we believe we are. You have to be able to look in the mirror and be okay with who's staring back at you."

Dean nodded, chomping away. "So how do we decide who we are?"

I wanted to give Dean a good answer. In a matter of months, this job had cost me friends and burned bridges. What had it given in return?

I put a hand on Dean's shoulder, urging him on down the trail. All in all, looking in the mirror had never been so easy.

"We look to our heroes."

The End

WHAT!?
RASH
CRASH!!
HMMMM

YEAH!!

WHAT!?
RASH
CRASH!!
HMMMMM

Acknowledgments

THIS BOOK IS the product of a heroic team effort.

In order of appearance:

To my Aunt Michelle, who fostered my love of heroes.

To my wife, who somehow loves listening to me monologue.

To the Clubhouse Gang, for keeping me at the keyboard.

Thanks to J.L. Delozier and her super story-vision.

Thanks to Jeff Wooten for providing expert insight.

And to Tammy DreamWriter and others who provided insights on perspectives outside my own.

Mel Pinsler's deep dive caught plenty I missed, including a major geography error.

To my wonderful agent Lucienne Diver, who, as always, went above and beyond.

Thanks to my editor, Helga Schier, who brings out my best.

Thanks to the CamCat team. Sue Arroyo never stops fighting the good fight. Maryann Appel absolutely nailed what I thought would be an impossible cover.

As always, any mistakes or shortcomings are mine, and mine alone.

About the Author

BORN NEAR DETROIT, J. A. Crawford wanted to grow up to be a superhero, before he found out it was more of a hobby. He's the first in his family to escape the factory line for college. Too chicken to major in writing, he studied Criminal Justice at Wayne State University instead, specializing in criminal procedure and interrogation.

Despite what his family thinks, J. A. is not a spy. When he isn't writing, he travels the country investigating disaster sites. Before that, he taught Criminal Justice, Montessori Kindergarten, and several martial arts. J. A. is an alum of the Pitch Wars program. In his spare time, he avoids carbohydrates and as many punches as possible. He loves the stories behind the stories and finds everything under the sun entirely too interesting.

J. A. splits his time between Michigan and California. He is married to his first and biggest fan, who is not allowed to bring home any more pets.

If you enjoyed

J. A. Crawford's *Heroes Ever Die*,

you'll enjoy

Ash Bishop's *Intergalactic Exterminators, Inc.*

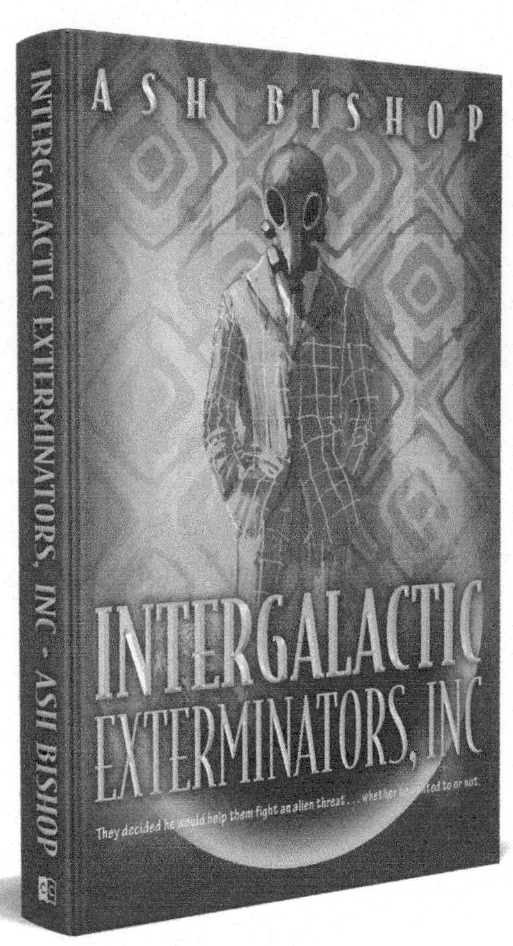

RUSS

RUSS WOKE UP lying flat against the ground, his mind foggy as hell. He could smell blood. When he reached forward, as gingerly as possible, his muscles screamed at the motion.

He was on his back. The forest trees waved down at him, blocking out the faint moonlight. He took a couple of deep breaths and reached his hand forward again, groping around in the darkness. His hand came back slick with blood and fur and leaves.

And then he heard voices.

". . . do you want to do this, then?"

"I just wouldn't call this tracking is all. The blood trail's three feet across. A tiny baby could follow this trail."

"Show me that baby."

"Shhh. Both of you, quiet. Something's registering on the heat index."

The confusion and pain made it hard to think. *Must be locals—teenagers . . .* he thought to himself. He fumbled in his pocket, looking for his flashlight, but also testing for further damage. His hand found the light. It illuminated the small clearing.

The deer's corpse was just a few feet away, right where he'd shot it, but it wasn't whole. Something had torn off its back legs, shearing straight through the muscle and bone.

Russ took a deep breath but didn't let his body or mind react to the sight of the carnage.

Seconds later, the strangers' flashlights found him.

"He's over here. To our left."

Russ heard three or four people hurrying through the brush toward him. A woman in all black stepped into the clearing. Her brown hair was tied back in a bun, and she had a long steel shotgun in her hands. An odd earring twinkled in her ear.

"You okay, son?" she asked, crouching down to place her hands on his chest. She stared into his eyes, examining him. "Looks like you're going into shock. Just stay on your back and concentrate on breathing."

A man followed shortly after her. He glanced around, holding up a funny-looking flashlight to cast out the darkness. "He's alone," the man confirmed. "Are you from around here?" he asked Russ.

"I'm from California," Russ groaned.

"I don't know what that means," the man said.

"Just hold still," the woman said. She pulled a gadget from her pack. The end telescoped out like an antenna.

Russ watched as an aqua blue light shone down from the device, running across his entire body. He flinched as it reached his face, and even that small movement caused his lungs to burst with pain.

"He's got four broken ribs, a hairline fracture in the left wrist and a torn hamstring. Did you see what hit you?" the woman asked him.

Russ tried to think. "No." The word was as much a groan as anything else.

"Tell us what you remember."

Russ rolled over onto his side. It hurt badly. Now that she'd pointed out the injuries, everything was localized. His ribs throbbed. His wrist felt hollow. His left leg was pierced with pain. "I was driving down Route Eighty-Nine, and a deer . . ." Russ pointed to the half deer corpse beside him. ". . . this deer dashed in front of my car. I knew I'd injured it by the sound it made when it hit the bumper, but I didn't think I'd have to chase it this far into the woods to put it out of its misery."

Russ took a minute to swallow. "After I shot it, I—I was kneeling, jacking out the leftover rifle shells. But then . . . I was flipping through the air. I think I hit that tree right behind me."

The woman looked back at the tree. "It's pretty splintered up."

"I was flying upside down. Backwards."

"Can you walk?" the man asked.

Two more women, dressed in the same black combat gear, entered the clearing. They both had long rifles slung over their backs.

Russ glanced at the newcomers, his eyes lingering on the guns. They weren't drunk teens. He could tell that much. "Who are you guys?"

"Just local hunters," one of the newcomers said.

"Sure," Russ gasped.

"Tell me what hit you," the first woman said firmly.

"I don't know. A meteor? A buffalo? Maybe . . . a . . . rig?"

The woman pulled a roll of pills from a MOLLE strap on her backpack. "Swallow two of these. They're going to kill the pain."

Russ chewed the pills. Their chalky taste filled his mouth and crept up into his nose.

"They won't cure any of the damage. You're going to feel fine, but you're not fine. Move carefully until you can get proper medical treatment. The road is two miles north. Can you reach it without help?"

Russ nodded. Whatever she gave him was blazing through his bloodstream, kicking the fog and ache off every organ that it passed.

"What'd I just eat?"

"Two miles north. Don't stop for any reason."

One of the newcomers, a well-muscled young woman with close-cropped brown hair, glanced at the half deer corpse lying next to Russ. Its blood sprayed a pattern across the splintered tree. "Look at the animal, Kendren," she said.

The guy, Kendren, shone his flashlight over the deer corpse. "Whoa," he said. "We definitely found what we're looking for."

"You really chummed the water with this stag," the short-haired woman told Russ.

"Kendren, Starland, mouths shut," the first woman said, making a slashing gesture. She pulled Russ to his feet. He gritted his teeth against the pain, but it was gone.

Kendren and Starland stayed huddled around the deer, crouched low, inspecting where the bone has been sheared off its hindquarters. Kendren looked at the deer's head and saw where Russ had shot it in the head.

"You make this shot?" he asked Russ. "In the dark?"

"Yeah."

"Was the deer already dead? Were you a foot away? Point-blank?"

"No. I was up on a ledge over by the river. Forty feet in that direction." Russ pointed up the gradual incline.

Kendren was still looking at the dead deer. "You shot it between the eyes, from forty feet, in the dark?"

"Yeah. I guess."

"Head on back to the highway," the woman said firmly. "You should start now. It might be dangerous to stay here."

The way she was looking at him, Russ kind of figured she meant that she was what was dangerous. If he didn't do what she said.

"I just need to find my grandpa's rifle first," Russ told her.

She grabbed him by the arm. Her grip was incredibly strong. In the light from her flashlight her eyes seemed almost purple.

"Start walking toward—"

Before she could finish her sentence, the third woman, who'd melted back into the darkness stepped forward again. "Cut the light," she hissed. "It's here."

Something came crashing through the brush, making a howling sound. It wasn't a sound Russ had ever heard before. It was a deep, rumbling growl, followed by a pitched screech that made the hair on his arms stand up. Branches were snapping, and he could hear the scrape of claws on rock. It was still thirty feet south, but it kind of scared the hell out of him.

"El Toreador. You're up," the woman hissed.

The girl they called El Toreador had been on lookout. She was far enough into the darkness that Russ could barely see her, just a wisp of thick brown hair bobbing in the darkness. That is, until she pounded a fist on her chest. Her whole vest lit up red, casting shadows across the trees. "My real name's Atara," she told Russ quickly. Then: "Don't look so worried. We're professionals."

"Starland, hit her with the hormone."

"The vest is enough," Atara growled.

Starland slipped back into the light. She was carrying some kind of tube. It looked like a pool toy. She pushed hard against the end, blasting thick goo all over the other woman.

"Hurry up. It's almost here."

Russ was scrambling around the brush, looking everywhere for his rifle when the creature burst through the perimeter glow of his tiny flashlight. Atara's vest reflected off its face, basking it in red light. It was all fangs and claws, huge, twice the size of a grizzly bear, but full of rippling muscles stretched out in terrifying feline grace. It leapt at Atara but midflight it caught the scent of the goo and reoriented to the left, bumping her off her feet but not harming her.

The huge cat-thing landed softly, immediately turning toward the fallen woman, sniffing in the air, growling, bobbing its head.

"It's got the scent. The big kitty's feeling amorous," Kendren yelled. He, Starland, and the other woman all had their rifles raised. They were tracking the cat, ready to fire. Atara looked pissed, sprawled on the ground with her legs splayed.

"Knock it down. We're authorized for lethal. What are you waiting for?" she shouted.

The creature was fully in the light now. It looked a lot like a tiger, but it was at least six times the size and with wavy, shaggy hair.

"What the hell is it?" Russ shouted.

The feline was practically straddling Atara. "I don't like how it's looking at me. Come on, shoot!" she demanded.

The creature batted at her, claws extended, and tore the glowing vest off her chest. It drew the vest up to its nose, sniffed, and started to growl again.

Then the huge beast paused, slowly turning away from Atara. It sniffed the air, shoulders hunched, fur on the scruff of its neck rising. As it turned, its deep onyx eyes looked squarely at Russ.

It growled and took a step toward him.

Russ thought his heart had been beating hard before, but as the huge cat glided toward him, the thudding in his chest was so loud it drowned out every other sound. He didn't even hear the discharge of Starland's shotgun, two feet away from the monster. The wad of pellets splashed against the creature's flank and it howled, tearing away into the darkness so fast Russ didn't even see it move.

Atara scrambled back to her feet and dropped her rifle. "Did you see that? A direct hit and no penetration. I told you Earth tech was garbage. What is this? The thirteenth century? I'm powering up."

The first woman glanced at Russ. The one with the purple eyes. She was short, wiry, with the powerful shoulders of a linebacker. Russ realized she was the leader of . . . whatever it was he'd run into.

"When are you going to learn to keep your mouth shut?" she asked Atara.

"You already used the CRC wand on him."

"Two hours of mandatory training videos. The second this is over."

"I'd rather be cat food than watch those again," Atara said.

"You skip the videos and I'll send you back through CERT training."

Atara wasn't really listening. She crashed off through the brush, headed in the direction of the big cat.

Nodding toward Russ, the woman shouted, "Kendren, you've got containment." Then she headed into the darkness. Starland drew a pistol from her belt and followed.

"Containment? More like babysitting," Kendren grumbled. "I should be the one doing the good stuff." He glanced in the direction they'd gone. Russ kind of agreed. Kendren was huge, at least six-five and covered head to toe with what Russ's cousin had always called "beach muscles." He had thick, wavy hair down to his shoulders.

Out in the darkness, Russ could see the others' flashlights bobbing up and down. They were headed up an incline, probably straight toward the bank of the river.

"Was it my imagination, or was the cat more interested in you than the vest covered in mating hormone?" Kendren asked.

At first, Russ didn't answer. Finally, he said, "What would make it do that?"

"No idea. It's supposed to follow the hormone. What's better than sex?" Kendren shook his head, seemingly unable to answer his own question. He frowned slightly. "The only thing I've seen them more interested in is an Obinz stone. You ever seen an Obinz stone? They're about this big," Kendren held his hands six inches apart, "usually green, with yellow veins running all along the edges? I don't think they're native to . . . this area." Kendren looked around in distaste. "But I've seen these cats jump planets just to get near one if it's in an unrefined state. An Obinz stone is basically intergalactic catnip."

"I—I've never seen one," Russ told him. He could feel his cheeks redden. He hoped it was too dark for Kendren to notice.

"Then we better shut this vest down," Kendren said. He stepped up onto a boulder and reached high into a tree, grabbing the vest from where the cat had tossed it. He folded the vest up and tucked it under his arm. "I'm not even sure how to turn it off," he said.

"That was a saber-toothed tiger, right? You guys cloning stuff? Is this Jurassic World or something?" Russ rubbed his temple. His questions were coming fast, jumbled in his mouth. Kendren had just said 'intergalactic,' and something about 'jumping planets,' but here in the dark Wyoming forest, six miles from his grandmother's house, he wasn't yet ready to face those pieces of information.

Kendren threw the vest on the ground and raised his rifle, pumping a slug into it. It kept glowing. "Damn. It's pretty important I get this thing turned off."

Starland's discarded rifle was just a few feet away. While Kendren kicked at the vest with his boot heel, Russ inched toward it.

"Touch the weapon and I'll shoot you in the face," Kendren said. He stomped on the vest again.

The flashlights were way north now, probably on the other side of the river. Russ could hear the distant voices bickering about which way the big cat went.

The voices were so loud, neither Kendren nor Russ heard the cat until it was right in front of them, growling, hissing, and spitting. It stalked into the circumference of the faint red light from the vest.

Kendren was still standing on the vest, his rifle slung over his shoulder. Beside him, the cat was enormous, twice as tall as a man. It crouched down and looked him straight in the eye.

"I'm dead," he said quietly.

The creature coiled back on its powerful flanks and threw itself forward like a bullet tearing out of a gun. Its wicked claws stretched out, razored edges slashing Kendren's neck and chest.

Russ kicked Starland*'s* gun off the ground, caught it, leveled it, and fired. The bullet split the cat's eye socket, ripping through its optic nerve and straight into its brain.

The dead body carried forward on its trajectory, smashing into Kendren and pinning him to the earth.

A few moments later, the rest of the team returned, clambering through the thick brush. The leader approached the enormous beast and nudged it with her boot.

"Is it dead, Bah'ren?" Atara asked, her gun still pointed at the fallen creature.

"Sure is," the leader, Bah'ren, told her.

The wind was starting to pick up, blowing the branches of the trees, shaking off a few dead leaves.

"How about Kendren?"

"Negative," Bah'ren said.

"Get it off me," Kendren demanded. "It's gotta weigh nine hundred pounds."

"How many intergalactic laws do you think we've broken here?" Atara asked. She moved next to Bah'ren, looking down at Kendren with an expression that was half pity and half amusement.

He had managed to sit up, but his legs were wedged under the huge carcass.

"Including the law about referencing intergalactic law on a tier-nine planet?" Bah'ren asked.

"You guys *are* being a little careless," Starland said.

"Not our fault this thing was a hundred miles off course. The MUPmap promised there wouldn't be any tier-nine bios in the vicinity."

"What are we supposed to do now?" Atara said, nodding toward Russ.

"Oh, we're conscripting him, for sure." Bah'ren said.

"Really?" Atara said. "We're getting another human?"

"Who? Who do you mean?" Russ asked. He glanced back in the direction of the highway. His eyes were starting to adjust to the dark again and he could make out a thick copse of trees just a dozen or so yards away.

"Get the huge beast off me," Kendren insisted.

Bah'ren moved to one side of the big cat and dug her powerful shoulders into it. Starland ran over to join her, wedging one arm against the creature's flank, but putting her other arm around the waist of the woman giving the orders. "Atara, come on. You, new guy, we could use your help too. It's heavy as hell."

Russ half ran over to them and dug his side into the creature. Its hairy skin sloshed around against the pressure, but the four of them eventually got it moving.

"Roll it the other way!" Kendren demanded. "Its penis is right next to my face."

They kept rolling, and Kendren kept protesting, as the great shaggy cat slowly grinded over his shoulders and face. Gravity finally caught hold of its weight and the corpse flopped to the ground. The three in black all chuckled as Kendren spit out the taste of cat testicle.

"Oh, that's what you meant. Sorry about that," Starland said, laughing.

Kendren crawled onto his knees, still hacking and spitting. His luxurious hair stood out in every direction. He stopped for a minute and looked at the cat's face, poking a finger in the thing's empty eye socket and wiggling it around. "Another hell of a shot."

"The debriefing wasn't just wrong about location," Atara said. "The creature's fur is like steel mesh. Our bullets were doing jackshit."

Kendren rolled up onto his knees, both hands propped on his thighs. "You saved my life," he told Russ.

"No problem," Russ said.

It was the last thing Russ said before he dropped the rifle and sprinted full speed back toward the safety of the trees. He was running as fast as he could, pumping his arms, banging his shins on rocks, bumping past pines, carelessly plunging through the dark.

He'd only gotten about twenty yards when something metal slapped around his ankle, yanking him off his feet. As he was running full speed, it tipped him off balance and, for the second time that night, he could feel himself careening head over heels.

He hit a tree, again, then slowly slipped out of consciousness.

MORE SUSPENSE FROM CAMCAT BOOKS

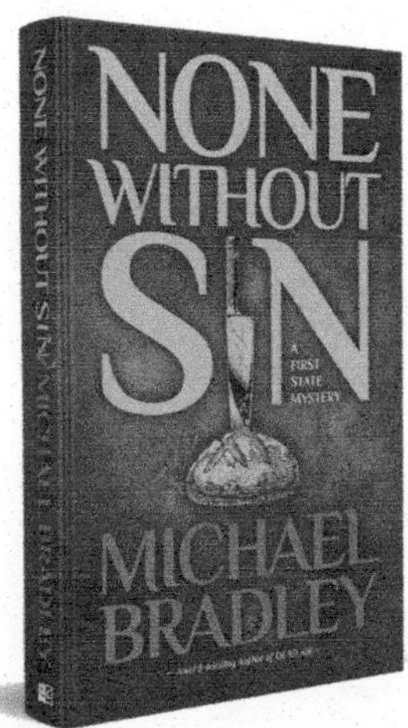

Available now, wherever books are sold.

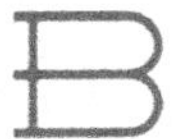